HOT
SOUTHERN
NIGHTS

HOT SOUTHERN NIGHTS

DIANNE CASTELL

BRAVA

KENSINGTON PUBLISHING CORP.
www.kensingtonbooks.com

BRAVA BOOKS are published by

Kensington Publishing Corp.
119 West 40th Street
New York, NY 10018

Copyright © 2010 Dianne Kruetzkamp

All Kensington titles, imprints, and distributed lines are available at special quantity discounts for bulk purchases for sales promotion, premiums, fund-raising, educational or institutional use.

Special book excerpts or customized printings can also be created to fit specific needs. For details, write or phone the office of the Kensington Special Sales Manager: Kensington Publishing Corp., 119 West 40th Street, New York, NY 10018. Attn. Special Sales Department. Phone: 1-800-221-2647.

Brava and the B logo are Reg. U.S. Pat. & TM Off.

ISBN-13: 978-0-7582-2363-0
ISBN-10: 0-7582-2363-3

First Kensington Trade Paperback Printing: May 2010

10 9 8 7 6 5 4 3 2 1

Printed in the United States of America

Chapter One

When Churchill McKenzie *stared down the business end of a sawed-off shotgun she swore that if she got out of that mess alive she'd get herself back to Savannah as fast as possible and never leave as long as she lived . . . which she hoped was more than the next two minutes.*

She meant that three weeks ago in Atlantic City, when the Jersey boys paid her a visit because she'd been asking too many questions about her '56 Chevy Bel Air that they just happened to borrow permanently, and she hadn't changed her mind. She was done with back alleys, big guns, badasses and black pinstripe suits.

Except—why was there always an *except* in her life— there she was again, standing in another back alley with Savannah's number one badass, Cal Davis. She knew the bad part firsthand because she'd had him thrown in jail three years ago. She knew the ass part because they did the deed on her twenty-first birthday in the back of his '67 red Mustang convertible.

"When did you get out?" Dumb thing to say to someone who hated her guts. You'd think since she was a librarian she'd have a better opening line. Faulkner would, Dickens would, Crichton not so much.

Cal folded his arms and gave her an f-you look. "When did you get back?"

She could say *I asked you first* but Cal didn't look like the kind of guy who needed to be messed with. Even in the dim light casting his face in shadows he looked pissed. Cal always looked pissed . . . except for that twenty minutes in the back of his Mustang. "I came home last week. I was in Jersey. Librarian, in the ancient history section."

"And here you are again," he sighed. "Whose life are you out to screw up tonight?"

"I was cutting through the alley on my way to your grandmother's." That warranted a bit of an arched brow. "Miss Ellie asked me to stop by and sit for a spell."

Cal took her arm. "I'm coming along. You show up and things go right to hell. Miss Ellie doesn't need that. None of us need that."

Churchill didn't budge. "I don't believe you were invited."

"I don't believe I give a damn."

But instead of leaving, he backed her against the side of a concrete block garage in the alley. Cupping her chin, he tilted her face to his then straightened her glasses, uncertainty in his eyes. They were more ice than the smoky blue she remembered. He was leaner, harder, tougher, and he'd been plenty tough before. Rhett Butler does Savannah.

"You have a scar on your chin."

"You have gray hair."

"Jerzee is a scary place."

He deliberately tucked a strand of her hair behind her right ear. To Churchill, that was about the sexiest thing a guy could do to a girl . . . other than rip both their clothes off and jump in the backseat of a Mustang.

"And here you are, Ace, back in Savannah, meaning I'm the one who should be scared." Before she had time to consider that he still called her Ace or that she wanted the clothes-ripping more than the hair-tucking, he kissed her. It was one of those terrific spontaneous kisses that scared the spit out of her because she was on fire for the bad boy again!

His lips devoured hers. He tasted like good sipping whiskey, delicious sex, and forbidden fruit. If an apple fell from the sky and a snake appeared she wouldn't have been surprised.

"How can someone be a librarian and be such a pain in the butt?" His mouth breathed the words against hers, sending heat clear to her toes and frying her brain. "It's the name. It's made you different. Churchill."

"I'm a British statesman with jowls?"

"You think too much, ask too many questions, and wind up in the middle of shit storms."

She pushed him away. "Okay, time out. That's it. I didn't stumble into that car theft ring in Jersey on purpose. They took my Chevy Bel-Air that Uncle Frank gave to me. The police said there was no hope of ever getting it back so I asked around. Suddenly there were men in pinstripe suits and black fedoras. For the record I didn't send you to prison, you sent yourself. You did the stealing. I just happened to be a witness."

"So many shit storms in so little time."

"Coincidences."

"Not when your name's Churchill." Sirens sounded. Not the kind in her brain that said *run, this guy's nothing but trouble*, but real ones of the red and blue flashing lights variety from a police cruiser rounding the corner. The car squealed to a stop in front of her and Cal, catching them both in the glare of headlights and police strobes.

"Davis," the police officer barked as he got out of the cruiser. "We want to talk to you down at the station."

Even in the dark she could see Cal's eyes narrow, his hands fist at his sides. "Do I need my lawyer?"

"Where were you tonight?"

"With me," Churchill blurted. "Least for the last fifteen minutes." Mentally he'd been with her for the last nine years. "We were—"

"I was at Willie's down on River Street. I'm heading back here to get my car. Ask the bartender."

The officer yanked open the back door of the cruiser. "Get in while we check it out."

"What's this about, Dempsey?"

"My being a cop and you being a no-good asshole who steals money meant for some poor old folks here in town. You haven't changed since high school."

"And you're still a prick in elevator shoes except now you're hiding behind a badge instead of your daddy, the principal."

Dempsey's brows pulled into one long furry line over his beady eyes that were getting lost in an angry red face. He touched the holster that held his gun. Churchill hated that more than anything. "We can go and do this the easy way or the hard way. It's up to you."

Cal turned to Churchill before climbing in the backseat. "Do me a favor and stay out of my life and stay the hell away from my family. I'm not kidding, Churchill, stay away. You're nothing but trouble." The cruiser faded into the night, leaving her with crickets, alley bugs, and singed lips. Cal wanted the kiss but didn't want anything to do with her. She wanted the kiss but nothing to do with him. Except— there was that word again—singed lips were a long way from nothing.

He told her to stay away from his family and of course that included Miss Ellie. Well too darn bad. She might be Cal's granny who pretty much raised him, but she was Churchill's friend, and friends didn't leave friends sitting alone when they promised to show up for a chat. She cut across the next alley to a garden walkway, a sliver of moonlight picking out crape myrtle lining the path. A chinaberry tree protected the screened porch from the blasting Savannah sun and summer jasmine scented the humid August air. In Jersey the overhead expressways kept out the sun and exhaust fumes scented the air.

"Well now," said a voice behind her. "I'd about given up on our getting together. I figured you buried your nose in some book and got carried away."

Churchill swung around to see Miss Ellie sitting on a white wrought iron bench. She had on Nike running shoes, pink Capri's, and a yellow T-shirt displaying a half-eaten Georgia peach and the words BITE ME.

"I didn't see you." Which seemed incredulous considering the getup. "Nice shoes."

Miss Ellie stuck out her Nike's with Pepto colored trim. "I'm still kicking. 'Course my son and his uppity wife think I'm dumb as a box of rocks because I can't quote Shakespeare. But then they can't quote Bono so the way I see it we're even." She gave a laugh that was more a cackle. "I hear you got mixed up with the wrong crowd and got yourself thrown out of Jersey. Your mama must be right proud."

"Margo's rafting the Amazon. Library work in any form isn't her idea of high adventure."

"So now that you're back, what do you think of a little Low Country adventure? Something to keep you on your toes."

"I'm all flats and flip-flops these days, Miss Ellie. The adventure gene did not get passed on. Believe me I know that for sure now."

"So, what about finding out some answers for me? You always were good at finding answers. That's what makes you so smart. I want you to prove my grandson didn't belong in jail after all. I want you to fix things right by Cal."

"Miss Ellie, I was there. I was the one who saw him

drive off in his Mustang. I saw Reverend Dodd run out of his big white revival tent in his pristine white you're-all—doomed-to-hell preaching suit. He was yelling at the top of his lungs that he'd been robbed and Cal was going straight to hell for stealing money from God."

"I'm here to tell you that if Dodd is God we're all in a heap of trouble. I don't care how many Bibles he waves around or what anyone else says, Cal did not take that money. I've had three years to think about all this and things just don't add up the way they should."

"Cal said he used the twenty-five grand to pay off gambling debts."

"See, there it is. I taught Cal how to play poker and he could beat the socks off anyone, including me. He works for what he wants, always has. Why steal in the middle of the day? Cal's way smarter than that. There's something else I've come across that's got me to thinking that someone else is involved in all this." She slid a heavy looking skeleton key from her pocket. "Cal gave me his Mustang to drive while he was in the slammer. One day last month I went to the drive-through at that McDonalds over there on Abercorn because they have this young stud working the pay window. I dropped my French fries when my cell phone started to vibrate. Had the thing in my blouse pocket. With all that tingling I thought I was having a heart attack right there under the golden arches. When I cleaned up the fries I found this here key under the seat. Cal said he didn't recognize it and I didn't say where I found it but it looks real important."

"Maybe one of his friends dropped it?"

"Now I ask you, Missy, does this look like the sort of thing one of Cal's car racing buddies would have? It's not an engine part or something to pry the top off a beer bottle, but it's real important looking with all those weird markings."

Churchill held the key up to the moonlight. "Actually the top does look like a bottle opener. It's like an upside down *U*. Omega."

"You owe me, sweet pea. You wanted to work in a big city and I introduced you to that library fella who has his summer house over on Hilton Head. He still calls me Stacks and he's not referring to books." Miss Ellie batted her eyes, fluffed her hair, and arched her chest. "That little nip and tuck last year did wonders. I want you to figure out who Cal's covering for and why this here key was in his car. I think they're connected."

"That's a pretty big jump, Miss Ellie. What would one have to do with the other?"

"Because they're two unanswered questions that came up at the same time and both have to do with Cal. No one's better at finding the answers to questions than you."

"Jersey lesson number one . . . asking questions short-ens life expectancy. I just want to live in Savannah and be a librarian." Churchill took Miss Ellie's hands in hers. "This city's been through pirates, plagues, and no-good Yankee plunders. Old is everywhere. That key is nothing special and maybe Cal did get into a gambling mess. It happens. But he's paid his dues now. He's back and he's safe and can move on with his life. You should too. Let it go, Miss Ellie."

"You've never been a granny. Moving on is something we don't do well when it comes to protecting our offspring. Besides, I know Cal and I'm thinking deep down you do, too. He's not a thief—especially taking money that was going to poor folk. I don't care what you saw." She marched past her chinaberry tree and into her gray clapboard house, the screen door slamming shut behind her.

So much for paying Miss Ellie back for getting Churchill the Jersey job. For a second she hated Cal for putting Miss Ellie through all that pain and putting Churchill smack-dab in the middle of . . . of a another shit storm.

Well, she was going to avoid that one. Her mama was the adventurer and Churchill was anything but. At times she thought she might be adopted except she had Margo's blue eyes and long legs.

Churchill headed across the alley and through Orleans Square with the boxwood edge and splashing urn fountain. Lamplight filtered through the live oaks as she passed the James Oglethorpe Founding Fathers Library. Built of Greek revival architecture, complete with stone oblique at the corners, it had a cornerstone of 1862. It was the oldest library in the city and she loved every stone and window in the place. Living next door was perfect.

She took the mossy brick steps up to her apartment that faintly smelled of mocha and cappuccino. Savannah Joe's Beanery, below, was new but the building was 1854. Old, interesting, historic with original plaster and woodwork. Not ancient but getting there.

It was a good day to end she decided when she got to the top landing and fished for her keys. Miss Ellie was mad at her and Cal made it clear he wanted nothing to do with her. Except—she was getting to hate that word—what about that kiss she couldn't forget? What about the sex she hadn't gotten over? There were all kinds—makeup sex, breakup sex, revenge sex. She wanted good-old-days sex, the kind in the back seat of a '67 Mustang convertible, with Cal Davis, with both of them naked as peeled apples. How she was going to get over that was the mystery of the ages.

Overhead lights glared off the deserted dirt track as Cal punched the gas, caught the cushion, then slung through the far turn, rear-end sliding, dirt flying, a cloud of exhaust billowing behind. Gas and oil fumes mixing with the odor of scorched rubber filled his lungs while his head throbbed with the roar of the big engine of the Late Model, a one hundred percent pure racing machine. Sweat trickled down his back and front, the fillings of his teeth hurt from the constant jarring, and dirt clung like a second layer of skin. Cal Davis was in heaven . . . till the car pulled right setting up a vibration in the steering wheel. Bad tire? Too tight? Not enough stick for a dirt track? He fought the wheel to keep the car out of a spin and—

"What the fucking hell!" He blinked to make sure he was seeing what he really was seeing and not just a glare of light. It wasn't a glare. Churchill McKenzie was running onto the track waving her arm at him like a crazy lunatic. Was that a dog on a leash with her? Maybe a small horse? Hard to tell. What were they doing on the track? Holy shit!

Cal lifted his right foot from the gas and eased the brake with his left. More burning rubber fumes and dust invaded the car. Mud Monkey did zero to seventy in under five seconds but stopping was a different matter. "Get off the damn track!" he yelled as he raced by giving her a wide berth so as not to cover her in grime. He knew she couldn't hear him but he had to do something. "You're going to get killed." If he wrecked Otto's pride and joy, Otto would kill him.

Cal pulled the car into pit alley, then slid feetfirst through the open window. "Are you out of your freaking mind! You could have been hurt."

"Well, I'm counting on you being a better driver than that," she yelled back.

Walking toward her he swiped the sweat from his forehead. "This isn't the parking lot at Macy's." The dog of questionable parentage wagged his tail setting the whole back side of his brown body in motion. "Where'd he come from?"

"Jersey," she panted, out of breath from running. She pushed her glasses up the bridge of her nose. "I don't know why you're bellowing your head off at me when you're the one driving around this circle of baked mud like a lunatic.

Did it ever occur to you that you're going nowhere fast? What is the point?"

"Did it ever occur to you that a lot of those books in that library of yours say pretty much the same damn thing so why have them all sitting around? What is the point?"

Instead of yelling another insult, Churchill's eyes clouded with worry and she gritted her teeth. "I came to tell you Miss Ellie was in the hospital. She has a broken arm." Churchill put her hand to her chest to catch her breath, flattening her blouse against nicely rounded breasts, which Cal noticed but shouldn't be thinking about. He was pissed but when had that ever stopped a man from staring?

"What the hell did you do to her last night?"

Churchill's black rimmed glasses slipped down her nose and she glared at him over the top as the dog ran around her legs tying her in loops. "For your information, Miss Ellie was fine when I left her. We talked about you. She thinks you're innocent as the driven snow and should never have gone to prison in the first place and . . . why can't I walk?"

"Because you've got a dog. Give me the damn leash." Shitfire, what was that all about? He was supposed to do his time behind bars, then it was over. Miss Ellie deserved better than a despised ex-con for a grandson, especially a grandson she pretty much raised. Carburetors, pistons, and crankshafts didn't have a place in his parents' house of quantum physics and economic anomalies. Miss Ellie, on the other hand, had Granddad's '62 Ford Falcon that he used to race at the speedway years ago, some land out on Whitemarsh Island, and crocks for neighbors who didn't care squat that Cal revved engines, squealed brakes, and sent mud flying.

He held the dog in place and unwound the leash from Churchill's long shapely legs that disappeared under a black skirt. She should look matronly and boring and not matter to him one lick, except Churchill McKenzie was anything but boring. She was standing in the middle of a dirt speed-way splattered with mud and looking damn beautiful. That was no way to keep her out of his life.

"What else is going on? You're fidgeting like a fish on a line," he said.

"I'm all dirty. That's enough to make any woman miser-able." She swiped at the grime. "Isn't your grandma with a broken arm enough right now?"

"Librarians are bad liars."

She took back the leash and said to the dog, "Sit." She looked to Cal and puffed out a sigh. "This is all my fault."

"You beat up Miss Ellie?"

"Oh for heaven's sake, no, but I am responsible all the same. She wanted me to prove you didn't do the robbery. We both know you did so it's a waste of time. I said I wouldn't help because there was no new evidence. It seems she went out on the town last night asking questions, it got late, and she got mugged—right there on Bay Street." Churchill pulled in a deep breath. "They knocked her down and took her purse." She looked pained. "If I had just been there with her—"

"You both would have gotten mugged."

"I take pilates three times a week. I could have pro-tected her. And I have a dog."

"Yeah, bet you're hell on wheels on your big blue ball and there's no holding back Killer here. Now there's a real menace to society." Cal retraced his steps to the car.

"Where are you going now?"

"To get my grandmother."

"She's at my place and she's doing just fine. She's proba-bly sleeping by now."

"But she's *my* grandmother." Cal kept walking till Churchill caught up to him and took his arm, the unex-pected light touch stopping him faster than any hard punch. She could still do that after so many years. What was it about Churchill that got to him? Auburn hair pulled back in a loose knot and held in place by a pencil? Her slim figure under the simple skirt and blouse? Her long legs? All of it, dammit, all of it. The whole uptight librarian package drove him nuts because he knew somewhere under all that uptightness there was something a little reckless and hot as hell.

"She's fine. I tried to call you about what happened but with all the racket coming out of that heap you call a car the world could have exploded and you wouldn't have heard a thing. Miss Ellie thinks I'm out getting dog food so I better get back in case she wakes up." Church let out a sigh and let go of Cal's arm. "That's not a lie. Seems I always have to get dog food except when he won't eat dog food and I have to fry chicken or scramble an egg or make quiche."

"You cook quiche for a dog?"

"He has separation anxiety. He liked Jersey." She didn't say anything for a moment and stared at him. Her blue eyes suddenly went dark and soft and too damn sensual for a hot summer night in Savannah with no one around but the two of them. "Did you take Dodd's money?"

He had to bring an end to the conversation before her damn questions and her ability to turn him upside down made him say something he'd regret and mess up everything he set in motion. "You want to know why the police hauled me in? One of the guys who worked pit here at the track three years ago wound up dead. They think I had something to do with it. I'm a felon and that means any crime within a fifty mile radius has my name on it. That should answer your question."

"Why would your robbery have anything to do with the dead person?"

"You aren't nearly as smart as people say you are, Ace."

She didn't scare off easy, he'd give her that. Bet those

Jersey boys had their hands full when Little Miss Know It All showed up wanting her car back. Churchill McKenzie didn't do "I don't know" well.

"Go home." He walked across the track. "Thanks for taking care of Miss Ellie," he added without turning around. He slid through the open window of Mud Monkey and gunned the engine to drown out any other questions or comments Churchill had. She shook her head at him and walked away till Killer ran ahead nearly pulling her off her feet. Who was taking who for a walk?

He stifled a laugh making him feel better than he had since . . . since he kissed her. Damn that kiss, why did he do that? Why did she have to be there? Why couldn't she have kept her job in Jersey? Everything was going okay, he had everything under control for a long time now and then Churchill came back to Savannah and talked to Miss Ellie. Cal had a bad feeling things would not end with one talk. He had to keep a clear head and stop her before she got involved.

Trouble was, when it came to Ace McKenzie there was not one thing clear at all. He was attracted to her and shouldn't be for a grocery list of reasons. They were opposites on every front, the librarian and the jailbird. The darling of Savannah—just ask anyone—and the devil—just ask anyone. The girl who graduated top of her class, the boy who finished dead last. They had nothing in common and yet there was that spring night nine years ago when everything fell together and they weren't opposites at all.

He could still see her walking barefoot down Highway 80, white high heels swinging from her left hand, pink dress and long hair swaying in the sea breeze. She'd left her own birthday party out on Tybee Island early because her date got falling down drunk and Cal gave her a ride home—eventually—after they stopped to watch shooting stars over the marsh which led to their making love. It *was* lovemaking.

He felt it when he held her sweet body and in the way she touched him. Churchill was all woman—deep, thoughtful, stronger than he realized, and too damn insightful. The two of them had a connection that night he'd never experienced before . . . or since. But that was a lifetime ago and he had to get over it, too much depended on it.

Cal drove Mud Monkey into the pit and turned off the engine as Silky Callahan ambled out the front door of the office. He headed Cal's way while sliding one red suspender onto his shoulder, then the other. The ponytail that he was probably born with was more gray than blond and hung down his back. His shoes were habitually covered in track dust. His usual ear-to-ear smile got bigger the closer he got to Cal meaning Silky intended to bust Cal's chops about Churchill being there. Terrific.

"Well now," Silky said. "Wasn't that the librarian who just moved back to town? Pretty little thing, isn't she? She'd make a good match for your brother. Didn't Tripp just get his PhD in some highfalutin science major with a lot of big words? She's just his type with all those brains between them."

"Sure, why not."

Silky chuckled and slapped the hood of the car. "Because if you grip that wrench any tighter you'll snap it in two, that's why not. Tripp my ass. He's nine years younger than you and spent his whole damn life buried in books. If it's not written down the boy doesn't have a clue. Miss Librarian isn't interested in Tripp, I can tell you that much. She's all woman, and she's interested in a man. She's interested in you. Don't have to be some genius to see that."

Silky patted Cal on the shoulder as he dropped the wrench into the tool box. "She came out to tell me that someone mugged Miss Ellie and broke her arm."

Silky sobered. "Well I'll be. Who'd do a dang-fool thing like that? Everyone in town knows Miss Ellie and they know you to be her kin and would not take kindly to something happening to her."

To get Churchill out of his mind Cal concentrated on the car, checking the lug nuts on the wheel. Maybe one came loose causing the vibration. He ran his hand over the tire. Maybe it was worn on one side. Air pressure? Maybe that was off. Or maybe the shock valves? Damn. "Miss Ellie was out late and some dopehead probably saw her as an easy mark. She's resting at Churchill's tonight, and tomorrow I'll get her to my place. Why's this damn tire pulling? Might be the tread." Why did he mention Churchill's name again? That was not the way to get her off his mind.

"Hell if I know. You're the mechanic partner around here now. My share of the place includes doing the books, ordering up the beer, and doing some fishing and boating out on Cabbage Island. I sure as hell think I got the better end of our little deal."

"Unless we run out of beer. Did you put the ad in the paper for the Young Gun Shoot-out here at the track? We got three sponsors lined up to kick in some money and with the take at the gate and entrance fees the purse should be about five grand. That will bring in the drivers. Folks always come out for a fifty-lapper with the late models. Lots of wreckin' and bettin' going on. The pretty girls who tend bar and wait tables down at Fanny Hill's saloon are paying us a visit to make the winner in victory lane feel right special."

"So, what are you going to do?"

"About the shootout? Hope we make some money and everyone has a hell of a good time."

"I mean about the librarian."

"Nothing."

Silky rested his hand on Cal's shoulder. "Yeah, that's what we all tell ourselves, boy, and it never quite happens that way. I'm guaranteeing you right now, with that cute as all get out little lady in your life, something's going to happen. You're a doomed man."

He was, dammit, in more ways than one. He had to figure a way out of it all before something happened that he couldn't fix.

Chapter Two

The morning sun nearly had the sidewalk to fry-an-egg-temperature as Churchill balanced three coffees in one hand. With the other she unlocked the lovely wood library door carved with magnolia blossoms. The aromas of books and old polished cyprus mingled with double latté, the smells of heaven. Kindles and the like were fine but nothing replaced a physical book. She loved the way it felt in her hand, the way it aged with dabs of peanut butter and jelly from one reader and cookie smears from another. All were signs of a really good book. Just opening a book cover meant adventure, a kind of adventure Margo never understood. If her mama couldn't climb it, cross it, jump into it, or yell, "yeeehaaaa," while doing it she had no use for it. Sometimes, deep down inside, late at night when Churchill had to be honest with herself, she wondered if she was included in that list. She'd tried the adventure route. Adventure camp at ten, space camp at thirteen, wilderness camp at fifteen, Himalaya Camp at twenty. Then she took the Jersey job hoping to add some adventure that Margo would approve of to her life. Big city, big library . . . then big problems and big trouble. She was done with big except for the big dog. Churchill McKenzie was finally content to be the poster girl for THERE'S NO PLACE LIKE HOME. Maybe she should change her name. She didn't deserve Churchill.

"You always beat me here," Michelle sing-songed as she skipped through the door. "But I'm still the good cousin 'cause I went and bought some of those low-fat blueberry scones from that new bakery over there on Bull Street. If you're right nice to me, I'm willing to share."

"I don't think you ever just walk anyplace these days. You're always dancing, even here in the library."

Michelle twirled, her yellow peasant skirt flowing out around her. "I dropped a hundred pounds thanks to Lap-Band and another two hundred pounds thanks to my divorce lawyer. This skirt's a size ten and and Tommy Lee Dempsey's lying ass was history three months ago today. I do indeed feel like kicking up my heels." Michelle handed Churchill a blueberry scone and Churchill handed Michelle a coffee.

"Speaking of men in our lives," Michelle said around a mouthful after licking her fingers, "word over at the bakery is that you've been spending time with the likes of one Cal Davis. My, oh my, what is that all about?" She cut her eyes to Churchill and batted her lashes.

"It is not what you think. Some people in this town need to get a life of their own, thank you very much. Miss Ellie was mugged last night right on Bay Street, of all places. I ran out to the speedway to tell Cal because I thought he should know. That's all there is to it—not one thing more—so put your mind at rest. Miss Ellie's staying at my place now. She has a broken arm but seemed better this morning when I left. And Storybook's there for protection."

"Protection? Storybook? The only time he barks is on command to get a doggie treat. Poor Miss Ellie." Michelle put her hand to her breasts that were considerably smaller than they had been since junior high. "Well, bless her heart. I must have missed the morning muggings report at the bakery and just caught the social report. Bet she pitched one big hissy. She's a feisty one." Michelle grinned. "But, honey, when it comes to you and Cal Davis together for any reason, there's always a lot more to it."

Pounding on the door made them jump. Churchill splashed coffee across the red mahogany checkout desk. "What in the world?"

Churchill got paper towel to clean up the mess as a man's voice yelled, "Michelle, girl. You get yourself out here right this very minute you hear me now? I know you're in there somewhere."

Michelle put her cup down on the glass case holding Richard Arnold's sword from that unfortunate Northern Aggression. "Well piss and vinegar, it's Tommy Lee. What a way to start the day. I don't think I'm ever going to be rid of that man, I swear." Heaving a sigh she brushed crumbs from her sweater then opened the door. "Merciful heavens, what do you want now?"

Tommy Lee's round face flushed and what was left of his hair stood on end. "Where is your son, woman? Can you answer me that?"

Michelle parked her hand on her hip. "Don't you *woman* me," she said, looking every inch a sexy woman. "Don't you mean *our* son? He's at summer school where he's supposed to be, taking algebra because he flunked it in regular school. He has a hard time with math."

"You better be guessing about all that again." Tommy Lee stepped aside. Tommy Junior sat in the backseat of his father's cruiser. "He was drag racing down Abercorn, between traffic lights. TJ was nowhere near summer school. He scared the crap out of half the Savannah population on their way to work. If you can't control him better than what you're doing I'm filing for full custody."

"Full custody? Ha!" Michelle stomped her foot on the black and white marble step, her curled hairdo not budging an inch thanks to Suave extra-hold. "Half the time you don't want any kind of custody because you're out carousing."

"I'm not having any son of mine who's carrying my name, running around Savannah causing trouble and getting himself killed. I'm assistant chief of police around here. How does that look?"

"It looks like you need to lose fifty pounds."

Tommy Lee sucked in his gut. "I'm taking away his car and sending him off to military school. It's what's best for him. I told him to get a job this summer and he didn't. I told him to make up that algebra class and he's not going. I told him to cut his hair and it's falling over his eyes like some sissy mama's boy. He hasn't done one thing I told him to." Dempsey stormed back to the cruiser, yanked Tommy Junior from the backseat, and hauled him toward the library door. "I'm filling out the papers today for Camp Hill Military so be packing his bags and saying your good-byes. By the end of the week he's gone from here."

Michelle pulled TJ inside and slammed the library door. Churchill found books to shelve on the balcony level as Michelle said to her son, "You were supposed to go to school, then go home and do the dishes and—"

"And what, read a book? I hate algebra, I hate reading, and I hate school. Dad's just mad because I want to work on my car and not go to that gun show in Beaufort on Friday. I hate guns."

"Boy, you're going to hate military school a lot more and that's where you're headed. You need to try and get along with your father. I have to work today and you're staying in this library with me so I can keep an eye on you."

"And do what?"

Michelle shoved a book at her son. "You can put this and the others away for starters and they better wind up in

the right places. Then you can polish the big cypress bookcases on the next floor up."

"You can't put me in military school. I won't go. I swear
I won't."

"Don't you go swearing at your mama about anything.
If your daddy's determined there's not much I can do to
stop him. You've messed up too many times, TJ, with losing the job over at Findley's Market, cutting classes, and
now not going to summer school like you were supposed
to." Michelle closed her eyes for a moment and added in a
lower voice, "How could you do this?" She sounded tired
and sad. "You're ruining your life, throwing it away."

"Well, it's my life to ruin any way I want."

"Except it's my life too. You're my son."

"I wish I wasn't!" Defiant look firmly in place, TJ
slammed books onto the old wood shelves as Michelle
slogged to the circulation desk not dancing at all. Churchill
considered taking one of the long thin books from the children's section and smacking TJ across his butt. Not that it
would do any good. This was between kid and parent, a
relationship she didn't handle all that well herself.

The door opened again and Cal Davis walked in wearing
soft worn jeans, a navy T-shirt draped over what Churchill
knew was a fine muscled chest and kicking her thoughts of
dysfunctional families to the curb. At least for the moment. As she returned to the main floor, he took off his black
Savannah Speedway baseball hat and his gaze met hers
causing her to drop an armful of books.

He set the hat and his keys on the desk next to *The Little
Engine That Could* and three Harry Potter books. He
scooped up *She Comes First, A Man's Guide to Pleasuring
a Woman*. Churchill's gaze fused again with Cal's over the
last book and she felt her face turn every shade of red since
she was eye-to-eye with the guy who could have written
the darn thing.

"I didn't check those out," she blurted. *Another brilliant statement by Churchill McKenzie.*

"I hear *The Little Engine*'s a real page-turner. I came to see my grandmother. Thanks for taking care of her. She doesn't get along all that well with my parents."

"Grandmother?" Something about that sounded familiar but her brain was too fogged with *A Man's Guide* to figure out what.

"Miss Ellie? Broken arm? At your apartment, wherever that is."

Churchill forced herself to stop staring at brown eyes, brown hair, and wonderful lips. "I live—*Think, Church, think, where the heck do you live?*—"next door. Yes, next door, that's it."

"I believe you." His eyes smiled but his lips—those wonderful lips—didn't budge. It was a business visit—all business. Well fine. She could do business.

"I'll take you. Storybook is there and you never know what he's going to do. Jump in your lap, lick your face, drool." The first two Churchill was considering herself. So much for it just being business. For her anything to do with Cal was personal. She walked toward the door as Michelle took the books from Churchill's arms, saying in a low voice and a twinkle in her eyes, "You won't be needing these, honey." She followed it with a this-guy-is-so-hot look.

Churchill tried for an I-don't-really-care look in return but some lies were too big to pull off, especially when under the influence of the guy. She led Cal out of the library and stopped dead, staring past the planters to a car parked at the curb across the street. The interior was white as the clouds overhead. The matching convertible top was down showing off the sharpest car in the universe. "You still have the Mustang."

"A lot of great memories in this car."

Churchill felt herself redden again to the color of the car. It was the second time in five minutes and more blushing than she'd done in the last three years.

Cal continued, "Memories like going to the beach, driving across the country after graduating high school, the first time I replaced brakes and struts on a car myself."

She was thinking the backseat, buck naked, Cal between her legs, and he was thinking road trips and car parts. "Right. Struts. Who could forget struts. Where would the world be without our struts to give us memories?" Whatever the heck struts were. She needed to get a life and quit obsessing over being naked with Cal. It was a long time ago, not likely to be repeated, and thinking about it was like clapping with one hand—not working and wasting a lot of energy.

Pulling her keys from her pocket, she climbed the brick steps to her apartment and unlocked the door to . . . to furniture upended, drawers dumped. Storybook eating hamburger and fries off a McDonald's bag, happy as a pig in mud. Miss Ellie tied to a kitchen chair, a big rope looped around her middle, broken arm and all. One of Churchill's new floral tea towels was stuffed in her mouth as a gag.

And Cal Davis was nowhere in sight. Where in holy hell had that man gone? He was right behind her a minute ago. Men! Were they ever around when you needed them?

She ran to Miss Ellie and pulled the towel from her mouth. "What happened? Are you okay?" She unwound the rope.

Miss Ellie looked frazzled but her voice was strong. "First I get my arm broken and then a man with a crooked nose breaks into your house, ties me up, and has the nerve to say I got ugly legs. Bad enough I got robbed but now I have to get insulted too, except he did apologize for the tying up part. Said he had to find that key and getting my arm broken was an accident."

"A crook with manners? Well, it is the South." Churchill looked down at Miss Ellie's doorknob kneecaps below neon green shorts. "You have great legs."

"Get me where I need to go. Now do you believe something's going on with Cal?"

"Cal? How does he figure into this?"

"Ugly Nose wanted the key I was flashing around the other night. I told him I didn't have it anymore. It was bad luck since I got my arm hurt so I threw that key in the Savannah River."

"Did you?"

Miss Ellie laughed—the one that was more cackle than humor. She reached under her T-shirt with a picture of a fish and the words KEEP YOUR MOUTH SHUT AND YOU WON'T GET CAUGHT and pulled out the key. "Had it between my boobies. Figured if I had to give it up least I'd get a quick feel out of the deal. What is with this here key? Something's sure going on. You got to see that now, honey, and you got to find out what it's all about."

"I'll ask Cal about it when he shows up. He was right behind me." Churchill went to the window and looked down at the street. "Good grief, someone stole Cal's Mustang and he's chasing it down the street."

"I declare nothing's safe in this city anymore. What's this world coming to?"

His lungs on fire, Cal ran flat out toward his retreating Mustang. The kid from the library was driving and had on Cal's Speedway hat that he'd set on the check-out desk beside his keys. The keys he'd forgotten to pick up because being near Churchill had turned his brain to motor oil.

Cal tore across the street, dodging a pickup and a honking VW. The Mustang got boxed in behind a delivery truck, a taxi, and a Land Rover giving Cal a chance to catch up. He jumped over the side of the car and into the passenger seat landing hard. He wasn't twenty anymore. Grabbing the keys, he turned off the car yelling, "What the hell are you doing? If you're going to steal a car at least know how to drive the damn thing!"

The kid didn't look at him but heaved a big sigh as he banged his forehead against the top of the steering wheel. "I can't even steal a car right. I can't do anything right." He held up his hand giving the *L* sign with his fingers. "I'm nothing but a loser."

Resisting the urge to strangle, Cal realized the kid was about his age when he'd had the same *L* feeling. Except it wasn't over driving a car—hell, he'd always been able to drive—but over *Wuthering Heights* and a book report with another D to add to a long list of the same grade in other subjects. He'd never been able to read worth a damn.

Cal waved the taxi around. "It's a sixties clutch on this car. It grabs in one spot and doesn't ease into gear like the new ones. The gears synchronize different. It takes practice to make it work. You have to keep an eye on the tack then make the shift."

The kid turned to face him, his eyes widening. "You're not going to break my face or something?"

"Believe me, it crossed my mind. You're tearing up the gears, dog rings, and syncro rings. I have to pull the whole damn engine to replace them. Now get the hell out of my car and go away."

"You're not going to call the cops?"

That didn't cross Cal's mind. "Not unless you insist." The kid smiled slowly, like he hadn't done it in a while and needed to get those muscles working again. "We're tying up traffic, kid."

"What if I wash your car and you teach me that clutch thing? Is it something special?"

"What if you get lost and we forget this happened. Gee, is that a cop car I see up ahead?"

"Cop? Holy crap, not the cops. Anything but the cops." Cal could relate to that part, too.

The kid pushed hard at the door, jumped out before it opened all the way, then ran across the street as if the devil himself did the chasing.

He climbed over the console, started the car, and moved the Mustang back to the curb. He switched off the engine, and pocketed the keys. How could he forget his damn keys? Was he out of him mind? Then he considered Churchill this morning, her navy skirt over nice slim hips, her crisp white blouse and all he could think about was messing her up! Undoing her hair, unbuttoning her blouse, sliding off her skirt and . . . No! No undoing or unbuttoning or sliding . . . definitely no sliding of anything, especially by him, anywhere.

His plan was to get to town this morning, get Miss Ellie, and get the hell away from Ace McKenzie before she asked any more questions. That's what he intended to do right now. When he was around her he didn't think straight, proven by the forgotten keys.

Cal walked back and took the brick steps two at a time to the apartment. He knocked, then opened the door as a black cast-iron frying pan came straight at him. His quick driving reflexes saved his not perfect nose from being considerably less perfect. He ducked, the pan whizzed over his head, and he caught Churchill around the waist before she fell over from the two-handed swing. He set her upright, her eyes huge. "Why the hell are you trying to kill me?"

"I'm trying to protect myself and your grandmother from more intruders and thought you were one of them." Who was going to protect him from Churchill nestled nicely in his arms? He wanted her so damn bad he hurt. He took a step back and sucked in a deep calming breath.

"Ace, intruders don't knock. What happened here? Unless this is a sample of your housekeeping."

Her brow narrowed, she held up the pan. "This time I won't miss and where the heck have you been?"

"Someone wanted my car and I needed to talk him out of it."

Miss Ellie sat at the kitchen table sipping something from a tea cup that Cal was willing to bet wasn't Earl Grey. "Someone came looking for that darn key again."

He pulled over a chair and sat down next to his grandmother. "Are you okay?"

"A man with a squashed face tied me up." Miss Ellie took another sip. "Least it looked all squashed under that there stocking mask he wore. Can you imagine putting a stocking over your head? Must be queen size for it to stretch that far. I bet it's real uncomfortable. Don't like those things on my legs much less on my face. He had a really big head but I have to say he was downright polite. Did manage to say please and thank you."

"Tied you up?" Cal studied the dog's head resting on his thigh, tail wagging, McDonald's QuarterPounder breath.

"But he didn't get what he was after," Miss Ellie continued. She tapped the brass key on the table. "I was flashing it around the other night at bars and restaurants and the bingos. Those gray-hairs at the bingos know everything, you see. I was asking questions when I got my arm broke and my purse stolen. Since I live on social security and my winnings from my bookie it sure wasn't money they were after." She picked the key off the table, sunlight slicing into the apartment turning it more gold than brass. "This is what's causing all the commotion all right." She looked at Cal. "Any guess why someone would want it?"

"Not a clue." He hoped he sounded more convincing than he felt. The key wasn't his but he had an idea who it belonged to. Cal stood to add some stern to what he was going to say. "You need to stay with Mom and Dad till this straightens out. They're due back from California soon.

Wright Square is pretty this time of year. You can have your own room and take walks there and—"

"And I'll have to listen to that NPR stuff they play all day long, bunch of commie liberals if you're asking me. That's what happens when you teach college and don't live in the real world. Not a chance. I can't live with them. Shame to say that my own son gives me hives. I've got Matilda at my place and I figure we'll be fine and dandy together now that I know to keep an eye out."

"Matilda Langford as in a housekeeper?" Cal said, knowing in his gut the answer wasn't so simple as that, but hoping for the best.

"Matilda Smith and Wesson as in what your granddaddy left me to shoot gaters that might find their way into the house. Dang it all if I haven't got some gaters now, after all these years."

Churchill rolled her eyes, looked faint, and smacked her palm against her forehead. Cal felt like doing the same. He said to Miss Ellie, "I'm taking you to my place out at the speedway. Silky Callahan owns the speedway. You remember Silky. Tall, good-looking, makes the best martinis in Savannah. Granddad used to race his Falcon at Silky's speedway. I think there's still a trophy out at that old cabin on Whitemarsh."

Her thin lips got thinner but there was a new twinkle in her eyes. "He pulled my pigtail and shoved me off my bicycle."

"That was seventy years ago. Maybe you can get him to apologize."

Miss Ellie fluffed her hair. "Guess I could give him a tumble. Make him happy in his old age. We younger women can do that, you know. He was a year ahead of me in school. I just bought myself some of that JLo perfume on that shopping network. Poor man won't stand a chance against that.

Melt him into a big old blob right there on his own speedway. I guess that could be fun for a while."

"Right, a blob. No doubt about it. We'll help Churchill
pick up this mess and then head on out—"

"I'll take care of it all. It's my place," Churchill added in
a rush as she walked by the table then stood at the door
holding it open. "You just hurry on and leave now. You
better get going. Take care of Miss Ellie and Matilda and
get them both out of town and settled."

He studied Churchill for a second across the mess.
"Thanks for your help, Ace." He'd nicknamed her that
years ago because she aced her way though high school,
but her brain power didn't stop at the classroom door like
a lot of smart people—like his brother. Tripp was all book-
brains and no street-brains. Ace McKenzie could connect
the dots in both worlds and right now that wasn't a good
thing.

It took longer than Cal thought to pack Miss Ellie's
bags and get her to his place. How many pairs of shoes did
an eighty-year-old woman need? And hats? What was
with hats and matching purses? And makeup? Silky Callahan had no idea what was coming his way.

Cal's cabin wasn't big but he'd fixed it up when he got
out of Costal State Prison and bought half of Savannah
Speedway from Silky. It was cedar and stone and probably
built as someone's fishing shack. It sat behind a stand of
pines removing it from the hustle of the racing cars and
crowd but close enough that he could walk to work at the
track and his garage next to the speedway.

The side porch overlooked the marshes with views of
sea oats, cranes, gulls, and the finest sunrises in Georgia.
After three years of concrete, bars, and metal he had new
appreciation. The upside of going to prison was you didn't
take things for granted. God knows there weren't many

upsides. He absently rubbed the scar on his chin that had taken twenty stitches to close. There were a lot of downsides.

Miss Ellie settled her things in the small guest bedroom. "I'm going to need an extra closet for my shoes and hats."

"There's one in the hall you can have. Next to my fishing gear."

"Not exactly what I had in mind."

After cranking up the AC he found some old movie Tom Cruise made in the good years and then warmed up the baked chicken, no skin and organic-grown peas and corn he'd cooked the night before. He kissed her on the top of her head. "I'll tell Silky you're here. He'll keep an eye on you."

"I'm counting on it. I'm armed and dangerous, boy, and we're not talking Matilda here." He started to walk off but she didn't let go of his hand, holding tighter, her expression sobering. "I don't rightly know why you went to prison. I'm not believing for a minute you're guilty for stealing money aimed for old folks so you can save your breath on that score. All I do know is you're here now, this key shows up, and stuff starts happening all over the place. There's a connection. I think you know what it is and for some reason you're keeping it all to yourself."

Cal got down on one knee in front of his grandmother. "I don't know anything, Miss Ellie. Whoever wants the damn key can have it. I've done my time. It's over with."

"But it's not over with, don't you see? Your reputation is ruined, Cal. Around here you're public enemy number one and I hate that."

He chuckled. "My reputation wasn't all that great in the first place, Miss Ellie. You and Silky are the only ones who ever had any good thoughts about me."

She looked at him hard as if considering something. "Now that's where you're wrong. There's someone else out there, someone a whole lot prettier and smart as a whip. She's always been that way, understands things others just don't get, like when some English teacher went and gave you poor grades when she should have been asking why you were having problems in the first place. As I remember hearing it that teacher said something about you being a dumb grease monkey and Churchill said something like . . . let me see now how did that go . . . stupid ignorant bitch."

"Churchill McKenzie called Miss Davenport—"

"And the school didn't like it one bit. It meant bye-bye Georgetown scholarship and hello Georgia State and student loans." Miss Ellie patted Cal's cheek. "See there. Just when you thought you had everything all figured out up pops the devil and you realize you don't know squat about a certain gal. I didn't see a reason to tell you before but now our little librarian's back and you're back and you need to know. You two have a connection."

"Had a connection."

"Not exactly. She took the key when she shooed us out of her place right quick today. I don't mind if she has it. She'll go snooping around like she always does and maybe come up with something new and set things right. Problem is if someone realizes she has the thing they could go after her too, just like they did me." Miss Ellie gave a sly grin. "So I guess you better go see what she's up to even if you don't have a mind to."

Cal stood and folded his arms. "You sure you just didn't give her that blasted key so I'd have to get involved like you want me to?"

"No, but it's a damn good idea now that you mention it. Sorry I didn't think of it myself."

Cal kissed Miss Ellie on the forehead then left, the last of the evening sun dropping behind the pines. Churchill had no idea what she was getting mixed up in . . . again. Another big shit storm headed right her way if he didn't stop it. Well hell. It was back to town, to Churchill, and the key. Damn the key! Why was she getting mixed up in it? Didn't she turn down Miss Ellie in the first place? Why didn't she just keep it that way and butt out?

He got in the Mustang and fired the engine. A few drivers at the Speedway did practice laps around the oval. The whine of the engines and squeal of the tires on dirt sounded like soul music. At least to him. At night in prison he'd close his eyes tight and try to remember those sounds and smells. It's what kept him sane. That Yankee Candle place needed to make a scent called Speedway. He'd buy it and so would every other car junkie out there.

He headed into town. The salt air whipped through his hair, the moon hung way out in the ocean as the Mustang growled along the highway, gobbling up the miles, the sound of heavy American metal. Nothing else like it anywhere. He loved cars, the driving, the independence, the connection between man and machine. Like Silky said, when he cut himself he bled motor oil.

Slowing down at the city limit Cal threaded his way around Johnson then Wright Square. Folks brave enough to venture into the Savannah muggy evening strolled about. Cal pulled to the curb in front of the library chasing a troop of black palmetto bugs to the bushes. There was a light in the front window of Churchill's apartment but there was also a light on in the back part of the library.

Ace McKenzie, resident ancient history librarian, was hard at work researching a very unusual key. Cal had no idea what the damn thing was all about but it was something important or people wouldn't be trying so hard to steal it. Miss Ellie found it in the Mustang. He didn't put it there but someone did—like the other person who drove the car the night Cal got arrested. That's why he'd get the damn key back and get rid of it.

But how was he going to get it? Maybe if he distracted

Ace, got her to think about something besides the key he could swipe it right out from under her. Under her? His heart gave a hard pound and his mouth went instantly dry. *Under Churchill* was a great place to be, a place he wanted to be instead of standing on the sidewalk thinking about her. Damn, he was distracted already and hard as concrete.

Walking slowly because at the moment it hurt like hell to walk fast—and why were those damn jeans always so small in the crotch?—he hobbled past the ivy planters, azaleas, and two big magnolias to the rear window, light spilling onto the grass and bushes. Churchill sat at a desk, a yellow ribbon around her neck, the key cradled between her breasts. He envied the damn key.

Piles of books, some leather bound with worn corners, some with frayed edges, sat on the desk along with a can of Mountain Dew and a bag of chips. She turned pages, then studied the key, looking happy, content, and focused, the way he probably looked when changing spark plugs, minus the pop and chips. He'd been watching her since high school, not in a creepy stalker way but a you-are-amazing kind of way. She read everything, always had her nose in a book, and didn't care diddly that the other kids called her a geek. He couldn't imagine the smartest girl in school having anything to do with the dumbest boy so he never got close . . . except for that time he changed her tire and she was so damn grateful she kissed him . . . and he kissed her back. Best damn thing that happened to him in high school.

The dog lay sprawled out next to the desk; if a dog could snore he was. Cal raised his hand to rap on the glass then stopped, a hot breath on his neck, a warm body right behind him. An *oh shit* moment, especially if it was the cops.

"What are you doing here?" came a voice. Cal turned.

It was that kid who tried to steal his car. There was a lot of stealing going on around there. Cal put his hand over the kid's mouth to keep him quiet, then pushed him between the magnolias out of sight of the window and the street.

"The library's closed, dude," the kid mumbled under Cal's hand.

Cal put his finger to his lips in *shhh* fashion then let the kid go. He whispered, "Why are you looking at Miss Churchill through the window? Got a thing for the library . . . or the librarian?"

"Someone broke into her apartment earlier and I wanted to make sure she's safe."

"You could ask her, you know. Knocking on the front door might work."

"She won't like it that I think she can't take care of herself."

A big smile rippled across the kid's face. "Well dang. I guess she'd get all mad at you and stuff if she knew you were out here checking up on her now. But don't you go and worry none, I won't rat you out 'cause you didn't rat me out. That seems real fair but there's a catch. You got to teach me to drive your car."

"Uh . . . What?"

"And give me a job so I don't get sent to military school. That's a good deal, don't you think?"

"I think you belong in military school."

"Is that any way to treat a new employee? Look, I'm desperate here. I'm not military school material. I'm race driver material. I got hot hands." He made like gripping a steering wheel and did some motor sounds. "I'm good at it, been driving the midgets since I was ten. My granddad took me out to the speedway till he passed on. My dad never did because he's not into racing. I know you're a good driver, probably the best around these parts. That's what everybody says. I've been asking about you because you let me go and all. That's not the normal thing to do."

"Then you know I'm nothing but trouble and you should keep your distance."

"You're the man behind the wheel! I want to be the man behind the wheel! I can *be* the man behind the wheel if you teach me how. I'm a gunner."

"You're a kid and you're a pain in the ass." Just like Cal was. Then his parents sent him to one of those bootcamps out west that was a lot more boot than camp.

"You teach me to drive and I won't be dragging on Abercorn."

"Or over on Pooler or Hwy 80. Did you have nitrous oxide tanks?"

"Couldn't afford it. Don't have a job."

Thank God. Cal knew first hand that using oxide was like getting shot out of a damn cannon. "Get yourself out to the speedway tomorrow. Wear dirty clothes because they're going to get dirtier. Make sure you clear it with your parents and if you even think about ditching school this fall with ideas of working the speedway full time you're done. You'll be working for Silky Callahan. Throwing my name around will get you nothing but grief. We just hired Daisy-Lou, a spit-fire of a gal to help out at the concession stand. Keep your eyes off her and on your work. Understand?"

The kid grabbed Cal's hand and shook it hard, pumping it up and down. "I'm a good worker, you'll see. You won't be sorry, I swear."

"Now get out of here."

"You coming?"

Like he had a choice? The key would have to wait till tomorrow. "Yeah, everything's peachy here. I'm right behind you." He watched the kid sprint across the street and realized he didn't even know his name, not that it mattered.

With a little luck there'd be one less kid wrapping himself around some phone pole. Cal took one more look at Churchill, a few wisps of auburn hair escaping from the rest held in place with the yellow number two pencil. Watching her was a piss-poor substitute for going inside and taking her right there on one of the old cypress library tables. Staying away from her was a hell of a price to pay for keeping his damn secret, maybe even worse than prison. But he had to do that, and get the damn key back.

Chapter Three

At nine sharp Michelle unlocked the library doors. The James Oglethorpe Founding Fathers Library was open for business. Finishing off the last drop of morning double espresso she sat down on one of the little wooden chairs with a beehive on the back and began pinning pictures the kids drew of Storybook, to the low bulletin board in the children's section. It had been one of those worry-yourself-into-a-stupor-over-TJ nights with no sleep.

"You know," she said over her shoulder to Churchill working at the end of the checkout desk, "This dog has single handedly, or is that single paw-edly, increased the attendance at story time by seventy-five percent and it's carried over to circulation, too. Kids are checking out books by the armful, most of them about dogs."

Storybook, aka Checkbook until they renamed him, wagged his tail and gave her a sloppy dog lick as if he knew exactly what she said and appreciated the compliment. Trying to explain to kids what a checkbook was hadn't worked and Storybook fit perfectly. Lumbering across the hardwood floor he made his way to his personalized blanket in the children's section, plopped down and fell asleep. It was a strenuous day in the life of the canine. If reincarnation was for real, Michelle wanted to come back as this dog.

"Mom," came TJ's voice from the doorway as he plowed through the double doors. "I have news."

Michelle's blood turned to ice and she felt faint. Her heart hammered in her chest that was now a fashionable thirty-six B instead of an overzealous forty-two D. "You were supposed to be at your grandmother's house last night, TJ, to help cut her grass. If you got caught drag racing again this morning or you wrecked a car I'm driving you to that blasted military school myself. And I will not be sending you cookies, you hear me!"

TJ grinned, looking happier than she'd seen him in years. "I got a job."

"You're smiling because you have to work? You never smile over work. You pout and sulk and make excuses and your grandmother probably had to cut her own grass." Michelle narrowed her brows. "What kind of happy pills did you take? Are you on dope? I bet you're on dope. I'm calling the paramedics right now and having your stomach pumped and—"

"I'm working at . . . a car parts place. Automotive supply. You know I love cars. This is all about cars and I get paid. I cut Grandma's grass early this morning and even did the trimming. I was up at six."

He'd promised before, lied before. She'd gotten her hopes up many, many times before. Michelle gave TJ the I'm-not-buying-this-crap-this-time beady eyed look.

"I start the job this afternoon, I swear. I just got back from my algebra class. I got a C- on a test but that's still a C. I asked my teacher if I can do makeup work for the classes I've missed and she said yes. Go ahead, call her. It's the truth, cross my heart and hope to die."

"Okay, what have you done with my son, the lazy one, the one making me gray before I'm forty? Did he get beamed up into a mother ship somewhere and I got you here with me instead?" She tried a little smile just to see how it felt and it felt great. But was it warranted? That was the big question. "I think I'll keep you. They can have the old TJ. Lordy, Lordy, I wonder if they know what they're in for."

"So, can you get Dad to drop the military school thing? I got a job, I'm passing, and I helped Grandma. I'm on a roll, here."

"I might persuade him to postpone the school. But if the other TJ is suddenly beamed back down he's going off to that school for sure." Michelle studied her son. "What in the world happened in one night? Is there a magic wand somewhere I don't know about?"

"Well you see there's this guy, Mom, who has this hot car and a thing for this lady. I helped him out of a jam so he got me a job. It's good. It is, I swear. The job's got real potential about stuff I love." TJ kissed her cheek and ran toward the library door nearly colliding into the black iron spiral stairs and yelling over his shoulder, "See you at supper time."

Churchill took one of the children's chairs beside Michelle. "The other night I caught Dodd on cable TV preaching that the age of miracles is not dead. I don't particularly like that man one bit but he got the miracle thing right. Yesterday Tommy dragged TJ in here by the scruff of his neck, threatening him with Alcatraz and Devil's Island and today we get this."

"I know." Michelle let what just happened sink in, then clapped her hands together and jumped up. "Heavenly days, if this don't beat all. My son who has been nothing but a wart on my behind since he turned fourteen has a job and is passing algebra. I can't believe I just said that. I wasn't sure if he could spell algebra. I have to say that you are looking at the happiest mama in Savannah right now." She hummed off key and didn't care as she danced around the library tables with their funny legs, the stained glass overhead catching the morning sun shining rainbows of colors over the floor. She twirled around the computer stand and the little carved beehive tables in the children's section doing some salsa steps she learned, shaking her backside, and wiggling her hips till—

A man with slicked back hair wearing baggy black slacks, a wrinkled white shirt, and pointy leather shoes snagged her at the waist. He hummed *on* key and spun her around right there between the chapter books and video games. He dipped her back over his arm like some TV dancing star then brought her up fast, her face to his face that really needed a shave. He smelled like used car and peppermint chewing gum, but he sure could dance. He did some fast little steps, twirling her in circles, her new peasant skirt swishing around her legs. Then he whipped her back into his arms that were stronger than she expected and she looked into his eyes—intense black with sparks of passion that made her catch her breath. He said, "So, Miss Librarian, how'd you get to be a terrific dancer?"

"Eight months of Salsa Sweat and Slim."

"I worked across the street from an Arthur Murray dance studio and watched all that twirling and stuff. Guess some of it stuck."

"Benny?" Churchill yelped. "Oh my goodness! I can't believe it's really you." Churchill ran across the library just as Reverend Dodd, in all his white suit glory and toting his ever present Bible, came in the front door. "Morning, ladies. The Lord sure has given us a mighty fine day here in Savannah, don't you agree? And good morning to you too, sir." Dodd nodded to Benny. "Are you from these parts? Don't believe I've had the pleasure."

"A friend of the family," Churchill rushed in. "He knows my mama, met her on one of her travels up east. Just passing through." Churchill handed Dodd a newspaper but he shook his head.

"Not today, my dear, not today. I'm here on the Lord's

mission. I'm here to find some information on helping the elderly and how to best meet their needs. Seems we have a lot of poor, older folks out there these days who thought they had enough money saved to see them into their later years, but it just isn't working out for them, bless their hearts. I hear Miss Ellie was hurt the other evening. How is she doing? Is she staying with you?"

"The books would be in finances and economics up on the balcony level. Arts and architecture are to the back so don't go that far." Churchill pointed to the spiral staircase by the front door. "As for Miss Ellie, she was staying with me but now she's with Cal out at the speedway. It's safer for her out there."

"Of course it is." Dodd smiled, then took the wrought iron stair. Churchill waited till he got to the top then stage whispered to Benny because the open center of the library let voices carry. "Whatever are you doing here?"

"I finished testify—"

Churchill flattened her hand over his mouth waiting for Dodd's footsteps to fade further into the library. She let go and asked, "Why did you show up on our doorstep?"

"I came looking for Checkbook."

"If you're not quiet, half the population of Savannah will know you're here. I don't think that's what you want since you're obviously on the run."

Michelle had no idea why her dance partner . . . Benny? . . . needed to keep a low profile, but what she did understand was that when he let her go she missed his arms around her more than she thought she would.

The guy jammed his hands in his pockets. He smiled at Storybook and Michelle realized she liked it when he smiled at her that way, too. He had one of those good smiles, the kind that went clear through to his eyes and said he actually cared. He gave a soft whistle. "Come here, boy. Come here, Checkbook."

Storybook pried open one sleepy eye then the other, then jumped up and galloped to Benny. His front paws landed on Benny's chest and he slurped his face, a reunion of man and beast. Both looked happy, but—

"Wait," Michelle said. "You're here to take Storybook?"

"Who's Storybook?" Benny managed between slurps and pats and hugs.

"This dog is and you can't have him. He's ours . . . the kids' . . . the library's. He's the children's hero since he found Jannie Brooks down by the river and guided her home when everyone feared she'd been kidnapped or drowned. Storybook lets the toddlers ride him around the library and the kids curl up with him and read to him. I think he's literate. He belongs here."

Benny scratched Checkbook behind the ears, a little to center, just where Benny knew he liked it. He'd been a pup when Benny pulled him out of that dumpster behind the Showboat Casino. "This here's a Jurzee dog. He was just visiting, right Church?"

"You shouldn't be here," Churchill whispered, her eyes darting back and forth. "We need to talk."

"I can talk. Sit," he told Checkbook as Church pulled him past some books to the deserted philosophy section on the other side away from the guy in the white suit. Guess not much philosophizing going on in Savannah. Her eyes were big and blue like he remembered but not in a good way. "So, what's the problem?"

"Me? I don't have a problem. I live here. What's wrong is you because you don't live here. You stick out like a neon sign," she said in a whisper that wanted to be more of a yell. "Have you lost your mind showing up like this?"

"I came for my dog."

"We could have met somewhere other than here and I could have handed him over."

"Yeah, but I'm glad I came. I gotta tell you that Michelle

is fine by me. I like the way she dances and her looks are okay, too. You know what I mean? I like a woman with some substance about her, something to hold on to."

"For heaven's sake, will you forget dancing with Michelle? Benny, look at me. You turned state's evidence, remember? You're the accountant who testified against the Jersey boys for money laundering and carjacking. Carlos is in the big house doing ten to twenty because of you. Pinstripes one and two are not happy campers that Pinstripe three is not having dinner at the family table tonight."

"Testifying seemed like a good idea at the time."

"It was a great idea. I came around asking questions about my Chevy and you realized there were two sets of books for Big City Auto Shop, meaning you're not the one doing ten to twenty. But now you've got to get lost, seriously lost. Am I making myself clear here?"

"Did you just speak Jerzee to me?" He grinned. "This here's a nice town, Church, I'm telling you. I see why you came back. Maybe I can set up a bookkeeping place of my own. Do some taxes, a few trusts, know what I mean? I could sell that. I could do some fitting in around here."

"Fit in? Benny, the first time you ask for a *cuppa cawfee* and a *baygal* the jig's up. The pinstripe duo will be looking for you. Once they know I have Checkbook they'll pay a visit and there you'll be. Everyone will say, 'Gee there's someone else here who talks funny just like you. That guy right over there doing our taxes,' and they'll be pointing to you and . . .you want to get killed?"

"K-killed?" Michelle stammered as she came up behind Churchill and stopped in her tracks. "Who's going to get killed? Well that's just plain terrible. What's this city coming to anyway?"

"Killed with kindness," Churchill said with a forced smile, trying to cover up their conversation. "That's what I'm trying to talk Benny into doing, killing us all with kindness by leaving Storybook here at the library and moving on. But that's not fair to him. Checkbook is his dog."

"But the kids will be heartbroken all to pieces and then some," Michelle whined. "Whatever do we tell them?"

Churchill bit at her bottom lip. "That Storybook had to go and help some other people. That he was on loan to us for a while. Benny has plans, places to go, people to see far, far away. Right, Benny?" Behind Michelle, Church did a shooting gun with her fingers then blew the make-believe smoke from the end to get her point across. And she was right. He didn't fit the Colonel Sanders image.

"I'm headed out of here, going far away. I got mixed up with some bad people in Jersey and I got to get going. It's not healthy for me to be here or for anyone I'm associated with. I can't be staying in one place too long. You get my drift?"

"Good, that's settled," Church said in a rush not giving him time to change his mind. He couldn't change his mind if he intended to keep on breathing. "I'll get Storybook's leash." She walked away but Michelle stayed behind, looking at him, her eyes getting a little misty.

"You're going to really miss my dog, aren't you?"

"My, yes. I truly am. We all are around here." Then she blushed.

He couldn't remember the last time he saw a woman do that for real.

"And we, you and me, were a mighty fine dance couple there for a few minutes. I never did dance much before except for exercising. Then you showed up here. It sure was fun while it lasted even if it was just for one little old dance in a library."

She gave him a smile that flipped his insides. She did it for real and not because she wanted something from him. Not her taxes done for free, not advice on how to hide Uncle Guido's money stash from the Feds, not how to get out of probate, nor screw cousin Larry out of his share of the estate. It was just a smile for a short, dumpy, not-so-handsome bean counter from Jersey.

He smiled back. He hadn't been doing much of that lately. "I had a real good time too, Michelle from Savannah. It's been a pleasure to meet you." He gave her a kiss on the cheek, then walked off to the front of the library. Churchill handed him the leash, Checkbook attached to the other end. "I gotta tell you, he's not looking too happy about all this. And neither are you." Church sniffed and Michelle came up beside her, tears in her eyes. He said, "I want to thank you both for taking real good care of Checkbook here. I appreciate it."

Michelle knelt down. "You be a good dog, now, okay?" She kissed Checkbook on the nose and scratched behind his ears a little to the center.

Church handed Benny a baggie of dog biscuits. "A few for the road. You did the right thing. It'll all work out." She handed him a paper and whispered, "This is the number of a library friend of mine in L.A. A big city's easy to get lost in. Savannah's like a goldfish bowl."

Michelle added, "Good luck."

Benny started for the door. Checkbook hesitated, looking back from Michelle to Church to his blanket. Head bent low and tail dragging he shuffled out the double doors into the Savannah heat, the library door closing behind them. Checkbook glanced up at Benny. "Don't look at me like that. What am I gonna do? I can't stay."

Checkbook licked Benny's hand.

"Did you have to go and do that?" Benny opened the library door. "You take care of yourself now." He beefed up his Jurzee speak just for Checkbook. "And you take care of those two good-looking broads in there. Don't tell 'em I called 'em broads 'cause they ain't going to like it none. Keep up on the reading. I hear that Harry Potter stuff is decent."

Benny closed the door behind Checkbook and walked on down Bull Street, Jurzee tough-guy attitude in place like always but inside feeling more alone than he had in his whole fucked up life.

Michelle clipped on Storybook's leash yelling to TJ in his room, "Are you finished with your algebra homework?"

TJ opened the door, looking tired to the bone, a new look for Mr. Sleep Till Noon. He grinned. "That other TJ, the old one, the one that got beamed up to the mother ship is still MIA. Low and behold, the new TJ did the supper dishes and his homework. The least I could do since somehow you went and talked Daddy into not sending me away." He studied her for a minute with eyes that looked a bit older. "So, how did you do that? How'd you get Dad to agree to give me another chance? I've had more than my share and messed them up plenty."

Michelle gave a little shrug. "I told him you were trying hard to make things right this time around, getting the job on your own and doing good in school. Your daddy's coming here for supper once a week from now on so we can all be together and talk things out. He can see how you're doing for himself."

"You bribed him with fried chicken?"

"And pecan pie and potato salad with bacon and hard-boiled eggs on top."

TJ grinned then sobered. "You're not thinking about trying to get back together with him are you, Mama? He lied to you, cheated on you, made you cry, a lot. Nothing's worth that, not even military school."

She patted TJ's cheek that was starting to need a shave from time to time. "Don't you go worrying yourself. Things change, people change just like you're doing and maybe your daddy's changing his ways, too. I've been thinking about it, your dad and I reconciling, and I want us to be a family, TJ. I want you to do well and if your daddy and I are both there for you that would be a good thing, wouldn't it? We've had our time apart and we've grown. He looks at me different lately, like today when we met up for coffee. I told him what you were doing. He was better."

"Because you look hot and you're doing well. You have a nice job and lots of friends. Everybody likes you, Mom. I want what's best for you." TJ's eyes weren't the only thing older, his brain and his heart were catching up.

"And I want what's best for you. You're my son, the most important person in my life. You seem to be at a good place right now, Lord be praised. Who could have thought an auto supply store could do all that? So now, where exactly is this here store?"

"Uh, out off of HWY 80." He looked at Storybook. "Dog sitting?"

"Churchill's working late at the library on something and asked me to walk Storybook for her." Michelle grinned at her son and it sure felt good after months and months of yelling, threatening and pleading. "Don't be cranking Keith Urban too loud while I'm gone. The neighbors will throw a hissy." She winked then closed the door of the yellow and white clapboard two-family house she bought after the divorce. It was a good purchase, helped pay the bills, and gave her and TJ a nice place to live. It was where she could be on her own. And being on her own was fine indeed. No more wondering when and if Tommy would come home or who's bed he was frequenting. But TJ was doing right-well and if she and Tommy could get back together to help him, she would do that. Tommy did seem better, a little. She had to take the chance for TJ.

As she walked Storybook the humidity closed in around her like an old August friend. Some hated it to pieces but to Michelle the weather was as much a part of Savannah as the azaleas in March, the magnolias in May, the no-see-ums in July. In August the city slowed, people sat a spell longer, chatted with their neighbors and savored their sweet tea on the back veranda with fireflies lighting up the bushes. If people wanted different than that they needed to move themselves to Chicago because Savannah was the South just as it always had been and with luck would continue right on.

The dim lights of Forsythe Park blinked on as she cut across Gaston Street and took the path that led around the big white tiered fountain. She spotted Reverend Dodd across the park with an elderly couple out for an evening stroll. Maybe some of the stuff he found in the books he checked out from the library would help. She didn't like the guy very much but he did have a way with the elderly. He seemed to be there for them when a spouse got sick or died and helped to set up their finances with the banks. It was one of the reasons Cal Davis was on everyone's shit list around there. He stole money Dodd had collected for the folks who were finding their social security checks stretched to the limit. On the Savannah popularity scale that put Cal one step below an IRS agent but still above politicians.

A band played in the gazebo. People sitting on the grass listened, a few danced on the concrete patio in front. She'd had her one time fling at impromptu dancing that day, probably for lots and lots of days. Tommy hated to dance.

Storybook plodded along looking just plain sad. "It's going to be okay," she soothed as they walked. "You'll get lots of love and attention from the kids and Churchill and me." But her words didn't seem to matter as Storybook slowed even more, then stopped all together and lay down right in the middle of the sidewalk.

"Come on, baby. Get up. Benny was good. He was great actually, but now he's gone and you still have all of us at the library." Michelle felt sad too, had been all day and not just because Storybook missed Benny but because she did, too. She liked him. She liked the way he danced for sure, and the way he smiled, and that he came all the way to Savannah to get his dog only to give Storybook back to the kids. She didn't know what business dealings he had in Jersey that got him into trouble but he sure was an okay guy in her book.

Storybook glanced up, his droopy brown eyes enough to break her heart. She felt guilty taking him away from his owner. And there was Benny to consider. He had to be hurting. Sitting down on the sidewalk beside Storybook she didn't care that the other strollers had to walk around them. She patted his paw and he rested his big head in her lap. "Come on now, things aren't so bad. The kids come in the library tomorrow for story hour and you like story hour. I'm reading *We're Going on a Bear Hunt*. There's a dog in it, a cute one with spots." She took out a dog cookie but Storybook wasn't interested. He should be since he hadn't touched his supper. She had even tried slipping him part of her chicken and she knew TJ did, too. Still he hadn't eaten. "I'll tell you what else. Come September we'll do story hours in all the schools and you can come along. I'll get you a new bandana to wear around your neck. What do you say? Won't that be fun?"

"If I get to sit next to the cute poodle with those pink bows, I'm in."

Michelle looked up to see Benny giving her that smile that lit up the world, at least her part of it. She hadn't realized just how much. She smiled back suddenly feeling much better than she did a moment ago. "Well my goodness, what are you doing here?"

Storybook sprang up, his eyes bright. He did the paw on the shoulders thing to Benny complete with messy slurps. Michelle stood and dusted herself off. "I have to say that's the happiest I've seen that dog since you left." She let out a sigh. "So what are we going to do about this? The situation is no good at all, Benny. We've got ourselves one dog that needs to be in two places and he's not going to be happy unless he is."

Storybook got down and jumped around yapping and playing. Michelle gave him the cookie he wouldn't eat before and he scarffed it down.

Benny said, "I'm out of here tomorrow morning. Checkbook will make an adjustment. He'll get used to the idea he's under new management. It will take some time but I'm telling you it'll happen. No big deal. It'll work. No long faces."

"I can't help it. It's just too sad."

"Can't stand seeing you sad, dollface." He winked. "You are a dollface, you know." Then he slid his arm around her waist and suddenly they were waltzing to some Strauss the band struck up. They circled the fountain with moonbeams dancing in the water, then waltzed into the trees, the fireflies lighting their way. They skirted the rose garden, the swing set, the red curvy slide, the sandbox. Storybook followed along jumping and turning in circles till the music ended with Michelle locked in Benny's arms. Both of them were breathless and happy, his dark eyes gazing down at her, a bit of waltz magic in the air. It was heaven, pure complete heaven.

"Bet you had your share of partners for those high school proms," Benny panted as out of breath as she. "You are some dancer."

"No proms for someone size double X."

"Girls didn't flock to crater-face kid either. Acne's a real turn off. But I have to tell you, I sure had a great time dancing with you here tonight. It more than makes up for all those dances I missed."

She gazed into his eyes smiling down at her. "Me too, Benny. Me too."

Her heart squeezed tight. As many times as it had been broken with no dates and mean cracks about her weight, that beautiful night in August made up for it all. The look on Benny's face told her he felt the same way. "The only thing missing is if I had on a pretty party dress."

"And if I gave you a corsage. And I need a tux. Never had one of those." He kissed her cheek and it felt wonderful. "Maybe next time."

"You're really a great guy, Benny, and I haven't had this much fun in who knows how long. I can't take your dog from you. That's just plain mean on my part. You deserve better."

"What are you talking about?"

"Checkbook's your friend. I can't just rip him out of your life like an old pair of socks. It's not right."

"How do you think I feel? I can't take Checkbook knowing there's a roomful of kiddies crying their eyes out with no Storybook around."

"Well . . . then . . . maybe . . . you should stay. Stay right here in Savannah." She held up her hand to stop his protests that were sure to come and give her brain a second to put some thoughts together that had been brewing since she met up with him. "Now you got to hear me out on this before you go interrupting. I know you said it's too dangerous to be here but what if you were suddenly not here, if you weren't anywhere. Gone. What if Benny just disappeared into thin air? Poof." She blew the tips of her fingers as if blowing dust into the darkness.

"You want to shoot me and throw me in the river, is that it?"

She giggled. "You're thinking Jersey. You need to think Southern. More flimflam and less bang bang. In fact, what I want to do is change you into a Southerner. Think about it. Benny the Southerner will make it so much easier for you to get lost for real."

"S-Southerner? Me? I-I . . . Dollface, I'm a Jerzee guy clear through. Something about a leopard not being able to change his spots. That's me."

"So, we'll paint 'em. I bet I can do it. I'll un-Jerseyfy you. Then you can stay right here in Savannah, we can both have Storybook, and he'll he happy. Keep in mind that if you don't change you'll be Jersey Benny forever. You'll be looking over your shoulder your whole life no matter where you go." Her finger traced a bull's-eye on his forehead to get her point across.

He stroked his chin. "I don't get it. You got me curious. Why would you do this?"

"Well now, that's easy as pie. Guilt." She pulled him down beside her on a wooden bench, Storybook lying across all four of their feet, tail wagging, looking happy. "I'm Baptist, you see, and no one does guilt better than Baptists. Some say Catholic or Jewish are good with the guilt thing but they're dead wrong. Baptist guilt trumps the Catholics and Jews every time. Here I am taking your dog away from you and I desperately need to be giving you something in return. If I don't, I'll be waking up at two in the morning thinking about how I'm going straight to hell for not doing the right thing in paying you back for your kindness. That can be very scary. Just ask any Baptist. So you'd be doing this all for me as much as for yourself."

"Churchill won't approve."

"Sweet man, Churchill won't know. Who's going to tell her? You? Me? Storybook's good with the reading but verbal communication's a showstopper. You'll be another Southern gent walking the street. I keep Storybook a lot of the time and we'll share him."

Benny held out his arms. "Look at me good here. I think she'll know."

"Not if we keep you hidden out of sight till you're ready

to make your debut. Fist we get rid of the black pointy shoes, then we—"

"But I like these shoes. They're Italian. Antonio made them special."

"Yeah, that's the problem. Then we cut your hair and make it fluffy. Southern men have fluffy hair that's a little long and seems to fall right across their forehead when they get active, be that in fighting or loving. Southern men do prefer the loving part unless provoked." Heat crept up her neck and she desperately hoped it was from the hot Southern night and not from thinking about Benny. Before considering which she rushed on, "I'll teach you how to say the rain in Savannah doesn't stay on any old plain but can be a mighty big gully-washer that's downright horrifying. You'll learn to say bless my soul and Lord have mercy and pass the okra and daddy's shotgun."

"Holy crap. That's a lot of Southernisms." Benny made a face.

"Better than don't make me come looking for you, end of story and today is revenge day. I watched the *Sopranos*. I know the talk and I'm telling you right now none of those people are Baptists because they don't have one single guilty bone in all their collective bodies. Amen."

"You're doing a Henry Higgins on me."

"Henrietta Higgins." She laughed. "I am a librarian so you get *Pygmalion* but I promise not to buy you a flower shop or put marbles in your mouth. Instead I'll feed you fried catfish, turnip and collard greens, and cornbread. You can stay at Miss Ellie's. She has a nice place over there on York. She's staying with her grandson right now and flirting with an old flame who pushed her off her bike when she was a kid. Southerners have long memories."

"I hear the Civil War is still a thing around here."

"You mean that there unfortunate Northern Aggression

when we hid our silver, art, and anything else worth a nickel so the damn Yankees wouldn't get their thieving hands on it? We have great-granddaddy's army sword mounted over the hearth as a reminder."

"That's one version of the Civil War, make that the unfortunate War of Northern Aggression, I've never heard before. Guess they left that out of my Jersey history book."

Michelle laughed. "So, how would you feel about a nice white suit?"

"Like a pimp."

"See, that's more Jersey. Think Colonel Sanders, the chicken guy, or Dodd that preacher guy who came into the library when you were there."

"Dollface, I gotta tell you. I'm a lot of things but preacher ain't one of 'em." She laughed at his sarcasm and he laughed too, trying to remember when he enjoyed a night more. Probably never.

"You just need to be Southern. I'm going to lend you my copy of *Gone with the Wind*. Memorize it and repeat damn Yankees ten times every hour to get your brain working proper. I have *Midnight in the Garden of Good and Evil* on a DVD. What you need to do is learn how to talk like Kevin Spacey and remember voodoo isn't for the tourists. It's for real, so watch what you stick pins into around here. We'll get you some boiled peanuts, a dozen or so pralines, and a bottle of Southern Comfort to make it all tolerable. And you'll be needing to come up with a new name."

"I got a name. Benny."

"You need to rebrand yourself head to toe. What about Jefferson after Jefferson Davis? Or Reese is good. I had an Uncle Reese in Beaufort but he drank a lot and never amounted to much. Forget Reese. What about Carver? Carver's a mighty fine Southern name, none better."

"Sounds like a mob name from Jersey like in Benny-the-book, because I kept the books. Carlo-the-carver because . . . well you get the picture."

Michelle's eyes rounded. "For the love of Pete, what kind of place did you come from?" She pursed her lips and thought of names. "What about Houston Elliott the Third, from Atlanta? Atlanta's good because the place is so big and spread out no one can find anyone. Proving who you are or aren't, will be simply impossible. You can say you lived on Peachtree something. I do declare the name of every street in that city has peachtree in it somewhere."

"The third what?"

"Now who cares? It sounds Southern because it means you have family with two others just like you coming before. Lineage counts, you can trust me on that. I'm going to call Miss Ellie right this very minute to get her landlord to let us in her place. She'll be tickled pink that my fourth cousin on my mom's side, my cousin Houston from Atlanta, is paying a little old visit and needing a place to stay. He'll keep an eye on things and water her prize African violets for her while she's at her grandson's."

"I'm going from working for the mob to watering some violets?"

"Better than pushing them up, if you get my drift." She tipped her chin. "This is a mighty fine idea on my part. I'm plum brilliant if I do say so. The kids get a library dog, you get a new life, and I don't feel so all-fired guilty and can sleep through the night."

Benny rubbed his forehead. Houston? A Southerner? What the hell! From Benny-the-book to Houston Elliott the Third? He was born in Jersey, went to school in Jersey, lived in the same damn twelve blocks all his freaking life. From now on it was sweet tea, driving so slow going backwards would be an improvement, and no snow. The last part he could live with. Not a problem.

"It's all set up, Yankee boy," Michelle said as she flipped

her phone closed. "I'll be dropping you off at Miss Ellie's
and then I'm making a visit to the mall. You can't come
along of course. You'll stick out like a bull snake in a bathtub the way you look now, even worse if you happen to
open your mouth and say something."

Michelle took his hand and smiled up at him, his heart
rate kicking up, his blood flowing faster. She said, "It's
going to work out fine, just you wait and see. But now the
big question is, are you going to do this with me or are you
going to cut and run?"

He'd seriously fucking doubted if anything was going to
work out except getting whacked by the Jersey brothers,
then along came Michelle from Savannah with her big smile,
sparkling eyes, and an insane idea. Not that he thought the
idea would work but the smile and eyes had him. Hell, she
could call him Houston or anything else and he'd wear
whatever freaking thing she brought for him from white
suit to a beanie with a propeller on top because . . . he
liked her, liked her a lot. She was different from any girl he'd
ever known. Michelle was honest and sweet. He didn't
know what that was exactly till he met her. She was a no
bullshit kind of person and where he came from bullshit
was a way of life. Everyone got fed so much of it in Jersey
that bullshit was one of the major food groups. He shrugged.
"I'm in."

Michelle threw her arms around him and the shock of
having her so near took his breath away as much as if
Hank The Hammer landed a punch, except it was a whole
lot nicer. "Why, Mr. Elliott, that is indeed good news. I'm
tickled to the tips of my toes and then some." Michelle
winked up at him. "Now that's how you need be talking,
lots and lots of words. You're in the South and we never
use one word when ten or so will do right nicely, thank
you very much."

She took the leash and hooked her arm through Benny's

as they strolled down the sidewalk away from the fountain and the band. All of it felt like living on another planet that moved at half speed and smelled a hell of a lot better. He couldn't remember the last time he strolled. He worked, he came home, knocked back a few shots, slept then started it all over again. Not a great life but it paid the bills and was better than living in that rat infested roach hole he'd lived in when he was a kid because his dad gambled away every nickel.

"You know how you just said you were in," Michelle offered, interrupting his thoughts . . . interrupting his life. "Well that's only two little old words. Mercy, around here we all just start listening to what's being said by the fourth word. The first three are mostly to get our attention. You need to say something like, Why, honey, I do believe that is the best idea I've heard all day. I'm mighty thankful to you for thinking of it for me."

She counted on her fingers. "See there, that's over twenty-five words you used, with a lot more feeling and gratitude attached to them than your two little teeny tiny words of 'I'm in'. Drama's good for the soul, just like minding your manners, knowing how to fry chicken up right, and rooting for the Georgia Bulldogs, like there is any other football team that matters at all."

They turned down York Street to homes that had steps going up to the front door, black wrought iron railings everywhere, trees with branches so big they touched across the street. A million flowers spilling out of window boxes. If it wasn't for the cockroaches on the sidewalk that were even bigger then their Jersey cousins, the place would be damn near perfect. Then again, Michelle was walking with him so maybe it was perfect after all.

"Here's Miss Ellie's place. It's a great apartment," Michelle said, nodding to a brick house with green shutters and lace curtains at the window. A bunch of purple flowers trailed out of big clay pots and there was a birdfeeder with the words, SNOWBIRDS WELCOME.

"When I came to Savannah to get Checkbook I never planned on any of this."

"Some things are meant to be."

"Yeah."

She gave him a slitty-eyed look.

"I mean . . . well now, the Lord sure does work in mysterious ways, don't you agree? We need to be mighty thankful that he does."

She laughed. "Why I do declare, Houston Elliott the Third, you do catch on right quick for one of those Yankee boys from way up North."

Not many people got a second chance at life and it was staring him in the face. The one making it all happen had big brown eyes, curls on top of her head, rosy cheeks, and the cutest damn accent on the planet. She was a woman he could fall ass over appetite in love with and was halfway there already.

She gave him a simple, soft kiss on the cheek that lingered a bit longer than a simple kiss and nothing had ever turned him on more. "Now tell me what your sizes are. I'm going to the shopping center to pick up a few things for you that don't scream I'm a Yankee boy, born and bred."

"You don't have to do that tonight. It can wait for another time."

"I need to be getting to the mall anyway and do a bit of shopping for myself. You see, I've decided to try and reconcile with my ex and if I'm going to do that I'm in desperate need of a few additions to my very practical wardrobe that don't smack quite so much of Miss Librarian, if you know what I mean." She blushed. "Tommy Lee, my ex, is in to flash, sparkle, and things low cut. I always feel so trashy when I wear low cut but if that makes him happy I'll do it."

"You're—you're going to reconcile?" Again he felt as if Hank The Hammer just worked him over.

"For our son's sake, you see. That boy's been through a rough patch lately and getting into trouble. He seems to be straightening himself out now. If his daddy and I can make it work between us and get back together that's more support for TJ. I have to try again for his sake. I figure I brought him into this world he has to be my priority. It's the least I can do as his mama."

Benny stuffed his hands in his pockets when what he really wanted to do was wrap his arms around Michelle and hold her tight, maybe dance up and down the sidewalk, and then kiss her. God, he really wanted that kiss, had wanted it all night. "Your son's lucky to have you. You're a good mom, Michelle. I admire that."

"The landlord has the door unlocked for you and the key is on the table. You make yourself at home now. I'll drop around tomorrow with new duds. You're going to be fine, Houston Elliott the Third. You just wait and see." He watched her walk off down the street. Michelle was the perfect woman in the perfect place and for a little while he sort of pretended she was his, and he was hers. He should have known she'd belong to someone else. Women like Michelle always did. The problem was how to keep focused on getting Southernized and not focus on getting Michelle. Hell, if he could do that he could do damn near anything. Even say y'all, eat greens, and wear a damn white suit.

Chapter Four

For the second night in a row, Cal parked the Mustang across the street from the library. He'd visited the place more in the last two days then in the last ten years. An auto supply store intimidated some people, for him it was the library. Not that he couldn't read, just that reading was hard, took time and a lot of effort.

Dyslexia was something his PhD college prof parents understood on an intellectual level but could never quite wrap their heads around on a real life level. How could two smart people produce a stupid son, is pretty much what ran though their minds. After Cal installed that Typhoon intake air filter on his dad's Volvo, and he got caught going ninety-five across the Talmadge Bridge and had to attend traffic school, it was all downhill from there. Good thing they produced Tripp.

The same window in the back of the library was lit again, the rest of the building dark. Keeping to the shadows Cal rounded the corner past the magnolias. Churchill was at the same desk. She'd draped the yellow ribbon with the key over the brass and floral desk light, a can of Diet Coke and a half-eaten Moonpie with strawberry filling next to it. The woman had the eating habits of a goat.

She was different than her usual buttoned up neat library

self. Her hair usually twisted back and held in place with the number two pencil had pulled loose. Her cream blouse gaped open at her throat exposing skin soft and golden in the dim light. She took off her black rimmed glasses and set them on the desk then yawned, stretching her arms up, pulling the silk tight across her breasts showing off her fine full figure nearly making him swallow his tongue. Holy hell, he hadn't expected that but his dick sure was damn appreciative and ready for more. Well guess what, there wasn't going to be any more, ever. He couldn't keep sneaking around. He'd get the key, tell Churchill it got stolen, and then throw the damn thing in the river.

Again, the big question was how to get the key. Churchill was reasonable so he'd go with that. He'd reason with her and get her to understand having the key was dangerous, that it would put her right in harm's way. She'd get that. It sounded good. Who the hell was he kidding? She'd never hand over the key if he told her that. He'd have to figure it out on the fly because he was determined to get the damn key one way or the other. He tapped the glass and her gaze instantly fused with his across the desk. At least she had the decency to look guilty. She hesitated then came around and slid up the sash. "What are you doing here?"

"Well now, how are you this evening, Churchill? Sure is lovely out here in the fresh air. Thought I'd stop by and pick up my key."

She pushed a few escaped curls from her face and tried an indignant expression to replace the guilty one. "It's not your key."

"It sure isn't yours. Miss Ellie asked me to stop by and get it for her, so here I am."

"It doesn't belong to her, either. In fact we don't know who it belongs to, do we? That's the whole point so I have as much right to that key as anyone, don't I? I think I'll just go and keep it for myself."

"It's not just the key, Ace. It's dangerous and has trouble written all over it. If anyone knows you have it you've got problems."

"No kidding. You showed up."

He grinned and slid the window up the rest of the way, then hoisted himself through the opening the same way he got in and out of race cars except he landed on his feet next to the desk instead of in a driver's seat behind a steering wheel. He noticed she was barefoot. She had pink toenail polish, no stockings, and smooth, tan, silky legs. He tapped one of the big books. "Find something interesting?"

"The key is for me like what's under the hood of a car is for you. When something's not right you got to look inside and see what it's all about. It just keeps bugging you until you pay attention to it. The key has ancient markings. It's not that old itself but the markings are. Besides, that's what I do. I read about old things. Why do you care about it anyway? What's it to you? If I've got it and no one knows but you, I'm safe, right?"

"Because it involves Miss Ellie and someone may come after her again. Let's throw it away."

"Or let's find out why they want it." Churchill looked tired to the bone. Her blue eyes were not so focused and intense, her body was relaxed, her clothes slightly mussed. Churchill the efficient librarian was always a turn-on in her prim dark skirts, white blouses, sensible shoes; Churchill late at night, barefoot, sleepy, and mussed was lethal. She drew in a resigned breath knowing he wasn't going to give up on the questioning. "There's an alpha on one side, an omega on the other, and *ad honorem* inscribed on one side of the shaft."

"For the honor."

"You know Latin?"

"Must have heard it somewhere. Prison maybe." He was an idiot . . . a horny, oversexed idiot who needed to spend less time thinking about Churchill's legs, breasts, and lovely face and more time thinking about the consequences of opening his big mouth, not censoring what came out. Churchill wasn't buying the prison excuse. He could tell and didn't blame her. He blamed himself. Not many inmates were Latin scholars but he wasn't ready to tell her he'd looked it up himself after Miss Ellie showed him the key a few weeks ago. She'd want to know why he was so all-fired interested and he wasn't about to get into that conversation.

He needed a distraction, something to keep her from thinking *gee, how'd he know that.* He slid the pencil from her hair letting the rest of the auburn curls tumble down around her face. She gasped, her lovely lips parting in surprise. Well good, it worked. He noticed a spark of fire behind the deep navy eyes that she slowly raised to meet his gaze. Her hands were at her back and she gripped the edge of the desk for support. Her cheeks were flushed, her chest rising and falling making his blood flow hot and fast. He didn't need hot and fast, he needed a level head. He had to think. He caged her in his arms, his hands on the desk next to hers, close to the light, bodies touching. He wanted more than touching. He wanted her on her back.

For a second the earth stopped and he thought of the other times they'd been together, alone, close like they were now. The faint tick of the library clock in the front room mixed with the hum of the occasional car passing by. He could hear her breathe, slow and steady and full of life. He couldn't believe he was there with her. He touched her cheek. "You turn me upside down with one look, you know that? You're gorgeous. You've always been gorgeous. I like it. I like you."

She touched his cheek. "You need a shave. You always need a shave." She swallowed. "I like it. And I like you too, more than I want to."

His fingers slid from her delicate face down her delicious neck, stopping at the V in her blouse. She swallowed but didn't pull away. She leaned toward him, then a little more. He undid the top button and then the next, the blouse parting to show cleavage and a black lacy bra that he never in a million year would have suspected. "Nice duds."

He could feel her skin getting warmer, making him harder and, truth be told, he didn't think that was possible. He traced his finger over the upper edge of the bra touching the softest skin. "You're just like I remember. Every inch of you is just like I remember."

"I remember you, too. A lot. Often. Too often. Cal, I sent you to prison. How can you, how can we . . .? You have to hate me. Isn't that an issue?"

"No."

"But it has to be," she breathed on a delicate sigh.

He slid his arms around her, resting his palm against the small indent of her back, guiding her away from the window. It was not window behavior and he had no intention of stopping the behavior any time soon. He kissed her and she kissed him back. No one kissed like Churchill. Just like everything else she did she gave it her full attention. His hand slipped under her blouse, the sweet touch of her warm skin against his fingertips incredible, bringing back so many memories. Her arms circled his neck, her thighs to his, his erection against the juncture of her legs. She leaned into him making their bodies closer, her breasts to his chest. It went way beyond what he intended when he first got there.

He sat her on a low bookcase, her skirt inching up, bare thighs circling his hips. He wanted the damn key but God help him he wanted her more. His head filled with the thudding of his heart . . . or maybe it wasn't his heart. Something more? Another kind of thudding? A banging? Oh damn, banging!

"Churchill," came a voice at the front door. "Church? I've got Storybook here with me now, honey. We had a nice walk and I'm bringing him back to you. Are you in there Churchill? I saw the light on, sweetie. I have to come in the front door because there's no handing him to you through the window. Can't imagine boosting his big bottom through the window, so you'll have to open the door if I can't find my key. Churchill? Are you there? Are you okay?"

Churchill's eyes got huge, his did the same, reality crashing back into their lives. "It's Michelle, the other librarian."

"We're consenting adults. It's okay."

"But we don't need to be consenting right here in the library and getting caught at it—like we're too horny to wait and get ourselves a room. It will be all over town by morning."

"You're embarrassed at being caught in here with the town bad boy?"

"I'm embarrassed to be caught fooling around in the back of the library." They jumped apart as Michelle came up the hallway saying, "Hope you got yourself something decent to eat and not that usual junk you call food. That stuff's going to kill you. Ever hear of free radicals and antioxidants? Did you know Cal's Mustang's parked across the street? Have you seen him . . ." She came into the room, looked from one to the other, and grinned hugely, putting her hand to her hip. "Well, I'll be darned. I guess you have seen him and it's about time. Hello, Cal. Fancy seeing you here. I got to say books aren't the only things that can be overdue in this place. You two sure do look good together."

Churchill pushed hair from her face and tried to straighten herself up. Necking in the stacks was so . . . juvenile. How many times had she caught kids sneaking a kiss and there she was doing the same thing and more. In a few minutes she'd be doing a whole lot more. "It's not what it looks like."

"Oh, honey, I sure hope it is."

Churchill twisted her hair back up. Where was the darn pencil that held it? This was a library, there was always a pencil around. She grabbed a pen and pinned her hair with it hoping it wouldn't explode giving her blue highlights. She put on her glasses. They always made her feel more in charge. Everyone should have a pair tucked away for when they needed a little boost of confidence. "We were discussing the key and the importance—"

"What key?"

"The key here on the . . . lamp." Churchill stopped dead, her gaze glued to the lamp with the delicate magnolia blossoms embedded in brass. It sat by the window and was where the key had been but wasn't. It was the bare brass lamp. She turned to Cal and looked him square in the eyes. "All right, Bubba, that's it. Strip."

Cal grinned, Michelle laughed, and Churchill blushed. Did she really just tell Cal to strip? Still laughing Michelle said, "Oh, this just keeps getting better and better. Who would have thought?"

"Cal has this key I was doing research on."

"If you say so," Michelle said

Cal winked at Michelle as she unclipped Storybook and dropped the leash on the desk. Storybook moseyed over to his blanket and Michelle moseyed out of the room heading for the front door saying, "I will leave you two alone to do whatever needs doing. I hope it's something good. Have fun with that key or whatever excuse you're making up to be here."

"Cal took it," Churchill called after her. "I know he did. I just want it back because, because he wants it and I want to know why."

"Honey, you just make up any story that suits you. I

don't have to know why you're here. Fact is I think I'll pretend I never saw you." Michelle smiled, then retraced her steps, and closed the main door behind her.

Cal parked himself on the edge of the desk and Churchill paced back and forth. Moving had a calming effect. Standing still had an I-wanna-kiss-you and to-heck-with-everything-else effect. She was losing it, probably because it was late, and he was there. He looked terrific and smelled good like he'd just showered. That's where the naked came from. *Snap out of it, McKenzie!* "The way I see it, you came here and got me all involved. Then when I wasn't paying attention you swiped the key. That's exactly what happened."

"You were paying great attention."

"I know you were making out with me to get what you wanted. That's what was going on here. You used me and I don't appreciate it but just give me the damn thing back and we'll forget this happened."

"Damn?"

"I'm tired, it's late, I'm pissed."

"Pissed?

She gave him an eat-dirt-and-die look.

"I don't think either of us will do much forgetting about tonight. And I wasn't using you. Enjoying you? Most definitely." He stood up and kicked off his gym shoes while unbuckling his belt. Holy crap he was really doing it. Cal Davis was taking off his clothes for her. Not voluntarily but she wasn't going to quibble. He unzipped and pulled his jeans off, one leg then the other leaving him in gray briefs. He pulled his T-shirt over his head and dropped it on top of the jeans, then leaned against the wall and folded his arms across his broad bare chest. "Do you want more?"

Oh my God! Oh my God! She was wide awake and heck yes she wanted more. What woman wouldn't? He had one of those golden tans from working outside with his shirt off, muscled arms, and firm six-pack abs that went clear down to gray briefs, then disappeared under the waistband. There was *the bulge* indicating the very male part of him was darn fit, too. Then again, she knew that firsthand and for the love of God, do *something besides stare, McKenzie!* She swiped his jeans off the floor and rummaged through his pockets, tossing his car keys onto the desk. His money clip and wallet followed. A blue foiled condom wrapper slid across the wood surface. Her gaze glued to his across the room and her heart stopped dead in her chest.

She wanted Cal Davis so damn bad her teeth ached. She had no idea what her teeth had to do with any of it but they ached anyway. It took every ounce of effort she could muster to keep from tackling him right there in the library, ripping those damn briefs right off his firm ass, and using the damn condom for the purpose for which it was intended. She tossed the wallet, condom, keys, and clip to him. "Get dressed and get yourself a new wallet. This one's falling apart. You've got electricians tape holding it together and it's not doing a very good job."

He picked up his shirt and nodded to the open window. "Here's what I think happened."

What happened? Nothing is what happened. She realized she hated *nothing* to pieces.

"I had other things on my mind besides the key and I'd like to think you did, too. We were out of sight from the window. Anyone could have reached in and snagged it off the desk." He slipped on the shirt and grabbed his jeans. She wanted to wring his neck. How could he be so calm and . . . unaffected? "It's bad that the key's gone but it's even worse that someone's watching you, Ace. Watching you damn close."

"Well they'll probably die of boredom if they're watching me but maybe they're watching you. Ever think of that? You're the one who crawled in my window."

"Except Miss Ellie wasn't staying at my place when

someone broke in. She was at your place. They didn't find the key there and figured you have it somewhere. You worked late and have a stack of old books lying around. Doesn't take Sherlock Holmes to add it all up, Ace." He pulled on the jeans. "There, I'm clothed." He touched her cheek and said in a low voice, "Next time it's your turn."

A little shock zinged through her at the thought of stripping for Cal, taking her clothes off just for him. Of them together intimately and something happening after her clothes were on the floor. Not like now when *nothing happened*. Blast him. "In your dreams." There was just so much frustration and disappointment a woman could take in one night.

He went over to the window and slammed it shut. He turned and his gaze met hers. The spark in his eyes said that he was thinking about her being naked, too. She could feel her heart beating fast, then faster, her legs getting wobbly, the place between them embarrassingly wet and hot. Couldn't she have Cal once more, just once more? Did the look on his face mean he wanted it as much as she did? *Does he want it tonight? Tonight would be good.* After all, the last time she had him was nine years ago. She was due. She was so due!

She took a step toward him just as he grabbed his shoe off the floor and sat down saying, "You don't have the key so I guess that's the end of figuring out what it's all about. Guess we're done here. You can go back to being a librarian and not stay late tomorrow."

He was still thinking about the damn key and being done and she was thinking of hot slippery bare-ass-naked sex! Another reason why it had been nine years! She snatched her notes from the desk. "Why does someone want this thing?"

He tied the second gym shoe. "Doesn't matter now, does

it? It's gone. Can't open something if you don't have the key, can you?"

"You seem awfully happy about that."

"Miss Ellie was hurt, someone was watching you but now you're all safe. Whoever has the key is welcome to the damn thing. I don't care about it."

She picked up her glasses and read the notes. "Well, all's not lost entirely. I sketched it out because keys like this don't come along every day. It's specially made for something. It's shaped like an *H* or an *I* depending how you look at it with one side longer to form the shaft. The bottom side of the opening has the Greek letter alpha imbedded, the top opening has the Greek letter Omega, the beginning and the end. These letters of the Greek alphabet usually symbolize forever, eternity, that sort of thing. The obelisk is a symbol for enlightenment and the crossed mallet and opened compass—the building kind of compass not the where-the-heck-am-I kind of compass—make up the teeth part of the key that opens whatever it opens."

Cal shrugged. "Meaning?"

She tossed the legal pad back on the desk and yawned, suddenly tired to the bone. "Meaning I have no idea where it all leads to. Some of these are universal symbols, some I have no idea, and right now I'm too tired to care. This is Savannah and not Greece so nothing fits."

"It could have been a prize in a Crackerjacks box or a box of cereal for all you know."

"Except people don't steal those and they're plastic, not brass."

He made ghost sounds and hummed the *Twilight Zone* theme but when he looked at her notes there wasn't a glimmer of amusement anywhere in his eyes. "I want you to promise me you're done with this."

She had another smartass answer but when he smoothed

back her hair and gently placed a kiss on her lips she forgot what she was going to say.

"I want you safe, Ace. And that's the God's honest truth. Out of everything that's going on I don't want anything to happen to you. Don't get mixed up in this. Leave it alone." He kissed her again, long and hard, his tongue doing to her mouth what she wanted done someplace else.

"You turn me on more than any other man I've ever met and I don't know why."

He kissed her on the forehead and said in a low steely voice, "Because I care. I always have and I want you to remember that." He kissed her again and pulled her hair loose for the second time. Slowly he ran his fingers though it, the curls tumbling around her face making her feel sexy as only Cal Davis could. He said in a low hushed voice that she'd only heard one other time, the time they made love, "I like your hair this way. It's the real you." He turned and left, his handsome strong silhouette fading into darkness then out the door. Her notes were gone right along with him.

For a minute he'd had her convinced that forgetting about the key was a good idea. After all, it was gone. Having it was nothing but trouble and she came back to Savannah to get away from trouble. But he took the notes and that simple act filled her brain with more questions. She started to run after Cal, beat him to a pulp, and demand to know what was going on. She didn't, because something most definitely was going on and the last person on earth to tell her was Cal Davis.

Why was he so interested in the key and anything associated with it? Why was he so hell-bent on her not knowing anything? And why, why, why could he set her on fire with one simple look and melt every bone in her body with one kiss?

She didn't know much but the one thing she'd bet the

bank on was that Cal wasn't the sort of man to steal anything—except maybe her heart. That wasn't his fault. It
was hers. Three years ago there was overwhelming evidence he stole money from Dodd. She saw what she saw
except—there was that word, that infuriating word that
kept her up at night and on edge all day—except there was
a lot more going on than just Cal running out of the tent
with Dodd in pursuit. She intended to find out what. Most
of all she wanted to know what made Cal Davis go to jail
for three years for a crime he didn't even commit.

Cal leaned over the fender of the stock car. There was a
miss, a hiccup somewhere and he couldn't figure out what
it was. He could hear it buried in the guts of the engine . . .
somewhere. "Give it the gas," he yelled at TJ inside the car.
The car hummed then accelerated to a louder roar, the sound
vibrating off the walls of the concrete block garage. He heard
the hiccup again. TJ let off the accelerator and joined Cal
up front, heads together under the hood. "I don't hear a
thing. She sounds good to me."

"Every engine has its own rhythm. I modified this one
so I know it. It's like if you were a Kenny Chesney fan, listened to his songs day after day, then suddenly he flubbed
a note. You'd hear it."

"A little miss that you can barely hear makes that much
difference?"

"When you're going wheel-to-wheel at a hundred and
sixty miles an hour everything makes a difference." He
patted TJ on the back. "I just picked up a totaled '09 Challenger over in Beaufort. It's wrecked all to hell and back.
I'm going to start putting her together. Help me out and
maybe you'll learn something."

"Me?"

That's all Cal had to hear to know he made a good decision. TJ didn't ask how much are you going to pay me or I

got a date so I can't be there on Saturday or any of the other million excuses kids had. All he said was, "me?"

"Monday after you finish work we can drag her out and take a look. She's really a mess."

"And we can fix her up. Bet it's a V-8. Goes like a bat out of hell."

"You got to learn how to drive the bat first so you don't wind up in hell."

TJ grabbed Cal's hand and shook it just like he did the other night. "You're the best, dude."

"Hey, Cal," came DaisyLou's voice from the open double garage doors. "Some nice-looking gentleman's here to see you."

Cal turned to the new concession gal they'd hired. She had on denim short-shorts and a red blouse tied in the middle showing off her pierced belly button. Her blond hair was piled on top of her head. Bright pink lipstick and blue eye shadow accented her face. He wasn't sure if DaisyLou was her given name or if she took it for the effect, but it fit and either way the speedway would sell a hell of a lot more beer.

"He says he's your brother but I told him he was way too cute to be related to the ugly likes of you." She smiled showing sparkling white teeth and she crinkled her cute nose. The girl could sell snowballs to Eskimos, especially male Eskimos.

Tripp came inside the garage and for a second Cal wasn't sure if it was really his brother. He wore beat-up loafers, khakis he could have slept in, and a faded navy polo that he probably used to wash his car. His hair was too long, uncombed. He hadn't shaved in days. Tripp was never a JCrew model but usually a few steps above Salvation Army. "Am I catching you at a bad time?" he asked.

Cal introduced Tripp and TJ then said to TJ, "Mind getting the blower and cleaning off the grandstands? People are going to start showing up for the qualifying laps. And help yourself to a Coke. It's hot out there."

DaisyLou touched Tripp's cheek. "Would you like me to get you something nice and cold to drink, sugar?"

"I'm fine."

"Oh my, you sure are." DaisyLou winked at Tripp and he turned the color of her shirt, making Cal smile. Silky had better order more beer.

DaisyLou sashayed out the door and Tripp said, "You're looking good, Cal." He stood on one foot, then the other, then walked in closer. "I should have come to see you more often while you were . . . away."

"I told you not to."

"I wrote, not enough but some. I just didn't know what to say."

"We both know how I just love to read." At least that got a mutual smile. "Heard you're nearly finished with your post doc at Duke. That's pretty damn terrific. You gotta be feeling real good right now."

Tripp raked his hair looking serious to the bone. Too serious. "It sucks. This all sucks. Me here, you there, what happened because I was stupid and then you . . . I should never have gone along with this. It's not right. It wasn't right then, it's not right now."

Cal sat down on a case of motor oil and braced his elbows on his knees. He looked up at Tripp. "I talked you into it, Tripp. This was all my idea, not yours. Now we forget it happened and I mean that. It's over. Hey, I'm doing fine. No worries. Look, I'm covered in grease and in my own shop. I'm a damn good mechanic and happy, which is more than I can say for you."

"How's business? Having the reputation of a thief can't be an asset."

Cal nodded out the door to the dirt track beyond. "I

had some money saved. I'm sort of Silky's silent partner. I keep a low profile. He's the front guy and you just got introduced to the new front gal."

"The parents are back from teaching that seminar at UCLA and I'm in town. I want us to have dinner together. We're family. I want us to be a family."

"You've been reading Dickens again?"

"The parents thought it was a great idea."

Cal gave him a sideways look.

"Okay not great but good. Yeah, good. They agreed that they wanted to see you, see how you're doing. The Pink House for lunch tomorrow? I know you have races here on Saturday night but can you do lunch?"

"For you it's family together. For them it's the obligatory in public we-stand-by-our-son meal. It's the way of the South. Our boy might be a complete fuckup all of his life but we're still talking to him, at least in public we are. Sure, let's get this over with." Cal stood. "Now I've got to get this car ready to race in two hours. I better get going. Bad for business if I turn out a clunker."

"Maybe they've changed."

"Sure." Cal sucker punched Tripp's thigh. "You been working out? You've got some meat on you."

"Putting on weight. Fat mostly. Not much exercise in a chem lab." Tripp puffed out a lungful of air, his face pale. "I don't know what I'm doing."

"Look at me, Tripp." Cal stood and put his hand on his younger brother's shoulders. He was bad, worse than Cal would have imagined, especially for someone who had the world by the tail. "You got your PhD at twenty three. You're a brain and you can do something with your life. Hell, you can do anything you want, research, consulting, go work for NASA, go to the goddamn moon for chrissake. You got to put what happened behind you. I did. I'm fine, you're fine. I'll be at the Pink House at noon just like you want and that will be fine, too. I'll even put on a coat and tie and check my attitude at the door. You're right, we are family."

Least in name, Cal thought to himself. If his parents could change that little inconvenience Cal felt sure they would. But for Tripp, Cal would do anything—from taking out a bully talking smack about his little geeky brother, to making sure Tripp ate when studying for his SATs, to anything else that came along. Cal may have been the ignored son, but Tripp had been the trained chimp, hauled around to perform and raised in a protective bubble. Ignored was easier to take than that. "See you tomorrow."

Tripp nodded, then headed toward the open garage doors. Cal stuck his head back under the hood of the car trying to figure out what was wrong. He noticed that Tripp stopped then turned around, a slight smile on his face, the first Cal had seen since Tripp got there. "Heard you were spending time with Churchill McKenzie."

Cal jumped up clunking his head on the raised hood. "What? Where'd you hear that?" He rubbed his head, a headache coming on from more than a whack on the head.

"Twitter. Twitter knows all."

"So I've heard. It's like gossiping on the front porch only it's a really big front porch."

Tripp laughed uneasily like he'd forgotten how. "You meeting up with a girl at the library is perfect. I love it." Cal threw a roll of paper towels hitting Tripp in the back of the head as he walked away. "I'm sure as hell tickled pink I brightened up your day, little brother."

"Me too." Tripp laughed harder and that alone made the gossip tolerable. It stood to reason if Cal saw the light on in the back library window others did, too. With the telltale Mustang parked across the street there wasn't much guessing who was where. Of course the gossips probably had some help from Michelle.

He studied the engine, taking it in all at once—the belts, pumps, hoses, pistons, carburetor, battery. He played the engine roar over in his mind running through the gears— first to second to third to fourth. He reached down and pulled a spark plug and checked the gap using the end of a matchbook as a gauge. He had a gapper, a real tool for just that purpose but the fist time he'd changed plugs that was how his granddad taught him. The gap was off. Too bad life wasn't more like a well tuned engine because when that got screwed up he knew how to fix it. Life was more of a hit-and-miss operation.

He thought of Tripp and how he was not himself at all. Cal had no idea what to do about it. Hell, he thought three years ago he'd fixed the problem. Truth be told things seemed worse all the way around but especially with Tripp. Maybe the parents had some idea how to help Tripp. They had to see that he wasn't himself. The three of them sort of lived on another plane in their own world of academics and books, writing papers and giving lectures, faculty meetings and symposiums, whatever the hell symposiums were. Cal had planned on doing lunch then getting the hell out of Dodge ASAP. But he needed to talk, really talk, to Ron and RuthAnn. He almost laughed. He couldn't even imagine that conversation beyond "Hi." But he'd find a way. He had to for Tripp.

Chapter Five

"TGIF," Churchill said to Michelle as Churchill closed the door of the library and turned the lock.

"No TGIF for you. You have to work tomorrow."

"But that means next week it's my turn for a weekend off. I'm TGIFing early." Churchill pulled her purse from the drawer and checked her watch.

"Hot date? Cal? Did you ever get him to take off his clothes?" Michelle slapped her hands over her mouth and mumbled, "I swore I wasn't going to ask because I didn't want to jinx anything that might be going on. I really hope something's going on—or off—as the case may be."

"Honey, you made it all the way to six o'clock without asking. That's pretty good. I'm impressed."

"Me too, but I'm busting a gut here. Did he go and do it? Was it good? I mean the man's delicious so it had to be good if he did it. So did he?"

If she said Cal was *sex walking* she'd never hear the end of a million other questions. "Do you really think Cal would take off his clothes right here in the library just because I said to?"

"Well, I remember some years ago, nine years to be exact, on your birthday. You were staying with us, Mama and me. Margo was . . . where was your mother that time? China?"

"That was her hike-the-Aztec-Trail period. She wrote those articles for the *World Traveler*."

"Whatever. I had to lie to Mama that you were sleeping and you weren't home yet. Then I looked out my bedroom window and lo and behold what did I see in the alleyway? You climbing out of a red Mustang convertible looking disheveled as all get out and Cal not looking one bit better." She fanned herself with her hand.

"Your point being?"

"Sometimes location isn't a priority."

"Well it was this time."

"That's downright depressing." She fidgeted. "I haven't had any since I started the divorce and that was a year ago. I'm needing to live vicariously through you. I'm a young vibrant red-blooded American woman. A little vicariousness would be nice here."

"I think it's time you started getting it on your own because nothing's happening in my neck of the woods. I don't have any woods. Desert, all desert." She studied Michelle who was suddenly very quiet and looking antsy. "Oh my, so something is happening with you. Spill it."

"I think I might be getting back together with Tommy Lee. Hear me out before you have a conniption fit, turn blue, and tell me I'm losing my everloving mind. That I need to get my head examined before I do something stupid. TJ is in such a better place lately. I think if Tommy and I were there for him it would help him along. So tomorrow Tommy's coming for dinner. We're going to talk about seeing more of each other and ironing out our differences."

"Tommy has a short attention span, honey. Fact is he's had lots of short attention spans all the while you were married. You were the only one not aware until one of his spans paid you a little visit. Gee, that was fun. Are you sure you want to set yourself up for this again?"

"Things are so much better now with TJ and I think it's because Tommy and I are more friendly-like." She bit at her bottom lip.

Churchill hugged Michelle. "You have to do what you have to do but don't get yourself hurt. I'm going to stop by Miss Ellie's and water her African violets then head on out to the speedway. Cal has something that belongs to me and I need to get it back before—"

"No!"

"No?"

"I mean you don't have to do that, water the flowers. Didn't I tell you a cousin of mine's visiting from Atlanta?" She rummaged in her purse looking intently for something. "A distant cousin, somebody you probably never heard me talk about, a real distant cousin, many, many times removed cousin. You've never seen him before. In fact till he showed up I never saw him before, he's that distant. He's staying at Miss Ellie's since she's staying out with Cal. Yep, working out just fine, it is. Fine indeed," Michelle gasped on her last drop of air. "And he's shy. Very, very shy. Painfully so. Doesn't say much. Nope, not a word sometimes. Nods a lot."

"That's the fastest I've ever heard you talk since I've known you and we've been best friends since I turned four and you came to my Indiana Jones birthday party. Mama cooked up cuy and all the kids freaked when they realized it was guinea pig."

"Margo had great plans for you."

"That she did."

"Well, I just didn't want you to waste your time going to Miss Ellie's to water her flowers, is all."

"I'll have your cousin over for dinner. Just you, me, TJ,

your cousin, and Tommy Lee. No guinea pig, maybe fried chicken and gravy. I'll buy it since pop tarts are my one and only specialty. Next week? Your cousin has to see some of Savannah while he's here, otherwise why bother to drive down. Want me to walk over with you for a visit now? You can introduce me and we can get acquainted and—"

"No. We can't do that. Houston . . . that's his name . . . Houston Elliott the Third is far too shy." Michelle grabbed Churchill's hand and hurried her out the door, then locked it. "Now I have to get home for dinner. Tommy Lee's stopping by. I'll introduce you to Houston later. He won't be so shy in a week or two, I hope. Least that's the plan. Trying to get over his shyness, I mean. Bye now, you hear."

Michelle hurried off toward her house and Churchill watched for a few moments to make sure she was okay. She was acting a little weird. Actually, she was acting nutty as squirrel bait but then getting back together with Tommy was enough to make anyone act that way. Tommy Dempsey was a ten course meal of total and complete jerk.

Evening sun starting to drop to the horizon and Churchill got Tic Tac out of the garage from behind the coffee shop. She strapped Storybook into his doggie seatbelt harness thing that cost entirely too much then drove for Highway 80. The white Prius was such a nice little car. She could see all the corners and it handled great. It was compact, neat, and small like a little Tic Tac. The gas gauge never moved and the engine turned off when she stopped for traffic lights, which totally freaked her out till she got used to it. The Prius was sleek and twenty-first century and without a doubt the single most boring car in God's universe.

She wanted her '56 Chevy Bel Air back! The one Uncle Frank left her in his will. It was robin's-egg blue with a white top and fenders. It had white leather interior and wide swaths of chrome that gleamed in the sunlight that made other drivers take a second look. It was standard shift, got eighteen miles per gallon, and had a bunch of stuff that seemed to impress the heck out of car enthusiasts. Basically she liked the color and she didn't care how girly that sounded because she loved . . . yes, loved . . . that car. Not that any of this mattered because Bluebell was history. She stifled a sniff.

The sun dropped further into the marshes as she turned off the highway toward the speedway, a roar of engines drowning out Rascal Flats blaring from the radio. Rascal? And people thought the name Churchill was strange. Well criminy. She didn't think about there being races tonight. Duh. Friday night in Savannah meant races! Really loud races. Didn't they ever hear of a muffler?

Up ahead a circle of lights glowed through the evening humidity that had droplets suspended in the air. When Savannah did humidity it didn't mess around.

She parked next to a big red pickup with fancy wheels and orange flames painted on the sides, probably Bluebell's boyfriend. People streamed by in denim, wearing T-shirts with sayings like SAVANNAH GIRL, GLOSSY LIPS AND CURVY HIPS, PRETTY IS AS PRETTY DOES and Churchill's personal favorite, HOTTIE WITH A BODY. Her black pencil skirt and white blouse didn't exactly fit in with the crowd. She was a nun at a lingerie convention. Maybe she should just go home and forget her great plan. And let Cal think he got away with taking the key and her notes? She unhooked Storybook, then locked Tic Tac. Did Fancy Wheels just suddenly snub her Prius? Pecking order of the car world.

She spied Miss Ellie on the other side of the track decked out in a pink baseball hat and matching jeans, her white cast done up in pink ribbons. Plaster makes a fashion statement at the speedway. Churchill paid her ten bucks and bought a Coke from a very popular Southern chickie who ran the concession stand looking better in short-shorts and heels than any woman had a right to. Churchill and Storybook climbed the bleachers, Churchill sitting on one side of Miss Ellie, Storybook on the other side taking licks from the lady's ice cream next to him. "How's the arm?" Churchill yelled as a car growled around the track right in front of them, killing hundreds of her hearing cells.

"I got to tell you it's fabulous. I get waited on hand and foot," Miss Ellie yelled back, then pointed to a man with a gray ponytail and red suspenders working on something electrical out by a big board in the middle. "That there's my Silky Callahan. He owns the place with Cal. Know why they call him Silky?" She had a sassy look in her eye. "Because he's so smooth." She giggled like a schoolgirl, the sound lost as number 73 whizzed by.

"I didn't know Cal was part of the speedway."

"He keeps a low profile but he does live here now. Has a nice little cabin around back right through that there stand of pines." She pointed toward the marsh area. "Silky built this track, you know. I think that heart of his is half car motor, half crankshaft, whatever a crankshaft is. I remember when he bulldozed the speedway himself back in '62. He used railroad ties to protect the crowd from the cars. No lights. Those didn't come till later and he had to buy liability insurance on a weekly basis 'cause that's how he could afford it. This year two drivers down at that Daytona 500 started at this here dirt track. But, what in the world are you doing here?"

"Paying Cal a little visit," Churchill yelled, the roar setting up shockwaves in her head. "I thought this was a race, why only one car at a time?"

"Time trials for pole positions. Cal's out there. The red car, number eighty-eight, waiting in line for his turn."

"He's racing? I thought he did engine motor stuff? A mechanic."

"He hasn't always been a mechanic. Started off racing. Tonight he's qualifying the car for Junior Darling. He went and broke his collar bone but wants the points for racing tonight. Cal's going to get the car qualified, then Junior will drive the race. Gives Junior a break from being behind the wheel so long though he will have to start in last position with the change of drivers. It's the rule."

"Junior's driving in this free-for-all with a broken collar bone? Is he out of his mind?"

"Honey, if they can have sex, they can drive. That's the way they see it and most of these guys would be having sex if they were wrapped in a full body cast." Another car tore up the track, mud flying, dust clogging the air. That was all very interesting information and not just the stuff about cars and drivers. Cal wasn't in his cabin. He was out there on the track, had no chance of showing up for a while, and Miss Ellie was there watching it all. "You know, Storybook looks hungry. I'm going to get him a hotdog. We'll bring you back some lemonade and chili fries."

"It'll take you forever to get through that crowd. Concessions here have never been so popular. I think that girl has leg implants along with a few other adjustments. I've never seen such long legs. I think I'm jealous."

Churchill climbed down the bleachers, not an easy feat in a pencil skirt and dress shoes with a big dog pulling her along. She headed for the concession stand just like she said in case Miss Ellie was watching but when Churchill got to the crowd she veered around to the back. "We'll get a hotdog later."

Storybook looked longingly at the concession stand. "I promise. Two hotdogs. Besides, you already had ice cream. We've been living together too long. Your eating habits are worse than mine."

Keeping to the shadows they headed for the pines. "You're the lookout, remember that. I don't spring for hotdogs for nothing." A porch light at the cabin made it easy to see in the dark. Together they stepped onto the porch and peeked in the open window. The night air ruffled the curtains. Story-book leaned his front paws on the sill and rested his head on them. "Guess Cal doesn't like AC. Is that a Pottery Barn couch? And hardwood floors with a chocolate brown area rug? Okay, where's the squashed leather La-Z-Boy? The mismatched oak furniture? Where are the deer antlers on the wall, the big fish over the hearth that sings obnoxious songs, and the beer cans and burger wrappers? Maybe Cal's gay. His taste is way too good for a straight guy."

She giggled, then felt Cal's strong arm slide around her waist, making her gasp as his hot breath scorched the back of her neck. "Guess what. I'm not gay."

She glanced at Storybook. "Some lookout you are."

"He's on my side. We guys hang together." Cal kissed the soft spot behind her left ear sending shivers down her spine and setting fire to her insides. She turned and faced him. His face wasn't the usual unshaven degree of handsomeness. It was bloody!

"Dear God in heaven and Lord have mercy, what happened to you?" She touched his cheek splattered with ooze and dirt.

"Accident." He reached around her and opened the door. She and Storybook followed him inside, over the wool area rug, the polished wood floor, and past a bookshelf that had more books on tape than the library ever thought about having. They went into the bathroom from Macy's Martha Stewart collection.

"I need to redecorate. My place is a pit compared to your house. Pottery Barn? Macys?"

"You weren't in prison for three years. I also make a mean risotto."

"Risotto?"

"Ever eat prison food?"

Storybook plopped down in the hall and Churchill said

to Cal, "You really are a mess. What kind of accident? I thought it was just qualifying laps."

"It looks worse than it is." He turned on the sink faucet and grabbed a washcloth. She grabbed it right back out of his hand. "You'll grind the dirt into the cuts and have infection. Get in the shower and let the water rinse out the cuts."

"Ace." He looked at her, one eye swelling shut. "I've been in wrecks before." But he didn't argue further and turned on the shower, kicked off his shoes, and pulled his shirt over his head. There were scrapes everywhere. Two bad looking cuts on his arms and his hands were skinned as if he'd slid along concrete.

"How could you wreck your car? You're a better driver than that, aren't you?"

He stepped in the shower, the water plastering his jeans to his legs, his very nice butt, his zipper area with an enticing bulge.

She handed him the white fluffy washcloth. She loved the white fluffy washcloth. "So what happened?"

"You're not going to let this go are you?"

"Me? You have to ask?"

He soaped the rag and dragged it over his face and arms. "I was out of the car and another car got too close. I got knocked into a wall. I'm not Mr. Popularity around here in case you missed the memo."

"Wait a minute. You're telling me someone went and did this to you on purpose? Someone tried to run you down and it wasn't an accident?"

"Shit happens."

She couldn't talk. She could barely stand. She saw red, blinding red light right there in front of her eyes. She headed for the door, at least what she could see of it through the rage. "I'm going out there and kill somebody."

"What? No you're not."

"I'm going to strangle them and—"

Before she could finish the sentence he lifted her up in one arm and took her into the shower with him sliding the shower door closed, trapping them inside.

"What are you doing? Let me out of here! People can't just go around beating other people up. This is not Jersey. This is Savannah and the reason I moved home." Water soaked her clothes clear through. Her hair streamed down around her face. Her shoes were ruined and she liked those shoes. But there were more issues at the moment so she poked him in his bare muscled chest sprinkled with fine brown hair. "If you think this is going to stop me from going after them you are so wrong."

"I don't care about the guys on the track." His eyes were dark as the sky outside, his forehead creased with concern. "I care about you and you're not going out there and get yourself in trouble. You side with me and people won't like it. You're staying here till you cool off."

"I don't care what people like and this"—she swiped at a smear of blood on his face—"is not going to happen." She tried to get around him but he blocked her way.

"I'm serious."

"So am I." She tried to push him out of the way and slipped. Cal caught her. "Why are you so pissed? Why in the hell do you give a crap about me? You sent me to jail and now you've got your panties in a twist because people think I'm guilty?"

"Because . . . because somehow, someway I was wrong and caused all this for you. If I hadn't seen what I did and talked to the police; if I'd just run off and kept my mouth shut, you wouldn't be here bleeding." She swiped her soaked hair from her face. "And because you stopped and changed my tire when no one else did. And you stood up for Tripp when he was twelve and in high school when the kids teased him, calling him Baby Einstein. You stood up for the other kids who were easy targets for the bullies and the jocks. Those kids were sort of under your protection. Everyone knew it and left them alone. I like who you are, Cal Davis, I always have and . . . and it's about damn time someone stood the hell up for you. I should never have testified and sent you to jail. None of this makes sense. You don't make sense."

She stopped and looked at him, not believing she actually said all that. Then she kissed him because she was out of words. She wanted him to know she meant every single word she said, though she probably couldn't beat up any of those guys on the racetrack no matter how hard she tried or how mad she was.

He kissed her back and she forgot all about the racetrack as he held her tight. Her hands slipped around his wonderful bare shoulders and across his strong back. God, she liked being there with him.

"I want you, Ace," he said in a husky voice. "And God knows I don't want much these days." His hand slid under her blouse, unsnapping her bra. He pulled down the back zipper of her skirt and peeled it over her hips, the soggy material pooling on the floor of the shower stall, the warm water falling over the two them. He snapped her up in his arms, surprising the heck out of her. "What are you doing?"

He nudged the door open and stepped out of the shower. "Showing you the West Elm bedroom."

"We'll get it wet."

"I hope so." *What happened to staying away,* Cal thought as he walked through the hall with Churchill McKenzie in his arms. What happened to not letting her get close and screwing up everything because she was too damn smart, too clever, asked too many damn questions? She'd walked into his house and wanted to take on half the rough asses in Savannah for him, that's what happened. He sure as hell hadn't counted on that. But Churchill was always surprising the hell out of him. She was in his arms all wet and wonderful and his great plan to keep them apart didn't seem so great at all. "Ah, fuck."

She looked up at him and smiled, making his head swim. "I think you talked me into it."

He laid her in the middle of his bed, on the new tan comforter. When he'd bought it he'd had no idea that Churchill McKenzie would be sharing it with him. But there she was, her long legs curled into the folds, her hair wet and wild. If he stopped to think what the hell he was doing he'd think his way right out of it. He was tired of thinking, tired of making decisions. For once, just this once, he wanted what he wanted—that perfectly proper woman in his bed waiting for him. Not taking his gaze from her— if he did she might vanish like she did so often in his dreams—he pulled off his jeans. "I want this to last, Ace. No rushing. I want to take my time with you, remember you, every inch of you."

Fresh air drifted in off the marsh. A nightingale sang in the distance accompanied by frogs and crickets. The roar of the speedway was muffled by the pines. He sat beside her and unbuttoned the top button of her blouse that was more see-through, a hint of nipple showing though the cotton fabric. He bent his head and licked the hard nub because he simply had to. The scent of her bare, heated skin filled his head till she suddenly grabbed him around the neck and pulled his face up to hers, his chest across hers. She panted, "You were naked in my library, you're naked now, and I'm pretty much naked in your bed. That's too much naked going on to be taking our time, not to mention that you're turning me on with the licking thing." She framed his face in her hands, her eyes boring into his, her cheeks heated. "I want it, I want you, your dick, now."

"Did you just say dick?"

"Frustration is a powerful motivator and I'm motivated more than you can imagine." She pushed him up, then sat beside him, and with one big tug ripped off her blouse, buttons springing across the room. How'd she get so strong? She wiggled out of her black lacy panties, her long legs stretched out, the dark patch at the juncture waiting for him. How'd she get so sexy? How'd he get so . . . horny.

She said, "I'm totally naked, now, so do something with it. But first . . ."

She scooted to the edge of the bed and his heart nearly gave out.

"You're leaving?"

She started tearing though his nightstand.

"What are you looking for?"

"It sure ain't a Bible." Her head jerked up and she snapped her fingers as if remembering something. Pulling his wallet from his soaked jeans on the floor, she plucked out the condom that had escaped across the library desk. Grinning, she held up the trophy then eyed his erection straining against the front of his briefs. "Just a guess on my part, but somebody there sure wants out."

"Where's the prim librarian I see over there on Bull Street? The one who wears skirts, white blouses, and sensible shoes? What kind of books have you been reading in that library of yours?"

"Really, really good books. Hence the frustration element." She licked her lips, then tore the end off the blue packet and handed the coiled latex to him. He'd been handed a lot of things in his life—a beer, a sandwich, a wrench, a screwdriver, but never a condom. He usually found it on his own in his own time. Someone was impatient and that knowledge turned him on even more. He disposed of his briefs, Churchill's eyes wide, round, and appreciative turning him on all the more. She watched him as he covered himself and he thought he'd have an orgasm right there on the spot.

"I don't remember it being so . . . big."

The orgasm possibility got more intense. "I do remember you being so beautiful." He kissed her, laying her back, smoothing hair from her face, his erection pressing into the cleavage of her legs, the soft mound of her sex teasing him more. He kissed her neck, her chin, her lips, then settled himself over her, gazing down into eyes he'd dreamed about for three long, long years. "How'd I get so damn lucky to find you in my life?"

"You're one of the good guys, Cal Davis." She ran her fingers over his face and across his chin stopping at the scar. She frowned, her eyes filled with apprehension. "I did this to you."

"No, that would be Fletcher Cunningham, two-fifty, six-foot-three who thought he should have my mashed potatoes."

"This over potatoes?" She closed her eyes and he felt her exhale in disbelief. Damn, he shouldn't have told her. It was going to take a while for him to adjust to the outside world. What was accepted as everyday in the slammer wasn't the norm in the real world. He had to remember that.

"Hey, I didn't want to upset you." He kissed her nose. "I'm fine. I'm here with you now and everything's perfect. That's all that matters." Then he kissed her delicious lips and slid into her, her legs circling his waist as she arched, taking him deep inside her sweet body.

She gasped as her lips parted. He took her again and again, still not believing he was with her. How many times had he dreamed of it, of Churchill? Every night in prison he dreamed of holding her, smelling her hair, her skin, the scent of their lovemaking filling his head. Every single night he thought of her.

He made love to her one last time, claiming her for the moment because it wouldn't last. They'd always been star-crossed and he knew when it all played out nothing would change to make that different. He'd used her and lied to her. When she realized it, no matter what reasons he had, the two of them would never be as innocent or giving again. But they were together and he'd always remember how he wanted it to be between them.

"How are you doing, Dad?" Cal said as he approached the table at the Pink House. Those five words were probably the only positive ones he'd get in for the next hour. He sat down between his parents, opposite Tripp. Cal straightened his tie and resisted the urge to order a double scotch on the rocks to get through the ordeal because it was more than just a lunch. Ron and RuthAnn had an agenda. He could tell because they had their lecture faces in place, the ones with plastered on superior smiles. That was okay. After they were done pontificating he'd talk to them about Tripp and how to get him back on track. That's why Cal agreed to lunch in the first place. Tripp.

"Your mother and I have news," Ron started, making Cal rethink the double scotch idea. Anything that started with *we* and *news* and both parents in Brooks Brothers suits was never good news for him. It meant they were plotting out his life . . . again.

"Dad," Tripp said, knowing the telltale signs of life-as-it-should-be-according-to-the-parents as well as Cal did. In fact, Tripp had probably been a victim more often than Cal. He was younger, more vulnerable. "This is just a friendly lunch to get us back together."

"Of course it is." Ron patted Cal on the back. "That's why we're all here but there is a bit more. You see, your mother and I have been working on Cal's behalf."

His behalf! It was worse than Cal thought.

"We talked to the maintenance department at the college and the groundskeeper is retiring next month. This would be a great opportunity for you."

"I have a job." Cal studied the menu already knowing what he'd order, she-crab soup with a side of arsenic and hemlock for dessert.

"But you'd be affiliated with the college," RuthAnn added.

Cal felt an aneurism coming on.

"That's the best part of all. The job comes with some prestige. You'd meet the right people. There are college functions that I'm sure they wouldn't mind if you attended, provided you came with us as our guest, of course. Many fine teachers and supporters are part of the college, their families reaching back to the days of Lee. With Jefferson Davis being a distant relative of ours that does put us in good standing with the community. It always has."

"Even for an ex-con groundskeeper? I don't think so."

"Well that's the whole point. They'd be giving an ex-con a second chance at a normal life here in the city." RuthAnn smiled too brightly.

Cal put down the menu. "I'm a charity?"

"Part of the prison outreach program." RuthAnn's perfect hair ruffled a little around the edges but she strained to keep a smile. He'd give her that. In all fairness, having a jailbird for a son wasn't easy. His parents had their pride, had worked hard for it. Then they had Cal, who never measured up. No, having a jailbird son was not easy for them and Cal hated that he was responsible for it. There wasn't much love between them but they were the parents and they didn't deserve the humiliation.

RuthAnn continued, "It's better than being with the no-good riffraff you run around with over at that speedway. Nothing but a bunch of rednecks, and that Callahan person you've spent time with, well, I have no idea how you got mixed up with him or why." RuthAnn tisked, her Southern drawl sneaking out more than usual. "I'm sure Miss Ellie is involved somehow and she is another person I do not understand at all." She gave Ron a subtle glare of disapproval for having such a mother. "You simply must take this job, Cal, for all our sakes."

"Look," he said, trying for a big dose of nice in his tone. "I like cars. Always have." Cal girded his loins for the response he'd get from his own next piece of news. "I'm half owner of the speedway, now."

"Oh no." RuthAnn shut her eyes, looking faint. "OhmyGod!" She flopped back against her chair, fanning herself with her napkin. Ron handed her a glass of water. "You're trying to kill me. Lord have mercy you truly are, I do declare. How could you come from this family and be so different from the rest of us? Our family has connections. Your father and Tripp belong to organizations, societies that have a purpose here in Savannah and—"

"Not now, dear," Ron interrupted in a hushed voce.

"Cal is who he is," Tripp said with a heavy sigh, his face more pale than ever. "He's doing what he wants to do. Can't we just have a peaceful lunch?"

"Works for me just fine." Cal studied the menu. "I'm starved. Anyone else starved?" He motioned to the waiter. "Can we have a bottle of wine here? A few bottles might be best and keep 'em coming."

"You have to make amends. Getting thrown into prison and humiliating us all is not acceptable," Ron hissed, trying to keep his voice down—and not doing a good job of it—as the waiter began to pour wine into their glasses. "Thank God Tripp came along."

"Yes," RuthAnn blurted. She downed her wine in one gulp. "He knows what this family stands for and is ready to carry on the traditions of being a proper Southern gentleman taking his place in society. There I said it and I'm not sorry. It's time you stopped embarrassing this family, Cal, and take responsibility for being a Davis. For years I've tried to explain you to our friends but I can't anymore. There aren't any more excuses left since you wound up in jail for stealing from Dodd and his charity for the poor elderly of the city." She shook her head. "You should be grateful the college will even consider you."

Cal knew there'd be days like this, even weeks and months, and more than likely an entire lifetime. He wasn't thrilled with the idea but it was a hell of a lot better than the alternative. He'd been through worse; he'd survive. It's what he did best. He folded his hands together on the table. "I'm not taking the job. I'm sorry I've hurt you and our family but I've done my time and it's over. That's all I can say."

RuthAnn stood. "Yes, I do believe this is over." Nose in the air she walked away. Ron followed, but Tripp remained at the table, looking worse than ever. He shook his head. "This is wrong. I'm going to—"

"Do nothing," Cal interjected as he leaned across the table to Tripp. "The parents will move on to teach new classes and being guest lecturers. Colleagues will commiserate with them on having a no-good son and reassure them that they did their best. All things considered, not that much has changed. The black sheep just got a little blacker, is all. I probably won't be invited to their Christmas party but you can save me an apple tart."

"This isn't funny, Cal." Tripp ran his hand through his disheveled hair. "I can't do this anymore."

"Yes, you can." Cal looked Tripp straight in the eyes. "Because nothing else makes sense at this stage of the game. It's over. Are you with me?"

"I hate this game." Tripp let out a long breath. "I'm going to find the parents and try to calm them down." He gave a little smile. "If you're not at the damn Christmas party I'll go freaking nuts. And you know I'll eat the tart before I ever get it to you."

Tripp left and Cal poured another glass of wine. Since he was stuck with the bill he might as well kill off the rest of the bottle. It would let the parents and Tripp get a head start. The worse part was Tripp was still a mess and Cal had no idea how to fix him. Cal reached for the Australian Riesling he'd picked. He was a beer man but every now and then . . . His thoughts died as Churchill McKenzie slid into the chair next to him. Holy damn. Just when he thought things couldn't get any worse, they did. Not that he minded being with Churchill but when she was around there were two things going on between them, sex and a never-ending barrage of questions. With this being a restaurant part two was the winner, unfortunately. She took his wine glass right out of his hand, drank it dry, then plopped it back on the table with a sold thunk. "Sex last night was really great."

Possibility idea one and two mixed together. Other patrons in the restaurant stared wide-eyed. They had to be thinking *Well dang, this conversation sure beat the heck out of the one making him a lawn maintenance man.* He leaned back in his chair. "Okay, I agree."

"Except," she went on, her eyes glassy, "I think it was a distraction like when you kissed me in the library and took the key and my notes." She gulped wine from the bottle, the waiter in the far corner nearly fainting dead away. Her eyes crossed now. "So, tell me, Cal, was the sex to keep me all dreamy-eyed so I'd forget about everything but you and me in the sack?"

"What are you doing here, Churchill?"

"Drinking my lunch and trying to make sense out of what's going on because I have to tell you, being sober wasn't working one little bit. I went with gin and tonic. Sherlock Holmes drank gin so I thought I'd give it a try." She hiccupped. "Let's see now, you went to prison and I put you there. Then this key situation turned up and nothing's been quite the way it should be. I know you're not going to level with me. I think you know something and that's okay if you don't want to share. I can figure things out on my own." She pointed to her head. "I have my notes memorized all right up here and put them together again."

"Let it go, Ace."

"I can't." She closed her eyes for a second. "You got cut on your face over potatoes. Last night some idiots tried to kill you or at least mess you up pretty bad. Today your parents treat you like a leper. See"—she held her arms wide open—"the problems is I can't live with myself if I'm the one who caused this and you weren't really guilty in the first place. Somehow, for some reason, that stupid key connects everything." She closed her eyes. "Damn it."

"I took the money. That's all there is to it."

"What would make a man give up three years of his life if he was innocent?"

"I'm not."

"I don't believe you, so there, and that is not the gin talking, it's me, all me. You know, I came back to Savannah to get away from trouble and lead a nice boring life and I intend to stay right here forever. I like boring. I truly do. Ask Margo, she'll tell you. She'll write you an epistle on the subject of her boring daughter. For me it's books go out, books come in. Easy peasy. But now I got a bad feeling I sent the wrong guy to prison." She hiccupped. "So I'm going to find out what this is all about and I'm going to start as soon as the room quits spinning. Then I can go back to my books out, books in way of life."

In a low voice, adding a bit of stern he hoped she'd pay attention to, he said, "You're getting in over your head."

She grabbed his tie and yanked his face to hers. "I did that nine years ago in the back of the Mustang. Next time I'm taking the damn bus."

Chapter Six

Michelle looped the handles of the shopping bag over her wrist, held on to Storybook's leash, then knocked on Miss Ellie's red door. No one answered. Where in the world was Benny? He had to be here. Surely he hadn't given up on their project and left. That would be terrible for . . . for Storybook. Yes, what would the poor dog do without Benny in his life? She knocked again a little more frantically and the door flew open to Benny on the other side. She started to breathe a sigh of relief until she noticed his black hair was wet from a shower, jeans hung from trim hips, and no shirt. Her relief died, replaced by interest. He hadn't expected to see her and she hadn't expected him to be partially dressed. Shorter did not mean scrawny and it certainly didn't mean fat.

"Sorry," he said raking his hand through his hair.

She wasn't sorry at all. She was downright grateful.

"I was in the shower after working out." Benny stepped aside and Michelle entered Miss Ellie's living room complete with chintz curtains, floral-patterned davenport, Savannah Spring china in the cabinet, and bench and weights in the corner. "Hope you don't mind," he said nodding at the bars and heavy disks. "Staying cooped up in this apartment was driving me crackers. I'll give the stuff to the thrift store when I move on, so that works. Had to work off a little energy."

He stretched a white T-shirt over his head and Michelle realized there was no flab overhang. No muffin top for Benny. In fact, the guy was ripped. "I'll be back in a minute. I'll get a dress shirt from the bedroom."

He turned and she took his arm, the connection between the two of them like an electric shock. That's what it probably was, static electricity from the carpet. "Wait. No more dress shirts unless you're going out for something special. You won't be needing so many layers down here in this heat. Light clothing and light colors. Like me in this little blue sundress. More casual, more friendly."

"Dollface, you look great. I'll give you that."

"You do, too." She blushed. "I mean staying inside hasn't been hard on you with staying fit and all. The T-shirt look is fine for you." *Very fine indeed. Oh Lordy, is it hot in here or what!* She unclipped Storybook and he did his paws on Benny's shoulders greeting. Thank heavens. One more minute looking at Benny and she'd be the one salivating instead of the dog. "I think you were missed."

"Goes both ways." Benny grinned and laughed. He had one of those deep friendly laughs that you like to hear. He scratched his dog and kissed him on his big black doggie nose. Storybook gave one more lick, then got down and wandered over to a rug by the door and plopped down. Benny said to her, "That doesn't look like normal library attire to me. New?"

"As a matter of fact, it is." He did a twirl motion with his index finger and she did a little spin. The skirt flowed out around her making her think of when they danced. Her skirt tickled her thighs making her feel feminine and sexy as all get out.

"Something special?"

She stood still, feeling breathless and not all from the twirling but from the slow smoldering all male look sliding into Benny's eyes. He didn't make a pass or even flash a sexy smile. He simply looked at her.

"I'm going out with . . ." Who the heck *was* she going out with? Churchill? The girls from the book club? She wouldn't dress like that for the book club gals. "Tommy. That's who it is. My ex."

Benny cut his gaze to the window and shoved his hands in his jean pockets. "How's the reconciliation going? Making progress?"

"Tommy likes my cooking."

Benny glanced back her way. "And?"

"And he's taking me to Savannah Bistro tonight. That's a mighty nice restaurant here in town. He brought the rolls for the dinner the other night when he came over. He and TJ talked some and I think it's going to all work out just fine between us." She nodded. "It just has to. TJ is better than he's ever been, even working overtime. He's doing the algebra and calling his daddy 'Sir.' Tommy likes that a lot. TJ's trying to make things work. He's looking at his daddy's gun catalog and he hates guns, so I need to try a little harder, too." She studied Benny for second. "What's wrong?"

"Sounds like a snow job."

"Excuse me."

"Like you're trying to convince yourself this is the thing to do and . . ." Benny shook his head hard. "Forget it. So, what you got here in the bag?"

Michelle put her hand to her hip. "Hold on a minute. I'm not forgetting anything. What do you mean snow job? I'll have you know Tommy and I are trying right hard to make things work. I know it's not going to be easy as pie or anything close but I'm going to do it, we're going to do it, so there. It's really none of your business anyway." She didn't mean that to sound so nasty. From sexy woman to harpy bitch in one minute flat. What was wrong with her?

"You're absolutely right," Benny said before she could apologize. He took a step back, sounding all business. "This is none of my business. What happens between you and Tommy is personal stuff and I overstepped. It won't happen again."

"I didn't mean to be—"

"You're one hundred percent right. This is none of my beeswax."

But that wasn't what she wanted either, Benny all formal and impersonal. She wanted friendly. He reached in the bag and pulled out khaki pants, deck shoes, and a navy polo.

"I thought it might be a good look for you."

"It's perfect." He grabbed his wallet from his back pocket and drew out some bills. "This should cover it."

"Benny, I apologize for being so snippy."

He gave her a half smile. "Dollface, you're never snippy. You have a family to take care of and I can appreciate that. I applaud it. You're just the kind of mom I expected you to be. You better go or you'll be late for your date."

"Have you been practicing your Southern talk?"

Benny cleared his throat. "Well now, I've been reading and watching that movie you went and brought over and I have to say the acting is mighty fine. Do you really believe that Jim fella went and did in his lover like they say he did? All seems mighty circumstantial to me. They're making up tall tales is all. Telling fibs like a fortune teller at a county fair. Look here at these pretty little old violets I've been tending for Miss Ellie. I figure it's the least I can do with her lending me her home and all. She even told me to make use of her car out back. Isn't that just like her. A truly fine woman." He gave Michelle a wink and she laughed. "Not perfect but I'm working on it."

"I do declare, Houston Elliott the Third. You do have a decent accent these days. A little more practice and you'll fit in like a little old pea in a pod. Oh, I almost forgot." She pulled a bag from her purse. "Hair dye."

Benny's eyes rounded. "What?"

"You need to change your appearance. This will lighten the black up a bit and you won't look so Jersey-ish. We need to dab a bit on your eyebrows. And here are some wire rim glasses." She thrust another bag at him. "Just clear glass but it'll help. You need to get outside in the sun, get yourself all tanned up."

"Do you not listen to the surgeon general? Tanning's a no-no."

"Getting dead is a bigger no-no. You're all pasty white, like some Yankee."

"I am a Yankee."

"Well, we can't all be perfect." She shook her head. "From here on you're Houston Elliott. That's what I'm going to call you. I'm not expecting you to dye your hair all by yourself you understand. I'll come over tomorrow and do it for you."

"But there's a woman on the front of this box."

"Hair's hair. A light brown will do nicely and then when you go outside put a little lemon juice on and it'll bleach out some of it to a dark blond."

"B-Blond? Me? You're talking third generation Italian here. You're making me into a damn weenie."

She took the glasses and slid them up his nose. "But you'll be a live weenie."

Benny glanced at himself in the mirror over the table by the wall. What had he gotten himself into? "I'm not sure it's worth it."

"Why sure it is, pumpkin." She went to him and patted his cheek, her eyes all fun-loving and full of life.

What he really wanted was for Michelle to kiss him, and not just on the cheek but on the lips, with a lot of tongue. Damn, he wanted her. The thought of her being out with another man was enough to turn his hair colors without one drop of dye. He folded his arms to keep from touching her—that's really what he wanted to do.

"I have to be going now. Tommy will pitch a fit if I'm late. He hates waiting for me." She headed for the door. "You take care now, you hear. I brought you *Gone With the Wind* on DVD, my very own collectors edition with extra footage. You treat it with the reverence it deserves and listen to the way they talk. But I must say, you are sounding more like a Southern gent these days."

Benny followed her outside and watched her take the steps to the sidewalk. She turned and gave him a cute smile, then realized what was going on, and shooed him back inside. "Whatever are you doing out here? You can't be exposing yourself like this. Now scoot."

"Yes, ma'am." Benny gave a little salute then closed the door, the apartment smaller than ever with Michelle not there, the silence deafening. He flipped on the TV but instead of being riveted by a rerun of *Antiques Road Show* he thought of Michelle. Hell, he constantly thought of Michelle. That's why he bought the weights, to try and pump off the frustration eating him up inside. She'd looked wonderful and she was off to have dinner with someone else. He couldn't stay in the apartment. He'd pumped iron till nearly exhausted and it wasn't helping. But he couldn't leave the apartment either.

What if he was in a car with the AC on and the windows rolled up. If he wore a hat, that might be enough of a disguise. He could at least drive around Savannah. "Come on, Checkbook, boy. How about a ride?"

The big brown dog pried one eye open for a second and then it slid shut. "Can't even get a date with my own dog." Where the hell would he find a man's hat in an elderly woman's apartment? He was stuck there.

Benny paced, thinking of Michelle, thinking of her on a date, thinking of her holding that guy's hand, her arms around his neck, kissing him and . . . "Enough!"

Benny picked up the box of dye. Better than a hat and it said on the front it only took ten minutes to work. He could do that. He'd seen commercials. Slap on goo, wait, shampoo goo out. Nothing to it.

The box said the goo stained so he found a roll of paper towels. He cleared the good terry towels out of the bathroom then stripped naked. He wasn't an idiot. The commercials showed no drips and everything easy but he was a dye virgin and accidents happened, especially with virgins. He read the instructions that told him to squeeze the color tube into the bottle of cream, then shake, and apply to hair.

He was a CPA. He could squeeze, shake, and apply. Hell, Marcy, the receptionist at Big City Auto in Jersey, who was dumb as a toad, dyed her hair. Not finding a scissors he bit the end of the tube. Dear God, it tasted terrible! And it burned his mouth! But he could stand the burning and the taste. He was a man. He could deal. Checkbook sat in the doorway as Benny squeezed the color into the bottle marked cream and shook, his mouth still burning and his eyes starting to water from the odor. "Holy shit! Holy shit! It smells like ammonia and boiled eggs! What the hell!"

His eyes watered more, his nose started to run, and he was drooling from the stuff in his mouth. But he could deal. He was a man. Using the corner of his right eye he could still see through, he changed the shake-top to the squirt-top. He squinted into the mirror through more tears that he was dealing with because he was a man. He'd do the middle of his head first then work his way down the sides. Sniffing and crying and drooling, he turned the bottle upside down over his head and all the goo came out at once. He forgot to screw on the fucking cap! The crap was dripping all over his head, down his face, and *onto his dick!*

And it burned! His dick was on goddamn fire! So were his eyes because the goo was dripping in them. Rubbing made it worse. He was going blind and becoming a eunuch all at the same time! He didn't know which end to grab first, his dick or his head! He ran water in the sink and splashed his eyes, then his dick, taking turns, not quite sure which he valued most, being Italian. With the miniscule bit of vision left he spied the bathtub.

The shower! Holding his dick that was throbbing and withered to the size of a cocktail weenie he hobbled into the tub. He turned on the water then the shower. The water was hot. Where the hell was the *cold?* He fumbled and slid, falling back on his butt. The damn stuff was slippery as hell. Not daring to get up he let the water beat down on his burning dick. He splashed some. Gradually the pain in his Johnson subsided. Blinking his vision began to clear. Checkbook's head rested on the side of the tub and if a dog could laugh his ass off, Checkbook's tail would be on the floor. Instead it was wagging. "What happened to man's best friend, huh?" Checkbook's tail wagged faster. Was he smiling?

Holding on to the side of the tub and still crying like a little girl, Benny stood slowly. Well damn, he was alive and all parts seemed to be working, at least as best he could tell at the moment. Bruised and beat-up as much as if caught in a back alley in Jersey, he climbed from the tub, dripping water everywhere. He grabbed the roll of towels that were soggy but better than nothing and dried himself off. He'd survived but for a minute or two there he'd had his doubts. He smiled and patted Checkbook. "All's well that ends well."

Benny grabbed another towel and swiped it across the bathroom mirror steamy from the hot shower but the towel wasn't cleaning the mirror very well, leaving behind orange streaks. He looked at the white cloth. It was still white and not orange. So where was all the orange stuff coming—"Oh shit." He turned and looked full into the mirror to his orange hair. Well, it wasn't all orange, just in the middle and then fading to kind of a copper tone on the sides. The orange streaked through his black eyebrows and across parts of the hair on his chest. He looked like an American flag, but instead of red and white stripes he was black and orange. Too bad Halloween was so far off. He had his costume. He laughed, a little at first then more because sometimes there just wasn't anything else to do but laugh and this was definitely one of those times. He most definitely had new respect for Marcy at Big City Auto. If he ever got out of the mess with Pinstripes one and two he'd send Marcy flowers of apology. The woman was a damn genius after all and he needed to tell her.

The good news was he didn't look Jersey anymore. Where he came from if you showed up with orange hair you would probably get the snot beat out of you just on general principles. He cleaned up the rest of the mess, then put on the new khakis and polo. He combed his hair, thankful that Nona Celeste wasn't there to see it. His grandmother would never understand messing with his black hair, no matter what excuse he had.

Benny backed Miss Ellie's sweet 1960 something white GTO from the garage, taking special care. That was some car and it got looks all right, but the guy with the orange hair got even more looks as he circled Reynolds Square, nearly causing two accidents. He headed down Congress where there were big Southern homes and massive trees.

An evening haze fell over the city and the streetlights flickered on as he stopped for a traffic light right in front of Savannah Bistro. There at a table by the window sat Michelle, *his* Michelle except she wasn't his at all. She was having dinner with some guy in shirt sleeves who was balding and had a paunch. At least from where Benny sat the guy looked paunchy. And he had bad table manners. Wasn't there something about good manners being part of the South? That guy didn't read the manual.

"Hey," came an angry voice next to him. "What are you doing with my grandmother's car?" A guy in his early twenties with sandy hair that needed to see a barber opened the passenger side and got in. "Are you trying to steal her car? I'm calling the police and—"

"Hold on. Miss Ellie lent it to me. I'm staying at her place over on York, watering her violets. She said it was okay, I swear it's true. You can call her. I'm Michelle's friend, I mean cousin. Yeah, cousin."

Damn, he didn't even know Michelle's last name. But before the guy could question him more, a horn blared behind them because the light turned and Benny moved the GTO forward. He was doing okay, getting along by himself till he actually saw Michelle with another guy. Now he just wanted to break something—except he had a passenger. "So, can I take you someplace?" he asked. Then he'd go break something.

"To my grandmother. Nice hair."

"I'm starting a trend."

The guy pointed out the window. "Take 80, it's up ahead. Miss Ellie's staying out at the speedway. Where the hell are you from?"

Oh crap, truth or lie? He had to lie. Time to start a new life. It was now or never. "Atlanta. Got family there."

"You sure don't sound like Atlanta. You sound a lot more Yankee."

Double crap. "Well now, that's because I spent a bit of time in New Jersey. You know how it is, you go someplace and lo and behold you just start talking like they do wherever you are. Happens to me all the time. Don't you agree? But now that I'm thinking about it, you don't sound like you're all that much from Savannah either."

"Duke. See that circle of lights off to the right? That's the speedway. Take the next right." They followed the gravel road, dust floating inside. With luck it would settle in his hair and tone it down to dull rust. Rust wasn't great but beat the heck out of crayon box orange. "Jeepers, is it always this crowded?"

"Jeepers? Did you say Jeepers? Now you sound like you're from Texas."

Would he ever get Southern speak right? It was nerve racking. "I mean, I see a place to park over there by that pick-up next to the concrete block building."

"That's the mechanic's garage for the race cars. My brother owns it."

"You have relatives everywhere."

"That's the way it is in the South, but then you already know that don't you, because you're from Atlanta." He gave Benny a disbelieving look as they pulled next to the garage. "Ah, hell."

"Hey, I didn't say anything this time." But the young guy was jumping out of the car even before it stopped. He headed to the open garage doors where some poor bastard was getting the hell beat out of him and he didn't even have orange hair. Benny hated one-sided fights. He'd always been the littlest kid in class and scrawny to boot.

He'd been picked on, pantsed, shoved in lockers, locked in bathroom stalls, stuffed in Dumpsters. You name it, it had happened—more often than he cared to think about. Well damn, he'd wanted to break something and from the looks of it this involved Miss Ellie's grandsons. Considering the fact that Benny was staying in her house and driving her car he owed her. That was as good an excuse as any to break something.

Benny swaggered up behind the younger guy, following him into the garage. Always good to do a little swaggering before things got bloody and it had potential with five good old boys against three. "Know what we call you guys in"—he almost said Jersey—"Atlanta. Chicken shits—too chicken to fight fair so you're nothing but shit."

The beat-up guy grinned, then sobered as his gaze fell on his younger brother. "Tripp, what the hell are you doing here? Get out of here. You don't belong here."

One of the bad guys said, "Tripp, this doesn't concern you none, boy. Go back to college and read some book. Leave us be."

Tripp looked confused for a second as if he didn't know what to do, one of those deer in the headlight expressions. "Scruck you."

"Huh?" The bad guys looked at each other. "What the hell's scruck, kid?"

The best Benny could tell it was a cross between fuck you and screw you by someone out of his element. He looked at Tripp, his hands smooth as a baby's butt. Make that two and a half against five. "Tripp," his brother yelled in that way older brothers do. "Get the hell out of here. I mean it, dammit. I can handle this."

"Do as your brother says, kid, before you get hurt. Beat it."

Slowly, Tripp backed out of the garage door which was probably a good thing. Duke was light years away from thugs in a garage looking for trouble. Except without Tripp it was two against five. Not good, but Benny had faced worse odds. One of the good old boys let out a mean laugh and looked at Benny. "Where the hell did you get the hair, Shorty?"

"My mama gave it to me. Wanna make something of it?" Benny swung at the guy and then all hell broke loose. He and Tripp's brother were getting beat up but giving as good as they got, almost. The five old boys could fight, all right. He'd give them that. Two grabbed Benny around the middle, then held his arms while another started beating on his ribs. Benny doubled over in pain and suddenly a shot rang out, echoing off the concrete walls. A little old lady in electric green jeans with a cast on her arm stood in the doorway, a smoking gun with an extra long barrel in her hand.

"I don't know what's going on but it don't look too fair a fight to me and Matilda here so I'm bringing it to an end right quick." She waved the gun at the good old boys. "Henry, Shortie, Billy, Donnie, Cletus, I'm going to get your mamas after you and you know what that means. Ganging up is no way to do things. Now you get yourselves out of here and if you ever show your faces again in this garage I'll be telling your grannies, too. Then there will be hell to pay. You won't be tasting fried chicken and corn bread for months. You should be ashamed of yourselves." She stuffed the gun that must be as old as she was back into her purse as the five filed past her and out of the garage looking more like grade school boys than thugs.

She said to Benny and Cal, "Now you two get your-selves cleaned up before you give this speedway a bad name. Silky will be plenty mad if he knows there's fighting going on. And you're making me miss my race."

"Miss Ellie," asked Tripp's brother still sitting on the floor. "How'd you know what was going on here?"

"That cute little thing you hired to serve up beer came and got me. Said she heard some guys talking smack and knew I was packing heat. Everybody knows I pack heat since I went and got my arm broke."

The brother scowled. "Well you weren't supposed to be."

"It's a darn good thing for you I was." She turned to Benny. "Nice hair. Brings out your eyes."

Benny didn't know what stunned him more, the woman walking out the door, her gun, or the hair comment. He stood up rubbing his ribs as the brother did the same, his eye swelling shut, a crust of blood on his lips. He held out his hand. "Thanks. The name's Cal."

"B—Houston, Houston Elliott the Third from Atlanta. Peachtree Street. What the hell did you do to those clowns to get into this mess?"

"Stole twenty-five grand from a preacher."

Benny studied Cal and considered how he wanted to protect his little brother and that Cal had a grandmother to protect him. He had his own shop that looked pretty lucrative and he seemed like he knew what he was doing with it. It didn't look like some front for something else. Benny grinned breaking open a cut on his lower lip. "You know, I've been around the block a time or two myself. I don't think you stole any money from some preacher. You're not the type."

Cal studied Benny the same way. "I've been around a couple of blocks myself and some guy with *the third* as part of his name never learned to fight like that in Atlanta on Peachtree Street." He shook Benny's hand. "Nice meeting you, whoever the hell you are."

The growl of the speedway echoed in the background as the moon dropped over the sea oats and grasses. Tripp stood perfectly still staring out at the marsh. It's what he used to do when the kids bullied him or called him names and Cal wasn't around and he'd had all he could take. He hurt inside, hurt a lot then like he hurt now. He didn't know what to do. He didn't want to be different anymore. When he was younger he'd hoped that if he stood perfectly still the Earth would open a crack, he could slide in, and the pain would go away. Of course he knew that was impossible, the bit about the Earth and the pain, but a tiny part of him wanted it to be true. He hated his life, he hated who he was. He was a chicken shit coward! He was a screwed up mess of a human being and he was getting worse.

"Hey, handsome, what are you doing out here all by your lonesome?" He turned around as the girl from the concession stand strolled down the path toward him. "Thought I saw you out here. Want some company?"

"Not really." He puffed out a breath of air. "I'm not good company right now. You should take off."

"You know, it's when you're not good company that you need company. Fact is, that's the time when my clients come see me most often. They need to talk and I listen. I'm a good listener." She sat down on a rock and looked up at him. "Wanna talk?"

"Cal sent you, didn't he? He's always taking care of me. Always."

She laughed. "This has nothing to do with Cal, sugar. It's just you and me being out here alone. Just the two of us talking and taking time out to enjoy one another on a beautiful August night."

"Why aren't you going after Cal? He's the smart one— smart where it counts. The handsome one, the one who has all the answers, and can take care of everything. Why are you out here? Let me guess, you're a psychiatrist in disguise drumming up business on the side. Or you're some kind of social worker going undercover to write a book. What the hell are you doing here? What the hell are you doing out here in the middle of nowhere with *me*?"

"I've been watching you, like when you came here the other day. You weren't happy then and you certainly aren't in a good way now. So, I've made you my project. I like smart men and you certainly are that. You just need reminding. I thought I'd come here and do that very thing."

He gave a dry laugh. "Excuse me? You really are a shrink? Well, save your breath. I've been to shrinks and counselors and therapists. They all tell me I'm fine, that I'm too smart for my own good, and will grow into my brain as I get older. I'll mature and be comfortable with who I am. Well, doc, I'm twenty-three and I don't like who I am at all. I'm crap. A big old turd who just ran away when he shouldn't have . . . again. A smart turd, I'll give you that, but a turd's a turd. There's no getting around it."

"So change."

He ran his hand over his face. "I don't know how." He looked back to the marsh. "I'm a damn coward. I've read tons of books and gone to school my whole life and I know nothing. Not a goddamn thing about who I want to be, but I know I want to be someone different. I don't know how to live. I walk off a college campus and I'm lost. It's like I'm on another planet. I don't know how to talk to people."

"You're talking to me just fine."

"You're a shrink. You don't count. I mean real people. I'm an adult and everybody takes care of me still. I'm like a ten-year-old and I don't know how to grow up, so I just go back and do more school."

She patted the rock beside her and he sat down, the moonlight making her hair shine like polished silver and her eyes dance.

"You sure don't look like any other shrink I've been to."

"That's because I'm different in a lot of ways." Then she kissed him full on the mouth, surprising the hell out of him and taking his breath away. No other shrink had ever done that before. She should smell of beer and hot dogs because she worked concession but instead the aroma of vanilla and springtime filled his head. Her fingers tracing a line across his chin and down his neck were a touch of heaven. Her lips pressed to his. As she opened her mouth his mouth opened too, and her soft, wet, warm tongue slid easily inside. Her mouth opened wider and her hot breath mixed with his. His tongue suddenly mated with hers and his body was on fire. "You're a good kisser, Tripp Davis," she said as she pulled back a fraction. "A very good kisser, indeed."

His heart was beating so fast he thought it might jump out of his chest, making breathing difficult. "Why did you do that?"

"So you'd remember you weren't ten."

"Point taken. It worked. Have you written a paper on this experiment?"

"Not exactly."

"Some new psychiatric study you're involved in?"

"You could say that. Confidence building. Do you feel more confident?"

"I feel something."

Her incredible lips smiled and it carried through to her eyes making him want to kiss her again. She was right, he never felt like that when he was ten. She took his left hand and put it on her breast, the warmth of her skin seeping though her blouse to his palm, the soft shape as if made for his hand and he suddenly knew exactly what he felt. Hard! Hard as a damn fencepost. She stood and the absence of touching made him dizzy. She undid the top button of her blouse, then the next till the material parted exposing a tiny ring pierced though her navel and her flat tan abdomen. The blouse slid off her shoulders onto a bush leaving her in a scrap of lace. Reaching behind, she undid it, freeing her breasts as the material fell away, the moonlight glistening on the loveliest skin he'd ever seen in his life. Not that he'd seen much.

"How do you feel," she whispered.

"I-I—"

"That's how a man feels, sugar, and you are all man, every inch of you. Here"—she touched his forehead—"here"—she touched his heart. "And here too." She placed her warm hand over his crotch. "You remember you're a man, you hear? The rest of life will come."

He stood looking into her dreamy eyes, her lovely body so near. "Can I touch you?"

She smiled and he went weak with awe. Again she took his hands and placed one on either side of her warm wonderful breasts. "You're not a virgin are you, sugar?"

"Define virgin. The few times I've had . . . It was never like this or with someone like you. Dear God, you are gorgeous. You're the woman men go to war over, write poetry for, compose songs and pen sonnets about, lock in golden towers so they have them all for themselves."

"My oh my, Tripp Davis, how you do go on about a woman." She kissed him again, his hands sliding to her bare back. He never knew a woman could feel like that. Janet Barrows from the chem lab didn't have skin like that. But then maybe she did and he didn't know how to appreciate it. Tonight he appreciated. Tonight he worshiped.

"Kiss me," she whispered in his ear sending chills down his spine. "Kiss me like a man kisses a woman he wants to be with. You know how to do this and do it well. Listen to your body. Feel it in your heart and in your soul. Let what you feel have its way."

And he did. He knew how to kiss her because she was special. He knew how to hold her softly but with enough strength to be serious but not overbearing or forceful. He tasted her and cherished her. "You are the most amazing woman. I feel as if I can do anything when I'm with you."

"And you are an amazing man. Male of the species in every way. Strong and powerful and able to do anything you set your mind to. You are master of your fate." She kissed him back. "Never forget that. Keep it with you always." She backed out of his arms and picked her bra from the bush where she'd draped it, then her blouse.

"You're leaving me with . . . with this?" He glanced at his crotch.

"This is just the beginning for you. Close your eyes and think about who you are and who you want to be. Come on, do it. For me, for you."

He did but the picture was a little fuzzy. He was still in college at his desk surrounded by books . . . and then he wasn't. He was standing with an incredibly beautiful woman in the woods, moonlight spilling across the grass and in to the trees. He opened his eyes and she was smiling at him. "You keep in touch now, you hear."

"But—"

"What you want to be, what you want to do will come to you just as you knew how to kiss me, touch me, and be with me tonight. It's inborn and it's all male. You just needed a reminder of what being a man felt like and I was happy to be the one to help you out. There are other things about being a man, of course, but this was a fine start." She smiled, turned, and walked away, then called over her shoulder, "If you feel you can do something, you can. You don't get that from reading books or giving lectures. You have to live it and do it all by yourself." She turned and blew him a kiss off the tips of her fingers. "Bye, sugar. You be sure to come see me sometime, you hear now."

Tripp sat down on the rock. That was the damnedest therapy session he'd ever encountered. Not that he was all that up on the latest psychiatric techniques. There were new procedures coming along all the time. He looked at the bulge in his pants. It was not shrinking. He wasn't sure how that new procedure worked in the long term or in real life but for the moment it got his attention. It made him realize he was indeed a man and not an academic monkey. And it sure as hell beat hoping the ground would swallow him up.

He started back toward town. He'd walk. He couldn't face Cal and that orange hair guy from Atlanta. He'd let them both down. He'd let himself down, been doing that for a long time, and that was the crappiest thing of all. That therapist was right. He was a man. He just had to figure out how to act like one, not just in the sex department, but in real life. It was do that or crawl back on to some college campus and stay there—safe, secure, and useless.

Chapter Seven

Holding her purse up in hopes of catching some light from the streetlamp, Churchill fished around inside the jumble of lipstick, comb, keys, box of red hot candies, and wallet for her library key. She'd intended to put all her keys together on one ring till she heard that the extra weight was bad for Tic Tac's ignition. So it was two key rings and she could never find the right one she needed when she needed it, especially when toasted.

"What in the world are you doing here on a Saturday evening? Don't you get enough of this place?" Michelle said from behind her.

"My brain is pickled. I need to get inside and can't figure out how to do it."

"I'm not exactly following you here, honey, but if you say so I'm believing you." Michelle took her own keys from her own purse and unlocked the door with the magnolias. "Your eyes look like roadmaps but those are really cute shorts. Where'd you get them?"

"Target, end of season sale. I took a nap at home but it didn't get rid of the killer headache and pukey stomach. My mouth tastes like the bottom of a birdcage and I think my teeth have fur."

"Thank you very much for that lovely description after

Tommy just made me try sushi at dinner. Why they don't cook the stuff is a mystery. Maybe put a little breading on it and mix it up in a batch of green and some okra. When Tommy went to the men's room I stuck the glob on a fork and cooked it over the table candle. It didn't help and smelled horrible. I need a hamburger. Why are you here?"

"Cal. Why are you here?"

"Walking home from dinner. Tommy had business at the station." Michelle closed the door. "The Cal comment covers a mighty big chunk of territory. Care to narrow it down a bit for me? Does it have anything to do with the pickled brain syndrome you're suffering from at the moment?"

Churchill turned on the main light and tossed her purse to the short end of the "I" shaped checkout counter. "He stole something from me. Something important, least I think it's important. Miss Ellie found it, then I stole it from her, and then he swiped my notes on it. Now I have a bunch of questions rattling around in my brain and I hate rattling questions. The reason I became a librarian is to answer questions, that and I like the smell of books. This all started when I saw Cal at lunch at the Pink House."

"A lunch you drank?"

"Gin. If it's good enough for Sherlock Holmes, it's good enough for me."

"Honey, he did cocaine and had depression, find another hero. Why do you have that dopey smile on your face?" Michelle sat on the bottom step of the spiral stairs with the ivy railing that went up to the balcony.

"Cal looked really good this afternoon. He had on a blue shirt and tan sports coat. He'd shaved. Don't know if I like him better that way or a little scruffy with the no-shave thing. Either way he sure is put together nice."

"Last week he was over on Bull Street, bending over to fix a fuel pump or something in IdaMay's car. What a butt.

Caused a three car pile up and they had to rush IdaMay to the hospital for heart palpitations."

"His parents were there for lunch too, with their disappointed looks and why-can't-you-be-more-like accusations along with I've-got-your-life-planned comments. I'm not exactly my mother's daughter. More like a jumbled bunch of recessive genes from housewives, farmers, and laborers back in my own ancestry so I understand how Cal felt." She tried to boost herself onto the desk but boosting was beyond her capabilities at the moment so she sat on the floor and leaned against the desk. "Did you know my grandfather was the youngest person to climb Kilimanjaro, and my grandmother swam the entire Mississippi River, and Uncle George climbed the major peaks in the Tetons in under nine hours? I'm an ancient history librarian who likes vintage cars, old houses, and antique furniture. Now there's disappointment for you, in spades. Anyway, I couldn't do anything to make the situation with Cal and his parents better but Cal didn't have to drink alone after they left in a huff. I could offer him a little diversion, so I did."

"You are a good Samaritan. I'm sure Cal is grateful. Why don't you just go on home tonight and get some sleep? You'll feel much better in the morning and the good thing is you'll only be seeing one of everything instead of doubles like you probably are now. You don't have to be here again till Monday morning. It's only Saturday night. That's early even by your standards."

"I need to look some stuff up before I forget it." A residual hiccup snuck out and Churchill slapped her hand over her mouth. "Sorry. Did you know that alcohol kills brain cells? What if it kills the stuff I have to remember and then all the information's gone? All I'll have are questions and no answers."

"I don't think alcohol works that way."

Churchill held her head to make sure it was still attached. "You don't know how much gin I drank. Then there was the wine from the bottle when I was with Cal, plus those nasty looks from the waiter. Australian, I think. The wine not the waiter." She closed her eyes and wobbled. "I think that's right."

"I missed all this for slimy bait food I had to cook myself." Michelle stood. "I need to get home to TJ. He was working late but should be in by now. Let me tell you that job has turned him around. He's a whole new TJ. I should go to that store and thank the guy who hired him. Are you okay here all alone?"

"It's a library. Noting happens in a library and my apartment's right next door. Where's Storybook? I thought you had him?"

"Uh, that cousin of mine that I told you all about, the one from Atlanta, is dog sitting. He and Storybook really hit it off."

"I can swing by and get him tomorrow."

"I'll drop him off at your place. Besides, I want to see how you're getting on." Michelle went to the door. "Lock this thing behind me, okay?"

"This is not the Denver mint. The most valuable thing we have is that old sword Richard Arnold gave to Grant when he went and took over Savannah, that damn Yankee come-here." Churchill stumbled to her feet and waved to Michelle as she left, then closed the door and turned the lock. The last rays of sun sliced through the stained glass windows above. She ambled her way toward the back to the research books. Ambling was as fast as she could go at the moment. Taking down two books she'd used before, she put them on the desk and turned on the little brass light with the flowers. Her purse was up front with her notebook and pen. She'd get them soon, very soon. She just needed to sit a spell and rest her head on top of *Brotherhood, Secrets of the South*.

When she opened her eyes her glasses were crooked on her nose. The library was dark, really dark, except for the little lamp casting a cone of light across her desk, the glow of the red emergency Exit sign in the far front corner, and the dim streetlight out front. Didn't she leave the light on in the main part of the library? Something creaked. The floor by the checkout desk was marble, the floor in the reading room was carpeted, and the floor from the main hall to the back was cypress. Marble was solid, carpet muffled, old cypress creaked. She jerked instantly awake.

For a second she considered yelling, *Who's there?* But whoever was there didn't want her to know or they would have knocked or made more noise. They would have called *Yoo-Hoo, anybody home?* There was also the little fact that she'd locked all the doors. She remembered doing that. Her iPhone was in her purse and *Brotherhood, Secrets of the South* made a poor weapon. Weapon? Did she need one? What happened to the library not being the Denver mint?

She doused the desk light. Knowing the library as well as her own apartment the dark gave her an advantage. She wasn't sure what advantage over whom but she wasn't hanging around to find out. Slinking out of the chair and onto the floor she huddled down against the side bookshelf. When the intruder came up the hall and into the room she'd crawl out of the room and down the hall, then run to the Exit door. It had one of those emergency push bars and she'd be out in a flash.

Another creak, closer. She prayed he didn't hear her heart beating because it sure was loud enough. *Why wasn't this happening to Margo? Margo would love this, probably write a best seller from the experience.* The figure passed right in front of Churchill. Men's shoes, Nike with that white outline of the checkmark glowing in the dark. Running shoes. Churchill didn't have on running shoes. She had on pink flip-flops that matched her cute shorts. Shoes that liked to slip on the marble floor. Her plight was not improving.

The guy came further into the room and she started to crawl into the hall. The floor creaked . . . under her. The guy turned, their eyes meeting across the darkness.

"Oh fuck! Oh fuck!" Did she just say fuck?

He took a step toward her and Churchill grabbed for a book behind her. The first one was too small, same for the second, but the third was big and fat. Thank God for wordy authors. She grabbed the spine and hurled it at the guy for all she was worth.

"Ugh!" He grabbed his face and Churchill jumped up like the scared little rabbit she was. She tore down the hall, sliding into the reading room and sprinting across the oriental carpet into the self-help section. She shoved the bar at the exit door and ran into the middle of the street. Two cars swerved, jamming on their brakes, the drivers looking totally pissed off. But she was safe. She didn't budge. The exasperated drivers drove around her, probably dialing 911 for the loony bin truck to come cart off the crazy woman in pink shorts.

Maybe she should call the cops herself. But she had bloodshot eyes and was wobbly. Half of Savannah must know that she'd been drinking wine straight from the bottle at the Pink House. It would be a while before she could show her face back there.

Her credibility was shot. The cops would think she imagined the intruder or maybe dreamed that someone broke into the library. After all, break into a library for what? Return an overdue book? Get your name first on the list for the latest Dan Brown offering?

She'd have to answer all those questions about the key, her notes, and what they were all about. She wasn't up for that since she didn't know squat. Any publicity would drive away Nike running shoe guy and she'd never find out who he was and what he wanted. That was another question unanswered.

A horn honked at her again. She really needed to get out of the middle of the street, but she felt safe there. Had she ever thought standing on a double yellow line would be a good thing? Then again did she ever think she'd guzzle half a bottle of wine? She'd go to Michelle's. Michelle needed to know about the break-in at the library since she worked there.

Churchill dodged her way to the sidewalk, looked back at the library, then started for Wright Square and on to Michelle's. Except . . . Stopping cold she turned again and looked up at her apartment. The door was wide open and there was no light in the window. That light was on a timer. She changed the bulb often. there was *always* a light in the window. Single women alone did things like that. Someone broke into the library scaring her to death and now her apartment? For the second time her apartment had been violated!

Enough was enough! She straightened her spine, jutted her chin and boobs—when you jutted one the other automatically followed—and crossed the street. Tip-toeing up the steps to her apartment she hid behind the open door. She might be angry but she wasn't stupid. Cautiously poking her head around the edge she peeked inside, the streetlight offering a little light through the open door. Someone was moving around. She snatched a pot of geraniums from the railing and, keeping to the edge, went in. The intruder was after information she had and not her. Right? No real danger. Right? She swallowed, dodged behind the coat rack with her dangling sweaters. Raising the pot and ready for action, she peeked around just as the intruder picked up her new white shrug that she'd just bought, and not off the sale rack. It cost the earth at White House/ Black Market.

"Put that down right now," came out of her mouth before she could even consider keeping it in. She hurled the clay pot, red flowers and all flying across the apartment, hitting the guy square in the head. She was getting really good at throwing things.

"Dammit!" He grabbed his head and faced her. Uh-oh. What had she done? Poked the bear? What if the bear didn't read the *no real danger* memo and he had a gun? Terror made every hair on her head stand straight up, then fall right back down. "Cal? What are you doing here?"

She flipped on the light at the table but it didn't work. "Why are you in my apartment? What happened to your face, again? You're a mess, again. This is getting to be a habit. You should consider getting a bodyguard."

"I can tell you what happened to my head. Next time try saying hello. Damn, woman." He rubbed his temple. "What in the hell are you wearing? Aren't those shorts a little skimpy?"

"Skimpy? This from the man who hired Miss Southern Sexpot? Why aren't you at the raceway where you belong? It's Saturday night. There are races. Why were you in the library tonight? Looking for more of my notes? Trying to see what I remember and get rid of that, too? What are you hiding from me, Cal?"

"You can find any damn thing you want. I was looking for Tripp and saw your door standing wide open. For the record it's not your library but I wasn't in it. Why in the heck would I be?"

"This afternoon in my slightly inebriated state, I told you I had all the notes memorized and only needed to reconstruct them. I went to the library tonight to look at the reference books again and someone came in. I threw a book at him, *General Oglethorpe's Georgia, Colonial Letters, Volume One.* I think. Anyway, I hit him in the face. You have a banged up face. A really banged up face."

"Someone came after you?"

"I outran him. I can move pretty fast when terrified. But you already know that since you're the one who was there in the library chasing me."

"Sweet pea, if I'd been chasing you I would have caught you." He touched his swollen eye. "This is from a little altercation in my garage, not the flying edition of *Colonial Letters, Volume One.* Ask Michelle's cousin from Atlanta. He was there and so was Miss Ellie. Fact is she broke up the fight with Matilda."

"Thought you got rid of Matilda."

"Southern women are not easily parted from their firearms. Tripp was at the garage, too. I didn't want him to get involved and I told him to get lost, that I'd take care of it. He has no business being in the middle of a fight. He's not himself lately and I wanted to make sure he was okay."

"Oh my God. Tripp. That's what this is all about. Tripp! Why didn't I think of him before? This is all starting to make sense."

"You know where he is?"

She closed the door, then sat down on her maroon sofa that she got from the second hand store. It was nowhere near as nice as Cal's from Pottery Barn. But that no longer mattered. What did matter were pieces of the what's-going-on-puzzle falling into place like that Tetris puzzle she played on her iPhone when no one was looking. "I think I get it," she said as much to herself as Cal. "It's Tripp. You've been protecting him all his life and something must have happened, something big. You're protecting him again."

Cal sat down beside her on the sofa. She looked at his calm, no-read face that was a little too calm and a little too blank as if he'd had a lot of practice in not giving anything away. She added, "I'm right. I know I'm right. You went to prison even though you were innocent. It was all to protect Tripp."

"You gave an eyewitness report, remember? You saw me take the money."

"I saw you run out of the tent. There's only one person you'd go off to jail for. Well, maybe three people now that I think about it, Miss Ellie, Silky, and Tripp. My vote is with Tripp because Miss Ellie and Silky probably know how to get away with anything they set their minds to. Tripp would do whatever you said because you're the big brother. You took the key and my notes because, well I don't know why but they have something to do with what's going on."

A dull thud landed in Cal's stomach. He'd been afraid she'd figure it out since the night he and Churchill ran into each other in the alley. When he'd kissed her he'd realized how difficult it was going to be to keep his feelings for Churchill out of the way and stay the hell away from her and her infernal questions. Cal pulled in a deep breath and shut his eyes for a minute. Maybe if he came clean about some parts she'd buy it. Dear God, she had to. So much was at stake.

"Tripp was never allowed to be a normal kid, you know that. No finger painting in kindergarten, no overnights at other kids' houses because they thought he was weird. When he was eight he went to Dillon Gallagher's house for dinner and did his dad's taxes. Got him a two thousand dollar refund. The parents kept Tripp insolated in schools with adults and other dysfunctional egghead types."

"He's not the only smart kid on the planet, Cal."

"Except he followed me. The baby genius followed the baby dunce."

"Hey, you're dyslexic. You're not stupid. everybody gets that difference these days."

"We're talking thirty years ago. Ron and RuthAnn are academics and I was, hell I still am, a bitter pill to swallow. They could read at three. I couldn't even write the alphabet at six. Nothing written made sense to me and I didn't make sense to my parents. For a little kid that's a damn lonely place to be. Then along comes the perfect kid. Ron and RuthAnn were thrilled beyond words and wrapped him in one big intellectual bubble. That was worse than being the family dummy because they left me alone and turned all their attention to Tripp.

"I escaped and found cars. Tripp never escaped. He was the Oscar on the mantel, the Olympic Gold Medal in the case. He was the one with the rotten life and didn't even know it, till now. He doesn't understand who he is at twenty-three anymore than I did when I was five. I don't know which is worse but I do know I need to help him. He's my brother."

She looked at him with big sad eyes. "I thought Margo and I were dysfunctional. I'm so sorry."

"No feeling sorry. I survived. I'm good at that." Cal took a deep breath, drained and shaky. That was more than he'd ever told anyone about being a little kid and the world being one confusing piece of shit. In fact it was probably more than he ever told himself. It just spilled out once he got going. "But that's the Tripp and me story. It has absolutely nothing to do with me and Dodd. The key is just some old piece of junk Miss Ellie found. It obviously means something to someone. Maybe you should get out of town for a while. Let the key thing blow over and all will settle down by the time you get back here."

He looked into her eyes, sleepy, sexy, dark blue. Her lips were soft and he wanted to give in to the temptation to hold her, kiss her, and make love to her. But the more important thing was, did Churchill buy what he said?

She looked right at him and asked, "What happened to make Tripp realize his life is screwed up?"

Damn! "Being twenty-three and being an adult. Everyone has to face it sometime."

She touched the scar across his chin and kissed him. "I like you, Cal. And you like me, but you're not leveling with me. I can feel it. We know each other even in the Biblical sense so we're not strangers. Oh, there's probably some truth mixed in with the bull crap you just spewed but right now I'm so darn tired, make that tired and hung over, I can't figure out what to believe. If I ever pick up a bottle of gin again, shoot me. It'll be less painful."

"Couldn't you have stopped at 'I like you'?"

"I had to tell you about the shooting part." He laughed and for the moment felt better. He let out a deep sigh and gathered her in his arms, holding her close, feeling the heat from her body mix with his as they settled back into the soft pillows on the sofa. For the moment they were simply two lovers in Savannah sitting on a davenport. No complications. How he wished falling in love was that simple. She kissed his cheek then rested her head on his chest. "I can hear your heart."

"Some don't think I have one."

"I think yours is too big for your own good and has a lot to do with you being in a big pile of doo-doo."

He hadn't expected her to say that. His heart swelled or did something that felt darn amazing. She always chose to believe the good side of him. How could he not be in love with Churchill McKenzie? She cared about him. She had for a long time. He'd give the world for that moment to last forever. He planted a soft kiss to her hair. "Let this go, Ace," he whispered into the quiet apartment. "Please, for the sake of a lot of people, just let it go. No good can come from stirring things up. Believe me on this."

"You're asking a lot, Cal."

"I know."

She brought her face to his and kissed him again, her tongue tracing the outline of his lips. "Am I hurting your mouth?"

"Only if you stop." He slipped off her glasses and took her beautiful face in his hands. "What are we doing?" He undid the pink ribbon holding her hair back. The long curls swayed free across her shoulders, the strands running through his fingers as her arms circled his neck.

"Making out. You're great at making out."

"Then what?"

"We'll think of something." She snuggled closer and he held her a little tighter. How could the one person who had the power to totally screw up everything be the one person he wanted most? "I keep thinking that if I make love to you just once more, I'll get over you, that I won't think of you anymore, that this obsession I have for you will go away, that we'll be done." Streetlight fell over her and he laid her back on the sofa, her hair tumbling over the edge. "We'll never be done, will we?"

She smiled up at him. "I do have a bed you know. New mattress, pillow-top, Target sheets. Best I can do on my salary."

"If we move we'll break the spell that we're the only two people on the planet."

"Like in the Mustang."

"I thought of you so often when I was in prison. Your face"—he touched her cheek—"your lips." He bent his head and kissed her. "Your blue eyes and how they're dark and stormy when you're angry, the color of the sky when you're happy, and lit with fire when we make love. I didn't know if I would ever see you again. But here you are." He kissed her, inhaling her scent of shampoo and soap, and that hint of musk when she was turned on. He gathered her T-shirt, then pulled it over her head, her nipples hard and pressing against the lacy bra. She grabbed his T-shirt and pulled it off, a sensual smile on her lips as she sailed it across the room. She ran the palms of her hands over his chest and around his shoulders, her eyes taking him in all the while.

"You're the reason I came back to Savannah." Her fingers raked the sprinkle of hair on his chest then slowly slid down his middle, making his solar plexus quiver. Then her hand crept lower and cupped his erection, her eyes midnight black, his dick instantly harder. She closed her eyes, a sigh of satisfaction escaping her lips as she applied a bit of pressure making him want her all the more. "Are all racecar drivers this well hung?"

"Flattery," he growled, then bent his head and tasted one nipple, sucking the nub through the material as he pushed down one bra strap, then the other. She hugged him close, her fingers digging into his back as her body arched to his, demanding more. A little sigh of happiness escaped her lips. He paid homage to her other hard bead then licked the warm heated flesh between the lush mounds as he slid the bra away.

"Cal." Her voice was a plea.

"Not yet, honey." Her velvety skin against his lips was an aphrodisiac from the gods and he planted kisses down her abdomen to her navel. He unbuttoned her shorts, then unzipped them. Holding her hips in his hands he was overwhelmed with his desire for her. "You're perfect, every inch of you." He knelt on the floor.

"Where are you going?"

"To hell. What you do to me is sinful." He slid her shorts down to the dark patch of her sex then stopped, his heart racing as he planted soft kisses there. He tossed her shorts onto a chair. "You are amazing."

She wound her arms around his neck, their noses touching. "And you are the sexiest man on earth. You ruined me for other men. You know that, don't you?"

"Ah, my plan worked." He snagged her around the waist and she gave a little yelp as he toppled them both to the floor. "Maybe we should have used that bed."

She gazed down at him, her hair tumbling forward in a wild tangle. "But I'm having a great time here." She straddled his thighs just below his throbbing dick, the thicket of auburn curls hiding her clit and sweet passage spread wide right in front of him. He couldn't see a thing, making her all the more mysterious.

"When you changed the tire on my car all those years ago—you were eighteen and I was sixteen—I nearly ripped off your clothes right there in the middle of the street because I wanted to see the rest of you. For the record, nothing's changed." She undid his belt, yanked it off then traced the outline of his erection through his jeans. Just when he was absolutely positive he could not get any harder, she planted a kiss on his dick covered by the denim and the heat from her lips nearly sent him over the edge.

She unzipped his fly, then stretched down the waistband of his briefs setting his dick free. "You're the one who's perfect." Taking his erection in her palm she massaged the length of him as he felt himself grow bigger, every muscle in his body hard and hungry for her. "Churchill, honey, that's enough."

"See, slow isn't all that great when the shoe is on the other foot, or in this case, the other hand on the other genital. You are so sexy, so very, very sexy."

Before he could figure out what kind of sexy she was talking about, she took his penis into her lovely mouth and he nearly passed out from the incredible sensation. He hadn't expected that. He knew her, and yet he didn't.

"Church-hill." He could barely say her name. "Honey." He swallowed, her tongue caressing him, teasing him, loving him. "You can't." But obviously she could and very well.

"Oh Cal," she said in a breathy voice that sounded as turned on as he felt.

He snagged her waist and flipped them both over, him on top, her face radiant in the moonlight streaming in the window. "I hate to be a cliché but damn you're the most beautiful woman I've ever seen."

"I want you inside me. I want to feel your release, to know I make you as happy as you make me."

"You do, sweetheart, and more. You can't imagine." He kicked off his shoes then retrieved a condom from his jean's pocket before taking them off. Her eyes smoldered, fixated on his erection. She wanted him and God knows he wanted her but most of all he wanted to give her pleasure, make her happy. He kissed her left delicious breast then took his time with the other. With deliberate care he licked and suckled his way to her navel. Gently he spread her legs, the sensual aroma of blistering hot sex drenching the air around them. He kissed her left thigh.

"Cal?"

"Let me make love to you." He licked the inside of her right thigh then kissed it, adding little love bites. Her legs quivered, her hips elevating in anticipation, wanting more from him. He kissed his way to her clit, tasting her heat there, savoring the moment. She gasped, her legs falling back, opening herself to him more as he placed his mouth to her. Her sweet moans filled the apartment and set him on fire as his tongue slid into her wet, waiting passage. He'd never felt more powerful or more wonderful in his life than satisfying the woman he cared most about in the world. "Let it happen. Let go." Her body tensed once more and she cried out his name. He nearly died from the exquisite sensation of making love to Churchill McKenzie.

He held her close, her head cradled on his chest, their legs intertwined. He soothed her, memorizing her in every way. "How can you do that?" she whispered as he kissed her eyes, and smoothed back her damp hair. "You're a wonderful lover. Tonight you're mine and you are magnificent." Her eyes were moist with tears.

"Because making love to you is astounding. You are an amazing woman." He placed himself over her, watching the fire of passion dance in her eyes, her lips full and moist from his kisses. He wanted to say, *I love you*, but it was not the time. There would never be a time but he wasn't going to think about that. He slid into her, her body waiting for him, wanting him, taking him deep.

"Again," she pleaded and he took once more, her legs locking at his back. Sweat beaded across his lip as he held on to the last bit of control wanting their lovemaking to last, to not let go of the moment. Once it was over, the real world would come crashing in. He hated the thought. All he wanted was to make Churchill happy. She deserved it. No one stood beside him the way she did or fought for him the way she did. He loved her, had for a long time, but never told her. He took her one last time knowing that soon memories of making love to Churchill would be all that was left of the two of them together.

Chapter Eight

Cal was hunkered down by the mangled Dodge Challenger, TJ beside him shaking his head at the mess. Silky was sitting in a chair, his legs propped on a case of Pennzoil, his eyes closed. Cars had always been Cal's salvation. Looking at the hunk of twisted metal, he tried to concentrate on that and not on the fact that he'd made love to Churchill. Not that he wanted to forget about it. Hell, that was the last thing he wanted to do, but it made his life even more complicated than before, if that was possible. He wanted to be with her more than he wanted air, but when they were together she asked questions and poked around in what was happening. That got her much too close to the truth. And the truth didn't set you free like it said in the Bible. The truth was a big pain in the ass he never dreamed would be so had to keep hidden.

TJ pulled at the car door and the whole thing fell to the floor of the garage with a loud bang, echoing off the concrete.

"Hey," Silky groused. "Some of us are trying right hard to catch up on our sleep over here since being up till two in the morning talking new paint and drapes with Ellie. Don't see anything wrong with the old paint and drapes in my place. Good enough for the last twenty years. Why in blazes is there a need to change now? I'll never understand women if I live to be a hundred."

"Sorry." TJ stifled a grin as he exchanged looks with Cal, then turned his attention back to the car. "She was brand new, only five thousand miles. What the heck happened?"

"Raced a train to a crossing and came in second. How are you doing in algebra?"

"I hate it but I'm doing okay."

Silky mumbled, "A lot of life can be that way, son." Cal smiled then said, "So what are we going to do about the car?"

TJ gave an obvious shrug. "Put her back together the way she was. She's a rear drive V8 muscle car with a high tech engine. Good machine."

"Nobody builds 'em better than De-troit," Silky added.

Cal said, "She gets about nine miles to the gallon in stop and go traffic, handles like driving a semi, and can't get out of her own way."

"So?" TJ kicked a mangled tire.

"So we can put her back together the way she was, or we can make her better."

"We?"

"Yeah, we. See anybody else here in this garage?" The kid beamed and Cal remembered what it was like when he rebuilt his first car, the red Mustang. "She's already got great suspension, that new electronic stability program, and traction control. If we shed weight, use some inexpensive parts, and a few ideas I picked up along the way at the tracks over the years we might just get her to out-run, out-stop, out-corner some of the superexotics that cost ten times as much."

TJ's jaw dropped. "We can do that?"

"And," interjected Silky without opening his eyes, "if you go with a few of those aerodynamic aids that aren't all that costly and that electronic drive system Cal's been working on for a while now, you can probably turn her into a parallel hybrid plug-in/solar/electric that burns no fuel at all in everyday driving out there on the road. Muscle car/eco car, best of both worlds. Pretty sweet if you ask me."

Cal laughed and looked at TJ. "So, what do you think? You up for it?"

TJ's eyes covered half his face. "Holy shit! This is going to be some car."

Cal patted the crumpled white fender, in his mind seeing the car as it was going to be. "Yeah," he said in a quiet voice. "That's pretty much what I think, too." He looked at TJ. "How come I've never seen you in the Kart races out here for the sixteen-year-olds?"

"My daddy's not exactly a racing fan."

More than likely TJ did his racing on a dirt road with no rules and no lighting. If a kid was going to race, a kid was going to race. He didn't stop because his or her parents said so. Cal knew that for fact.

DaisyLou strolled into the garage, wearing hot-pink shortshorts and a white halter top, a bright smile in place. "Put your eyes back in your head," Cal whispered to TJ making him blush.

"Sugar," she said to Cal. "You really need to be carrying your cell phone with you. A lady's been trying and trying to get hold of you. Since she couldn't she had to drive herself all the way out here and she is in a state."

Churchill? What did she find out now? Was that why she drove out here? "Tell Churchill I'll be up at the office in a minute."

"This here's a Miss Michelle."

TJ jumped up. "Well, you better go see her. It sounds real important. I'll stay here and start taking the car apart. I'll keep everything straight and number it all. Now you better go up there where she is."

"You're kind of jumpy. Anything wrong?"

TJ dragged the door across the floor, metal grinding against concrete. Silky pried one eye open then the next looking exasperated as TJ added, "I can't wait to get started. I'm getting to work right this minute."

Cal followed DaisyLou to Michelle pacing in front of the concession stand. As soon as she saw Cal she blurted, "She's gone. I checked on her yesterday, even took Storybook. No one answered her apartment and I just thought she must be sleeping off her hangover. But when she didn't come to work today, and her purse was in the library, and I found this note taped to the front of the library door saying she was taking a vacation I panicked. Where is Churchill?"

She handed the note to Cal that said Churchill would be gone for a couple days and not to worry but to be careful because someone had broken into the library. Did she really take his advice? Decide to go away till things blew over? "Maybe she is taking a vacation."

"Without her purse? She wouldn't leave me all by myself to work the library if something was dangerous about it. I think someone's got her. She's been working on something and now she's gone. When she came back to Savannah after leaving Jersey she said she'd never leave here again and I believe her."

"Okay, so she didn't go to Jersey."

"I don't like this Cal, not one little bit. It's not like her to run off."

Cal raked his hair, a bad feeling in his gut that hadn't been there a minute ago. He didn't think Churchill had been abducted but he did think she was up to something. Too many questions unanswered and if there was one thing Churchill McKenzie hated more than an overdue book it was an unanswered question.

"I can tell by that look on your face you're worried, too. What do we do?"

"I met that cousin of yours, Houston. You got to admire

a guy who goes out in public with orange hair. He has a decent left hook. Get him to stay in the library with you just in case."

"I fixed his hair. It's not orange anymore."

"Too bad. I kind of like it. I'll check around and see if anyone's seen Churchill. And don't worry. She's fine. I'm sure of it."

"Going away is not her thing, Cal. That girl intends to live and die in Savannah." Michelle slapped her hands over her mouth and mumbled, "Forget I said anything about dying, okay. No bad karma."

"No bad karma." He kissed Michelle on the cheek. "I'll keep in touch." Michelle walked back to the parking lot and Cal sat on the bottom bleacher, staring at pit alley across the way, the August sun baking the red dirt track to hard brick. So, where the hell *was* Churchill? Someone could have abducted her but a better answer seemed to be that she was up to something. Cal had the key and he had her notes so she wasn't doing research on those. She suspected that Cal was protecting Tripp. She could have gone to find him except Tripp had pretty much vanished off the face of the earth. Hopefully he'd found a man-cave somewhere for the summer and was off swilling beer, eating pork rinds, and watching NASCAR. Cal couldn't even picture that scene but he could always hope.

If there was no key, no notes, no Tripp for Churchill to go after, that left Dodd. Would Churchill go talk to him? If she suspected Cal was innocent she would. Dodd was holding a revival under the big white tent down by the river that evening. If Churchill went to the revival and started asking Dodd questions it would stir things up again and blow everything to pieces. He didn't need that. What he needed was for Churchill to stay away from Dodd.

For the rest of the afternoon he and TJ, under the sleepy eye of Silky, tore at the car, stacking and labeling parts, what to keep, what to recycle for cash. By five o'clock they were tired to the bone, except for Silky who seemed well rested.

TJ left. Cal grabbed a shower, ate some leftover polenta he'd made the night before, then closed the door to the cabin behind him just as Miss Ellie stepped onto the porch. He gave her a kiss on the cheek and she said, "Well now, you're all gussied up, so I'm thinking you got yourself a hot date. But don't you think maybe you should stand a bit closer to the razor? You're looking a little scruffy."

"I'm off to see the Reverend Dodd."

"Honey, you sure you want to do that?"

"He has a revival tonight on"—Cal pulled a flyer from his back pocket—"Sin and Sinners, Redemption of the Damned. I think he's calling my name."

"Have you done lost your ever-loving mind?"

"Churchill's MIA and I don't much think that she's missing so much as gone off to do some thinking. I'm afraid that might take her to Dodd."

Miss Ellie smiled. "I'd say she knows that you shouldn't have gone to prison and she's trying to find out what got you there. What do you have to say about that?"

"That you're both dead wrong and the reason I'm going to the revival is to make sure Churchill doesn't go stirring up any trouble by asking Dodd a lot of questions. I'll find her and head her off. I'll never get this prison stigma behind me if she keeps stirring things up."

"She thinks you're innocent."

"And you think my going to prison is somehow connected to that key you found. Anyone could have dropped it in my car, accidently or on purpose. I always have the top down. Tourists have even gotten in the Mustang for a photo op. All I do know is that I have no connection to it."

"And all I know is someone broke my arm to get it and ransacked Churchill's apartment looking for it. You didn't want it around so you stole it and probably have it hidden over in that garage of yours somewhere. You can save your breath about there being no connection. I'm not buying it. You are innocent and that key leads us to why you won't tell us what's going on."

She looked at the flyer. "The place will be packed. Dodd draws a heck of a crowd these days, especially the elderly."

"He's probably setting himself up as executor of their estates, then bleeding them dry."

"Lord knows I don't have any use for the man, but my friends Miss Rose and Miss Emily showed his advice to a lawyer and he said it was sound. Dodd suggests simple things like stay off the credit cards, deal with cash, pay off mortgages, because they're used to that. Even goes to the bank with them and sets things up. A teller over at Darby Bank and Trust said he's right helpful."

"With his name on all their accounts."

"Doesn't seem to be. No legal mumbo jumbo. Fact is, people have looked into Dodd and his dealings with the elderly and he's clean as the driven snow."

Cal raked his hair. "The only thing driven with Dodd is greed." Cal gave Miss Ellie another quick kiss then took off. He drove onto 80 heading back to the city but took a detour that went to the fairgrounds by the river. In the distance the big white tent billowed out with a gentle breeze coming off the water. Cal thought of the last time he was at Dodd's tent. The revival was right in the heart of Savannah then. The tent was packed, people spilling out the sides and back. The Savannah merchants had a fit because traffic was terrible. Even then the media came to catch the commotion and taped Dodd in his all-damned glory.

Cal parked the Mustang and looked around for Churchill's white Prius. Not a lot of those around, more Chevy-this and Ford-that. Not seeing the car, Cal made his way to the tent with the crowd, men in shirts and ties, women in going-to-church hats and purses, and kids in their Sunday school best attire. One went to Dodd's revivals as much to be seen as to see Dodd. Ushers directed people to available seating and Cal scanned the tent for Churchill. Still nothing so he found his way to a wood folding chair in the back. Musicians were playing old time religion songs, many of the attendees singing along from books provided, many others knowing the words by heart. The heat from the day began to fade. Big fans circulated what little breeze came off the river, cooling the crowd and chasing away mosquitoes and no-see-ums.

A path led down to the river's edge, with steps descending into the water. The front of the tent was laden with mountains of white lilies, green ferns, and lit candles. There was an oak pulpit in the midst, a white cloth across the center, and recording equipment to the side.

Still no Churchill but the tent was filled beyond capacity. Mrs. Sweeny, Mrs. Curtis, Mrs. Marin, all recent widows were in the front rows. Extra chairs were brought out and there were people sitting on the grass. A choir in red robes that had to nearly send them in to heatstroke stood on a platform in front, their songs lively with clapping and swaying as the crowd joined in.

The songs became more animated, charging the crowd even more. When "Show Us The Way" started up Dodd made his entrance. He came in from the back of the tent and walked down the center aisle, shaking hands, touching folks, and loudly welcoming people personally. Seemed everyone wanted to exchange a word or a nod. The music and singing intensified, whipping the crowd to fever pitch.

Cal had to give the devil his due. Dodd had his revival con down to a science. He was a pro and knew exactly what he was doing. He took the pulpit and held up the Bible, the crowd responding with loud echoes of, "amen," and, "praise be." Everyone stayed standing as Dodd roared out, "We are all sinners. We must repent."

Churchill must not be in a repenting mood because she was still a no-show. That was good. The reason Cal was there was to keep Churchill from asking questions and stirring up trouble so he could put all his troubles behind him. He'd like to leave but there was no escaping the throng. To walk away would draw attention and for sure he didn't want that.

For an hour and a half Dodd preached, becoming hoarse with determination and conviction. His voice was loud, commanding, and damning. Sweat trickled down his face, his white suit soaked through. The crowd added more amens and praise be's with some alleluias thrown in. The collection plate circulated, brimming with bills and not of the George Washington variety but more Jackson, Grant and Franklin. Then Dodd finished and the choir belted out "Save Us." Some folks went forward to Dodd and he put his hands on their head or shoulders. The crowd started to thin, the ushers holding out the collection plates once again and Cal gave one last look around for Churchill. Suddenly he was staring straight at Dodd, their eyes connecting across the tangle of wood chairs and meandering people.

"Glory be," Dodd bellowed in his rough voice, strong enough to get the attention of the remaining crowd. He raised his arms high. "We do indeed have a repentant sinner among us tonight. Is that why you are here, brother?"

Oh, fuck, Cal thought. That was the last thing he wanted to happen. He came here to keep Churchill from causing a ruckus and now he'd brought on a bigger one.

"Walk forward, brother, to be washed in the river and cleanse your soul."

Brother? Crap. He didn't move.

"Then I will come to you. It is my mission to heal those

who are in need, those who are misguided." Dodd came up the aisle to Cal, a band of people trailing behind. "Those who have sinned know in their heart they must make amends. Is that why you have come to us, Cal Davis, to make amends?"

"Amends? For what?"

"For the money you stole from this here congregation those three years ago. Money from these hard working people laboring in the vineyard of life."

"I didn't take your money, Dodd. There was no twenty-five thousand dollars. You didn't take in that much tonight and your crowds three years ago were smaller. You made it all up to get these hard working people to drop money into your thieving hands to make up for the money that was never stolen in the first place. You're a crook, a con."

Everyone gasped and Cal continued, "I know it, you know it, and now everyone does." Though the crowd didn't look as if they believed one word of what he said. Hell, why should they? Cal was the one who went to prison.

"Repent and be saved. Make straight your path. It is not too late to change for salvation is at hand." Dodd waved his Bible as Cal walked away, people staring and mumbling while he made his way to the Mustang parked in the grassy field. Why did he have to go and open his big mouth? Because he was tired of being accused of something he didn't do. It just spilled out. All things considered it was probably okay. No one believed there never was any money stolen. He'd be seen as an ex-con proclaiming his innocence like so many others. There would be no repercussions, just more people hating his guts because they adored Dodd.

All that because he came here to find Churchill, who never showed. So where the hell was she? What was she up to? He'd go into Savannah and check out Churchill's apartment. Michelle was right about Churchill not ever intending to leave Savannah again. There was a good chance she was holed up at her place or at the library. She wasn't far away. He knew that much for sure. When he found her he had to keep her off balance, off track. Since he had the key and the notes soon all her leads would simply dry up and blow away. And he wished with all his heart that his feelings for her would do the same. But that was never going to happen. He liked her, was damn crazy about her. He just could never ever have her.

Churchill killed the lights on Tic Tac when she turned off Highway 80 and on to the gravel road that led to the speedway. It wasn't a race night but according to Miss Ellie the drivers did test laps during the week and worked on their cars. The now familiar rumble sounded in the distance, a dust cloud hovering over the track. But she wasn't here to see cars race, she was here to get back what belonged to her. She needed her notes for some details she couldn't remember and she wanted the damn key even if it didn't belong to her. Cal insisted that going to jail, Tripp, and finding the key had no connection.

Everything that had gone on since she got home said otherwise.

Tonight she'd planned on going to hear Dodd, see what he was like as a preacher, and maybe ask him about the twenty-five thousand. Talking to Dodd was a good place to start in trying to figure this all out. But when she got to the revival she spotted Cal's Mustang. He'd never let her within talking distance of Dodd, even if he had to bind and gag her and toss her over his shoulder. So she decided that while the cat was away the mouse would get her cheese back. Easier than getting bound and gagged but the getting tossed over Cal's shoulder part had definite appeal. Heck, getting tossed over Cal's anything had definite appeal.

Churchill parked behind some shrubs, started for the

cabin, then stopped as her gaze landed on the concrete block building on the other side. Cal's garage. If she were Cal that's where she'd hide stuff, not in the cabin where a snooping librarian might come, and where a snooping grandmother already lived.

Keeping in the shadows and brush, and totally ruining her new skirt from JCrew on a sticker bush—she'd planned on going to a revival, not on breaking and entering or she would have on jeans . . . maybe—Churchill made her way to the garage. A light on a phone pole illuminated the side door that was locked and had a lizard thing crawling up the frame. If it got on her she'd scream her head off. The heavy garage doors in front wouldn't budge. She tugged on one window, then the next, with no luck.

"Try these."

She jumped and would have sworn all her hair turned gray at once. "Miss Ellie?"

She dangled a ring of keys in front of Churchill. "Bet these might help."

"How'd you know I was here?"

"Didn't know till I saw you." She pointed to the light with moths and other flying things swarming around. She laughed, the one that was more of a cackle. "I was heading this way myself to look see if Cal had my brass key hidden away in this here garage because he sure enough doesn't have it hid over there in that cabin of his. Since he's off to see Dodd, this was as good a chance as any, and then, lo and behold, here you are sneaking around, too. Imagine that. Great minds think alike."

"Wonder if they'll think alike when the cops arrest us. Why did Cal go to see Dodd?"

"To make sure you didn't. Said you'd stir things up with a bunch of questions, like you always do. I think he's trying to get this whole prison thing to die down a bit. But between you and me that's not going to happen until we find out what's going on and something sure is. The boy's hiding something, all right." Miss Ellie started off till Churchill took her hand, stopping her.

"What if the thing Cal's hiding involves Tripp? Besides you and Silky he's the one person Cal would do anything for, even cover for and go to prison."

Miss Ellie patted Churchill's hand. "You are right as rain in that Cal would do anything for his little brother, but the worst thing Tripp's ever done is not brush his teeth before he went to bed. He's simply not the bad boy type and there's no reason for him to be involved in any of this robbery stuff. He goes to college, lives at college, and has a bunch of old-fart men for friends. Him involved in illegal doings doesn't fit. I know my grandsons."

That sounds right, Churchill thought as she followed Miss Ellie back to the side door. But if she ruled out Tripp as the person Cal was protecting, who else was there? Miss Ellie pulled out a penlight.

"You're good at this B and E stuff."

"We all have our talents, honey. Trouble is we're out here under this dang light bulb for all the world to see us." She pulled Matilda from the pocket of her yellow jeans and blasted the bulb, shattering it all to hell and scaring ten years of life right out of Churchill. "Holy mother, what if somebody hears?"

"With all that racket going on over there you can't hear squat and if they did hear us they'd think it was nothing but a car backfire." She put Matilda away and jabbed a key into the lock. When that didn't work she tried another until the third fit. "I think we're in." She shined the light around, the smell of oil, gas, and metal mixing with the humidity from hell.

"I think a car exploded in here. There's car everywhere."

"I imagine Cal's rebuilding something that needed rebuilding. See that workbench over on the other side? I say we start there. That key isn't very big at all. Cal could have hid it anywhere."

"I'll follow you so I don't get lost behind a piston or alternator or something."

"You don't know much about cars, do you, honey?"

"Where to put the gas about covers it." Miss Ellie threaded their way through a bunch of metal things that somehow made a car. Amazing. Churchill gazed at the assortment of stuff on the workbench trying to figure out if she recognized anything. Hammer, saw, screwdrivers, done. A whole new world of let's build a car.

"Uh-oh," Miss Ellie said from beside her, her voice a lot more serious than darn-I-got-a-spot-on-my-new-blouse. She pointed out the window and Churchill followed her finger.

"OhmyGod, the cabin's on fire!" Flames poured out the front windows and door, gray smoke billowed overhead. Churchill grabbed Miss Ellie's arm. "Cal hadn't come home yet, right? No one's in the cabin like Silky or anybody else, right?"

"Not when I left, but isn't that Cal's Mustang down by the track? Cal could be there or in the cabin right now. I don't know."

Churchill felt her blood turn to ice. Stumbling over who knows what all on the floor—why couldn't they clean up that place—she tripped her way to the nearest window, fumbled with the lock, and pried the window open. Standing on a case of something automotive she wiggled herself up and out, falling to the ground headfirst in a heap. Then she ran. The closer she got to the heat from the fire the more her face hurt and her eyes stung. Smoke billowed in black clouds mixing with the night. She looked for a place to get in. "Cal!" she screamed as she got closer.

Others gathered at the front of the cabin but Cal wasn't with them. She couldn't see him anywhere. Fire ate at the front door and steps but the back wasn't totally engulfed yet. She headed in that direction and climbed over the porch railing, thin lines of flames starting down the freshly painted blue floorboards toward her. Pushing against the screen she dropped inside to the kitchen floor. Flames eerily danced across the ceiling. The heat felt like being inside an oven. *Oh fuck, oh fuck, oh fuck.* "Cal?" Where could he be?

The bedroom, the shower. After having anything to do with Dodd she'd what to scrub in the shower. Choking, coughing, and rubbing her eyes, she started for the hall then heard a deafening crash behind her, a collapsed rafter scattering fire across the floor. She stared at the inferno blocking her exit and to Cal on the other side. "What the hell are you doing?" he yelled.

"Looking for you in the shower."

For a split second he grinned, then jumped through the fire. He swept her up in his arms and ran to the window. He shoved her out as another beam crashed down onto Cal knocking him back into the kitchen, the beam busting apart, her heart doing the same. "Cal!"

She dove back into the kitchen. Was that Tripp right behind her? Never had she been so thankful to see another human being. Using his shirt he hoisted up the not charred end of the beam and Churchill scooted Cal free. Grabbing Cal's shoulders, Tripp pulled him to the window and together they shoved Cal out. Then Churchill climbed out with Tripp right behind her as more timbers crashed down, the kitchen covered in flames. The porch ceiling creaked and they dragged Cal into the grass beyond, both collapsing beside him in a panting heap of bodies, but they were live bodies.

"Are you okay?" Tripp asked through coughs and gasps of air.

"Are you?" Churchill looked down at Cal, her heart hammering at her ribs. "Oh, God, he's so burned."

Tripp pushed himself up, looked at Cal's hands, then swiped at his face. "Soot mostly."

Cal opened his eyes and Churchill felt her insides go to jelly with relief. "Say something. Who am I?"

"Loaded question," he croaked, his blistered lips upturned a fraction. "How'd you get me out?"

Churchill yanked Tripp into Cal's view. "The Marines landed."

His mostly gone eyebrows arched. "Well I'll be damned."

"In about two more seconds you would have been," Tripp said without much humor. "But since that didn't work out, you need to stay with me here. Focus, Cal. Stay awake."

In the distance sirens sounded. Churchill sat beside Cal, Tripp on the other side, and they helped him sit up. The front part of the cabin roof collapsed with a loud crash sending sparks and flames skyward, lighting up the night. "Who the hell did you piss off now?" Tripp asked.

Cal looked dazed.

"This is arson, the pure and simple kind. No fancy wiring, just a match and gasoline. Take it from a PhD in chemistry. Only an accelerant burns that hot and that fast, unless it's an explosion and there's no evidence of that. Someone hates your guts, big brother. And they aren't fooling around. This was meant to kill."

Silky came over, his arm around Miss Ellie. He touched the back of Cal's head. "Well you got a nice crack there, boy. Gonna need some stitching up. You need to get yourself to the hospital." He gazed at the cabin, the back part of the roof giving way with another crash, the scene more surreal than real as the cabin caved in on itself. "You had guys working on that place before you came home," Silky said, sounding miserable to the core. "Damn shame."

Cal touched his head. "When they say you can't go home again I suppose they're right."

Miss Ellie cupped her hand under his chin so he had to look at her. "That was said by some dang fool who didn't have family or good friends. You look around here, Cal Davis. Life may not be a big old bowl of cherries for you right now but it ain't a pile of poop either. You got friends and family who care plenty about you here and that there's who you come home to, not things. Now you go get yourself to the hospital, get yourself looked at, and this will take care of itself. You fixed it once, you can fix it again, and we're here to help. That's what life's all about."

"Yes, ma'am." Cal forced a smile for Miss Ellie's sake. He stood, wobbled, and kissed Miss Ellie on the cheek. "You always do know the right thing to say."

"That's 'cause I'm your granny and got to keep you in line," but her voice broke and her eyes filled with tears. "Who would do something like this to you?" She touched his cheek. "Some sick, sick person." She sniffed and stood tall. "Churchill's going to get that peanut little car of hers and take you to a doctor and Silky and I will deal with the fire department and police."

"I'll hang around too," Tripp said. "We'll let you know what they say."

"And for the love of God," Miss Ellie pleaded, "stay out of trouble for a while and give me a break." A tear slid down her wrinkled cheek.

"They're going to say the fire was deliberate," Tripp offered. "And then they'll probably ask if you have any enemies who would want to do something like this on purpose."

Cal gave a dry laugh. "An hour ago I just called Dodd a liar to his face in front of witnesses at his own revival. That should cover a lot of territory."

Charred and sooty and smelling like something run over and baked in the summer sun on the highway, Churchill paced the waiting room of the hospital. The few other people there at one o'clock in the morning and the nurses, orderlies, and doctors who ventured beyond the restricted double door sign stared. She felt like that "Pig-Pen" character in the Charlie Brown comic, the one that everywhere he walked a trail of dirt followed. Yeah, she was the "Pig-Pen" of Savannah, all right, which was better than being another stop on the Savannah ghost tours.

It was easier to think about all that superfluous crap than the terrible hell that had happened. A sick feeling turned her stomach. She'd wanted Cal, had for years, and she almost lost him in the blink of an eye without him knowing. She'd wasted so much time when they could have been together. Stupid stuff got in the way. Stupid stuff that didn't matter one lick when you're in the waiting room of a hospital wondering about a person you care for, if they are okay or not. What if Cal wasn't okay? What if there was something seriously wrong with him? Something that couldn't be fixed. She sat down because her legs simply wouldn't support her.

"Churchill?" Cal said, standing next to her. "You were a million miles away. Are you okay? Maybe you should get looked at, too."

"I've been looked at plenty tonight, thank you very much. Dear God, what are you wearing? Where'd that getup come from?"

His hands were blistered, his face raw in places, most of his eyebrows and some eyelashes gone. His nose was scabbed and his hair was the consistency of straw. It was easier to talk about the clothes. If she mentioned the other stuff she'd cry.

Cal held out his green stretch polyester pants that were huge and a too-small blue T-shirt. "I think these are clothes people leave behind."

"Oh Lordy, like when they die?"

"Like the lost and found, stuff that gets forgotten here in the waiting room. That's the story I'm going with." He waved discharge papers. "I got sprung."

"More like you said you were leaving and you didn't give a rat's patootie what anybody said. I can tell because they gave you such nice clothes as a departing gift."

He smiled, then all traces of humor vanished. "Some night." He held out his hand to her and she nearly sobbed, her emotions paper thin. She wound her fingers into his, taking care not to hold too tight. He looked into her eyes, his bloodshot and irritated. Standing on tiptoes she kissed his eyes, thanking God he still had them. He draped his arm around her and slowly, together, they headed out the exit doors. Cal stopped and looked up at the sky holding her tight, breathing deeply.

"That was close," he said in a whisper. "Too damn close." He wrapped both his strong arms around her right there beside the big red Emergency entrance sign. He held her so tight breathing was difficult. "I did this to you," he said in a grief-stricken voice that was also riddled with guilt. "This could have been tragic." She felt him shiver. "The fire was because of me. I could have killed you."

"You have to quit thinking like that. You didn't set the fire. You aren't responsible for any of this. It's not your fault. We're okay and that's the main thing."

"It is but—"

"No buts tonight. We're so lucky, Cal. So, so lucky." She took his hand and led him to an EMS truck parked off to the side that had been there since they came in. She opened the back door and climbed in. "I want to make love to you. I want you to know how much you mean to me. I need to be with you right now. We came so close to losing each other. I don't want to wait another minute. We nearly didn't have another minute."

"Protection?"

"Got it covered." She blushed. "That didn't come out right."

"Just when I think I know everything about Churchill McKenzie, I realize I don't." His eyes turned black and her insides blazed hotter then the fire they just left. "God I want you." His voice was nearly a growl. He climbed in the truck and tore off his pants as she whipped off her skirt. Then he was inside her, her legs around him, their climax instant, intense, life confirming, amazing. He was alive. He was with her, and she never wanted to let him go again.

Chapter Nine

Tripp walked up the neat brick path to the townhouse and knocked on the red door of 22 Delilah Avenue. A lawn sprinkler cut a graceful arch over the perfectly trimmed grass and a cat napped on a white wicker chair. Tripp knocked again and DaisyLou opened the door but instead of being dressed in shorts and a halter top she had on a yellow sundress and heels. She smelled of heaven once again.

"Well, sugar, whatever are you doing here?" She glanced around as if looking for someone.

Tripp felt himself redden. "I called but no one answered and I thought I'd come over and take my chances. I was in Silky's office and your folder was on his desk. You were so helpful the other night I thought I'd find you this morning and see if you have any openings."

"Openings?"

"Therapy sessions. I did something I'd never thought I'd have the guts to do and I think it's because you helped me see, feel, and think of things as a man. You helped me a lot. But now what should I do? Where do I go from here?"

She gave him a big smile. "Therapy. Right. Of course. Well now I just finished up with a client and I'm thinking I can maybe squeeze you in before the next one comes along. I think I have a little time available. Come on in."

"Really? That's terrific. I appreciate you seeing me on such short notice. So do we use charts or spreadsheets to plan what course of action I need to follow? I've been working on a program of cross components to optimize parallel data to arrive at a favorable outcome. We can use that to plan strategy. Or a formula or algorithm? Is there an algorithm you prefer?" Tripp followed DaisyLou who never seemed to simply walk anywhere but glide. "The kitchen? We're going to have a therapy session in the kitchen? Nice plants."

There were plants everywhere. Blue and white African violets on the windowsill, a bamboo palm, two Chinese evergreens, English ivy, three pots of red and orange gerbera daisies, and a vase of white peace lilies on the table.

"They freshen up the air and the soul. I do so enjoy watching things grow." She took his hand. "It's a passion of mine, sort of a hobby you might say." Looking into his eyes she ran her palm over his shoulder and down the length of his arm, then held his hand again, hers soft and delicate. "Where would we be without passion, don't you agree?"

His heart kicked up a notch and parallel data vanished from his brain. "Agreed."

"Now then, do you remember what you had for breakfast this fine morning?"

He was still thinking about passion. "Cereal, juice, toast, a Flintstone vitamin."

"Do you know what you had for breakfast when you were ten?"

"Cereal, juice, toast, a Flintstone vitamin."

DaisyLou laughed, her sweet sound filling the kitchen. "We're going to change your preferences from when you were ten to you being a man. Make you aware that there's a difference." Music came on. "That's *Nights in White Satin*, one of my favorites. You like?"

He nodded because he could suddenly see DaisyLou at night, dressed all in white satin. He felt lightheaded. He'd never thought of a woman like that before. Once he pictured the head of the chem lab dressed in fig leaves but that was after four Jell-O shots at a faculty party. He'd figured anything with Jell-O was just . . . Jell-O.

DaisyLou pulled two small pans from the cabinet and put them on the stove. Then she took out two containers and retrieved a bowl of big red strawberries from the refrigerator. She found a bottle of Kahlua and a bottle of brandy.

"All men need to know how to cook beyond opening a box of Cheerios or tossing dead cow on the grill." She framed his face in her cool, soft, smooth hands, her nails perfect with red polish. Her fiery green eyes bore into his eyes. "Something more. Something memorable that fits the moment, the occasion, the woman, the way you feel about her. Something warm, a little decadent, delicious, firm, intoxicating. Moist." She kissed him lightly, her tongue touching his. "Wet." Her red lips stayed parted, the word hanging in the air, mixing with the soulful sounds.

He was so turned on he couldn't move. He could barely breathe. His heart thundered. Standing behind him she reached around and tied on an apron, red. He turned around to see DaisyLou's dress draped over a chair. She had on an apron too, red over white satin bra and panties. "Nice apron."

"I'm tickled you think so, sugar." She faced the stove, her backside to him, her little scrap of panties across her lovely round, tanned derriere making his mouth go completely dry. *How did she get tan there?* He didn't want to think about that. Then he did think about that and about how DaisyLou was probably tan all over. His eyes crossed. How did he get so lucky to find this type of therapy?

She sprinkled dark chocolate drops in one pan, white

chocolate drops in the other, added butter, vanilla and turned on the heat. She handed him a spoon, then poured a good amount of Kahlua into the dark chocolate and brandy into the white chocolate. The heady aromas swirled around them, filling the kitchen.

"You stir like this," she said, moving behind him, her breasts pressed to his back, her warm soft patch against his butt. Her fingers joined his on the wooden spoon and together their hands moved around and around and around. The chocolate melted, the scents mingled, and their bodies got closer imitating the movement of the spoon. She held up a flute of golden champagne. "To not being ten." She sipped, leaving her red lip print deliberately on the glass then handed it to him. "This is for you."

He sipped. She stirred. The white chocolate and the aged oaken bouquet of the brandy made his mouth hungry with anticipation for . . . for whatever came next. Holding the stem of one deep red lush strawberry she swirled it into the dark chocolate and brought it to his lips. "For you, too. Just for you."

He bit, the sweet juice dripping down his chin. The warm chocolate on his lips and the Kahlua took his breath away. The gorgeous woman was a feast for his senses. Her tongue stole the juice from his chin then slid into his mouth. He kissed her, the flavors of strawberry, chocolate, liqueur, and woman more delicious than he could have ever imagined.

"Your turn," she said in a low breathy voice.

He swirled a strawberry into the white chocolate, splashing some on his fingers.

DaisyLou took the berry, her eyes soft, beckoning. "Did you burn yourself, sugar?" She held his two fingers up straight then licked slowly, deliberately bottom to top, one side then the other then drew them deep into her mouth, her tongue massaging and stroking, making him so horny he couldn't see for a moment.

"All better?" she asked, her voice a murmur. She took the strawberry coated in white chocolate and bit, the thick red juice mixing with the red of her lips.

Never had a strawberry looked so delicious and he had to taste it. He had to taste her. He kissed her again, the juice flowing into his mouth, the sweet taste of chocolate and Kahlua warming him all over.

"Do you like cooking?"

"I think I'm a fan."

She ran her finger along his jaw to his lip. Taking a bit of chocolate from there she brought it to her mouth, her tongue licking the dark spot. "So smooth, so sweet, so sinful." She placed her finger over his lips. "So much a man. What do you want to do as a man, Tripp? You have to make that decision. It's all up to you."

"Making love to you right here on your white granite counter top seems like a great place to start."

"But that would only be a start. This is all about you and the future. Your plans, your dreams. Where do you want to go from here? Did you ever see the movie *Moonstruck*? Where the woman slaps the guy and says, '*snap out of it.*'" DaisyLou waved her graceful hand over the kitchen and their cooking. "This is all about snapping out of it, but nicer. So much nicer." She kissd him, then slid her arm through his and led him down the hall to the door. "See you later, Tripp Davis."

"I have to go? Now?"

She raked her fingers slowly through his hair. "Keep in touch. Like this." She brought his hands around her waist to her back and below, the feel of her bare skin mixed with smooth satin panties turned his insides to an inferno that was nothing like the one Dante talked about. This inferno was good, damn good.

"You have to leave, Tripp."

"Leave? But—"

"Therapy. This is just therapy to get you in tune with the real Tripp, with what he wants and what he's about. What are your passions? What do you feel right now, Tripp?"

"Does horny count?"

She grinned. "That is only part of being a man. I've found that nothing gets a man's attention like sex. Now you feel the things a man feels. Now you have to figure out what to do as a smart man beyond studying and being in a classroom. Beyond cereal, juice, and toast."

She opened the door and nudged him outside while she slid off his apron. Gently she closed the door behind him, the click of the latch bringing him back to the real world.

Okay, how was he supposed to walk? Hell, he couldn't walk. His penis was in the way. He never really understood the third leg reference till now because it had never been in the way before, except the other night when he had the other therapy session. Some guy was making his way up the sidewalk toward him. Tripp couldn't just stand there in front of DaisyLou's house with a big hard bulge in his pants. He looked like a damn pervert.

He turned and made his way as best he could to his Volvo. *Now what,* he thought as he got in. What was something a man would do? A twenty-three-year-old man. Something that didn't involve books, lectures, papers, charts, or formulas.

He'd helped Cal and Churchill the night before but that wasn't planned. He went to see Cal, found the fire, and helped out. But now what? The therapy with DaisyLou was good, make that incredible, but it didn't answer any questions. What great plan was he supposed to come up with? What was that term people used? Man up. How was he supposed to man up? What *was* manning up? Crap, he had no idea. What he did know was that it wasn't running away.

*   *   *

Michelle knocked on Benny's door. She was early but she'd brought Benny, make that Houston, a few more things to wear, the latest issue of *Southern Living* magazine, and a real Savannah home-cooked dinner. It was the least she could do since he helped Cal out of that fight the other day. Considering the fire Cal needed all the friends he could get. And maybe a little part of her wanted to see Benny and have dinner with him.

Benny opened the door, shirt off again, smile spreading across his handsome face.

"Michelle?" Did he ever have his darn shirt on? Then again she was early and he'd been working out. He looked terrific. *Do not stare,* she ordered herself. "I didn't figure on you being here for another hour. What's that all about?"

She gave him an evil look.

"Right." He cleared his throat. "Why, good evening to you, Michelle, and a mighty fine evening it is, too. How's your mama doing? And that very fine son of yours? He sure is getting big. Butter my butt and call me a biscuit if you ain't prettier than a peach blossom in that there new dress you have on."

"By George, I think he's got it." She laughed and went inside. Storybook wandered over to check out the food and Benny slid on a shirt. Thank God. Benny was well built before but every day he seemed to be even better—tighter abs, muscled arms, stronger. She handed him the clothes. "Just a few things till you can get out and shop on your own. I wasn't sure if you were ready for that or not. And . . ." She could feel herself start to redden.

"And what?"

"And I like shopping for you. You look great in blue shirts. That's the *in* color this summer. I found this sweater and jeans."

"No white suit?" he teased. "How will I ever fit in without one?" He lifted the bags from her and set them on the table. "But you did get yourself a new dress." He took her hand and twirled her around in little circles till she tripped over Storybook. Then she twirled right into Benny's arms, their eyes connecting, their bodies doing the same, making her warm and radiant, happy to be exactly where she was. "Pink looks great on you."

His breath kissed her cheek and for a moment she thought he might do the same thing. She wanted him to. She wanted it a lot. No, that was not right! She had her family to consider. She took a step back. "Another attempt at getting rid of my librarian look. Trying to be a little more fashionable"—she busied herself with unpacking the food she'd brought—"so I bought this dress and a blue skirt."

"Right. Tommy." The mention of his name sucked all the fun right out of the room and replaced it with an awkward silence till Benny filled it with, "Well, I have to say, something sure smells mighty terrific."

"I'll have you know this is real Southern goodness here. It's my mama's recipe that goes back a long, long time." Michelle got two plates and Benny pulled out flatware and glasses. They were two people in tune with each other, knowing each other's moves as if they'd been doing it for years. She was comfortable being with Benny. Easy. "Your eye isn't so swollen from the other night." She touched it and Benny took her fingers from his face and kissed them.

"Ah, damn. I was trying to be real good and then I go and do something like this. I'm sorry. God, I'm sorry," he said and took a step away. "I shouldn't have. I swore I wouldn't. I know you're getting back together with Tommy and I respect that, I do. I hope to hell he knows what a lucky son of a bitch he is to get a second chance with you." Benny tweaked her nose and smiled. Then he walked across the kitchen, his back to her, putting space between them that she hated.

"Maybe I shouldn't come anymore. I mean, you've got

the Southern gent down pretty good and you're not orange anymore. You can shop for yourself. You really don't need me. We can pass Storybook between us at the library. I don't really have to come here if it causes problems."

He came over to her and gently put his hand on her arm. "No problems, I swear. I promise to mind my manners," he said in a rush. "My new Southern manners. I don't want you to stop coming around. I like being with you, Michelle, talking to you, seeing your new dresses even if you're getting all prettied up for somebody else." He held up his hands in surrender. "I get it. Hands off. It won't happen again." Benny sat down at the table and peeked into one of the containers. "Gravy? I love gravy. Put it on everything."

"Redeye gravy. It's made from the drippings of pan fried country ham and black coffee."

"Coffee?"

"Unless you're from Mississippi, of course. They're all uppity over there and use wine but coffee's the secret." She swiped her finger in the sauce and held it up to his lips. "Taste." He did and she nearly melted into a blob right there in the kitchen. Her gaze met his, generating enough electricity to light Savannah for a week.

"I think I died and went to food heaven," he said in an even voice as if nothing happened. Except his hand still held hers and he didn't seem as if he wanted to let her go. His eyes got darker and her insides got hotter. That was not a good thing.

"I wanted to thank you for helping Cal the other night when those thugs came after him in the garage." She took her hand back and filled plates for the two of them, concentrating on that and not looking at Benny. "I suppose you heard his cabin burned." Diversion. Diversion was good.

"That man has his share of enemies and then some. But I don't think he stole money from a preacher, like he says he did. It's not in him. I know crooks, been around them enough. Cal Davis is no crook." Benny sat down at the table and Michelle took the chair across from him. "Thanks for making me dinner. This is incredible."

"Thanks for saying thanks."

He gave her a questioning look. To Benny that probably seemed like a dumb comment but she truly meant it. "Tommy's not one for giving out compliments or even saying *thank you*. In fact, in all eighteen years of being with him I don't think he ever did either to me. It's just his way, of course. He expects everyone to do their job. I think it comes from being an efficient cop like he is. He has high expectations of others like he does of himself. He's a good cop. Works a ton. He's working again tonight." Okay, that was way over the top. She had to stop comparing Benny and Tommy. She was back with Tommy. Tommy, Tommy, Tommy. What was wrong with her? Why did she babble on like she did about his shortcomings? Everybody had shortcomings, even Benny . . . somewhere. And Lord knows she was no saint.

"Are you okay?"

"It's the Fresh Meat syndrome. That's exactly what this is, I saw it on *Oprah* once."

Benny put down his fork. "Excuse me?"

Oh dear, Lord, now what had she started? "That's what all this is between you and me. We're Fresh Meat to each other. Being together, doing this makeover of you, and saving you from bad guys is new and exciting. We're in that discovery mode where we think all the little quirks that will one day drive us crazy about each other are now so endearing and intriguing. That's why we have this attraction to each other. We're New Meat."

"*Fresh* Meat. Did you say attraction?" His eyes lit and he smiled.

Rats, she hated when he looked at her like that. Well,

she loved it actually but it wasn't good. It was bad, all bad. "Yes, darn it, attraction. You, me, tripping over each other like teenagers. The way I get when I'm around you—"

"How do you get when you're around me?"

"And . . . and I have another date with Tommy on Friday and it's going to be terrific and you and me are just meat, nothing more. We can't be."

Benny nodded and looked back to his plate. "I'm glad we got that straightened out." He picked up his fork and shoved food around. "So, how are things going between you two? Are you working things out?"

"TJ is doing so well. I almost hate to say anything because I'll jinx it and the old TJ will come back. I'm so proud of him. He got a B on his last algebra test and does the dishes every night without being nagged. He's happy. Just plain happy, like he used to be. I think it has a lot to do with the job. He's really into business."

"His dad's proud of him, too, I'm sure."

"Of course. Right now he's very proud of the Braves being in the play-offs. He wants me to take his mother to bingo tonight because he has to work, then pick up his laundry, shine his shoes, get a few things for him at the grocery, and drop them off." She stood. "I have to go. Bingo. I have to get Tommy's mom to the bingo on Abercorn. If she misses any games she gets all upset."

Benny walked Michelle to the door when what he really wanted to do was pick her up and carry her off to his bedroom. She was nothing but a damn maid to the biggest asshole on God's green earth. "Whatthehellareyoudoing! He's using you!"

"What are you talking about?"

"Tommy the fucking jerk. He doesn't take care of you and treat you with the respect you deserve. Oh, damn." Benny raked his fingers though his hair wishing he could eat the words he just blurted out. What was wrong with him? "I shouldn't have said that. This is none of my business."

"I'm not coming back," Michelle said in formal voice that tore at his heart because he knew she meant it. What had he done? He'd screwed up everything.

"Michelle, I'm sorry."

"You, me . . . this isn't working. I'm going. You can drop Storybook off at the library tomorrow and we'll make exchanges there from now on."

"But—"

"No." She held up her hand. "I need to get my life together and I need to stay away from you. If I keep telling myself this marriage will work out, it will. I need to stay focused and positive and when I'm with you that's impossible because all I think about is you."

He watched her nearly run down the steps, get into her car, and drive off in a rush. No waving to him, no backward glances. She just left. He couldn't blame her. He was an idiot, a dumb stupid idiot. Just because he didn't like Tommy he had no right to blow up like that. Friends stood by friends and Michelle was his friend. She helped him, shopped for him, and cooked for him.

Except he wasn't simply Michelle's friend. In his mind he was more, had been since that day in the library when he saw her dancing around the tables and he gathered her into his arms and danced, too. He didn't know if love at first sight existed but with him and Michelle it was definitely something at first sight. He couldn't let it go. Thoughts of her ate at him constantly. All he thought about was Michelle, how she walked, talked, and smiled. She had an incredible smile. She was kind and sweet to everyone and she loved her kid above everything else. A good mom was a good person clear through.

He had to start making plans to leave. It was too hard to stay in Savannah. All he'd get to do was see Michelle from afar and talk to her at the library like anyone else who came in looking for a book. No more just the two of them. He had to face that he had no chance with Michelle. He had to get out of the apartment. If he stayed there any longer and kept thinking about all that he'd go crazy. "Come on Storybook, let's take a walk."

Storybook put his paws up on the counter and got his leash. Benny clipped it to his collar and they stepped out into the clammy evening. The two of them walked aimlessly like they used to back in Jersey, not really knowing where they were going. The streets got a little rougher, the evening fading into night. People dressed in out-to-dinner clothes morphed into people hanging out on street corners in the projects. A blue Budweiser sign and the red neon of Danny's Den lit a dingy intersection and Benny walked in. He asked the bartender, "Okay if I have my dog in here?"

Cal Davis came over and unclipped Storybook. "Now he's a customer with bad hair. Three Rolling Rocks, Danny." Benny took a stool, Storybook on one side of him, Cal on the other. Cal said, "Of all the gin joints. What are you doing here in this neck of the woods?"

"Getting drunk. Heard about the fire. Damn sorry. I know my way around insurance forms so they don't screw you out of what's coming to you. It gets tricky."

Cal clinked his Rolling Rock to Benny's. "I appreciate it. How well do you know your way around women?"

Benny snickered. "I just royally pissed off the only woman I've ever cared about. I need to be putting her behind me and move on."

"And I *need* to piss off the only woman I've ever cared about and get this all behind me and move on. I need to get her out of my life for good, for her sake as well as a lot of other people involved, and I don't know how to do it." He took a gulp of beer. "If you don't mind me asking, who's the woman?"

"The ex-wife of the bozo sitting way back in that corner over there with the hooker."

Cal arched his brow that wasn't there and glanced in the mirror, the reflection showing Tommy's back and his balding head. "Well, damn. The scum of the earth, always has been always will be. You think he's working undercover?"

"I think he's working both sides of the street. Michelle's going to get hurt all over again and that's not right. She wants to get back with him for her son's sake. Seems he was ten miles of bad road then suddenly shaped up. Michelle thinks reuniting the family will make her kid happy, keep him on the right path, and make them into a Norman Rockwell painting."

"I need to introduce her to Ron and RuthAnn. My parents are joined at the hip and I'm so far different from what they want it boggles the mind. Kids are who they are. So, what are you going to do now? You got a look about you that says you're not letting this go."

Benny signaled for another beer. "Finish this off, then Tommy and I are going to have the talk."

Cal chuckled. "Where in the hell are you from?"

Benny smiled. "When you find out who torched your place you look me up. We'll deal with them."

"You can count on it."

Benny finished off the last of the Rolling Rock and ambled over to the back booth. He stood over the woman in a blue spandex top, a white skirt about the size of a wide belt, with hair the color of Danny's sign. "Excuse me. You got an important phone call at the bar."

"Get lost."

Benny took her hand, held it just a little tight, and gave her the Jerzee stare, the one the Pinstripe brothers used when someone didn't pay for their car on time. "Believe me when I tell you it's important."

She looked at Benny her eyes widening in understanding.

"Right." She snatched her purse from the table and hurried away. Benny took her place and Tommy hissed, "Who the hell are you? Do you know who I am? I'm the goddamn police around here and I can have you thrown in jail and—"

Quick as lightning, Benny reached across the table and bent back Tommy's thumb making him double over in pain. "Pay attention," Benny said in a low precise voice. "You are to treat Michelle with the respect she deserves. You are done fooling around on her. You will take care of her and treat her nice, give her compliments, take her out. You will not make her get your laundry, get your mother, or get anything else you're too lazy to take of yourself. If I find out otherwise I'll hunt you down, tear off your balls, both your thumbs, and stuff them down your goddamn throat. Where I come from that's how we do things. Do I make myself clear?"

Benny let go, Tommy collapsing across the table holding his hand, whimpering. Benny whistled for Storybook and together they walked out of the bar.

Michelle checked her watch and hustled a little faster out of the Piggly Wiggly so as not to be late getting Tommy's mom from the bingo that was across town. Michelle read through the grocery list Tommy gave her. Did she get everything? Lordy, she hoped so. Tommy was good at getting all pissy if she forgot something. She wouldn't be able to get it to him till tomorrow and that was never soon enough. She so wanted to keep peace, just get along, try harder than the last time, and make their marriage work.

She wasn't stupid. She knew she'd be the one doing most of the changing—that Tommy wouldn't—but that was okay. She was going into it with her eyes wide open. She was doing it for TJ. Tommy wasn't the best dad ever but he did love TJ in his own way. That's what TJ needed in his life, his parents around him for support.

She put the bags in the back of her little Saturn next to the laundry she'd picked up for Tommy at Mildred Kinkaid's. Like Tommy said she should, she told Mildred she'd be doing Tommy's laundry from here on out. That would save a few bucks for Tommy and make him happy. She had ten minutes to get back to the VFW hall on Abercorn. It was going to be tight. If she was late Tommy's mama would get all pissy just like Tommy did. The apple didn't fall far from the tree with those two. She smiled, then suddenly didn't feel much like smiling at all. Tommy's mama never did think Michelle was good enough for her baby boy and nothing had changed over the years.

A police car with flashing lights and sirens blaring pulled into the Pig parking lot and stopped beside her, making everyone in the lot and in the store stare at her. Good Lord almighty, what had she done? Did a deodorant fall in her purse and she not pay for it? That happened once a few years ago. She drove all the way back to the store and apologized profusely as she handed over the two dollars and fifty-nine cents. She still remembered how embarrassing it was. There she was, getting embarrassed again. Tommy would have a conniption when he found out.

Frantically she searched through her purse as the door of the police cruiser flew open and Tommy jumped out with flowers in his hands and a wide-eyed look on his face. "Tommy?"

"Michelle, I'm so glad I found you and caught up with you." He thrust the huge bouquet at her, then handed her a box of candy. "I'm sorry," he blurted in a nervous voice she'd never heard before.

She looked around for a minute wondering who in the world Tommy was talking to. Maybe she was supposed to hand the candy and all those flowers to them. But, she was the only one nearby, though others in the parking lot were staring. What was this all about? Tommy had never said he was sorry for anything in his whole life and he never sounded nervous when talking to her. He usually sounded apathetic, or had that strained tolerance in his voice, or he was angry for whatever thing he didn't like that she happened to do. Suddenly he was apologizing?

"I'll go and fetch mama."

"You'll—"

"From bingo." He looked into her car, then pulled out the grocery bags and tossed them into the cruiser, the bread, cheese, and pork rinds spilling across the backseat and onto the floor. He grabbed his laundry and tossed it on top of the groceries and slammed the door shut. "You'll not be doing my laundry."

"I already told—"

"I'll do my laundry, and yours. Yeah, I can do yours, too. I'll fold it up real nice and use that there softener you like. We'll get you a maid for the house. Yeah, that's it, we'll get you a housekeeper too, so you don't have to be cleaning after a hard day at the library. How's that sound to you, Michelle? And maybe a driver so if you get tired of driving around you can call him right up on the phone and he'll come get you and—"

"What the heck have you been drinking, Tommy Lee Dempsey? And when you're on duty, too. What's going on? You're going to lose your job."

"Nothing's going on, honey, I—"

"Honey?"

"I swear. It's me, Michelle. Just me. Well the better, new and improved me. I'm different now. I've been thinking. I've not been a good husband to you the way I should and that's going to change. I want to take care of you, treat you good, and give you the respect you deserve. I'm going to be doing better by you, Michelle. I swear I can. You're looking at a changed man here. I'm going to make you happy, I swear it. You're going to be happy with me. Happy as a pig in mud. I promise with all my heart. You go on home now and take a nice bubble bath and get some rest. Tomorrow I got reservations for us at the Pink House." He kissed her cheek as if it were a privilege.

"I'll pick you up tomorrow at seven sharp. I won't be late anymore or keep you waiting. We'll have a good time. I ordered that nice wine you like, had it put on ice for us. From now on I am paying attention, going to take good care of you."

Michelle clutched the flowers and candy and watched Tommy drive out of the parking lot. That was not Tommy coming to the realization on his own, that he was a jerk, that he needed to treat her better, treat her with the respect she deserved. That was Jersey talk. She'd heard it for days and knew the difference. It was all a blast of reality from someone who cared, really cared about her.

She got into her car, drove to York Street, and took the steps to Miss Ellie's apartment. She knocked and Benny opened the door. "Michelle?"

"I want you to hear me out on this and then I'm going to go. I know what you did. Well not the particulars of course but I can imagine. I don't know whether to thank you or be furious with you for interfering. The only thing I do know is that what you did made my life easier and that hasn't happened for a long while. I have to stick with Tommy. There's nothing else I can do." She gave him a quick kiss on the cheek, then walked back down the steps, got in her car, and drove off feeling sad, miserable, and lonely to the bone.

Chapter Ten

The sounds of the speedway hummed in the background and the fluorescent lights mixed with dust and dirt off the track as Cal stared at the charred remains of his home. When he was in his cell he used to think about the place he'd want to live in when he got out. Focus on the future, that's how he planned to get through three years of hell. Then Silky started signing him up for all those stupid magazines as a joke. And suddenly it wasn't a joke. There were ads and articles on furniture, fixtures, window treatments, linens, and rugs. All of his life that stuff never mattered until he was suddenly looking at concrete walls and floors, bars for doors, a metal bed, and a toilet right out in the open. Three years of that and creature comforts took on a whole new importance. Places like Pottery Barn, West Elm, Restoration Hardware were Mecca.

And it was all gone. But what mattered most of all, more than any rug, couch, or towel was that Churchill could have been in the middle of the fire. She could be dead and all because she'd gone back into the flames looking for him. His insides hurt at the thought and he could barely breathe. If he ever doubted it before he knew it for certain now. He was no good for her. Never had been. Knowing him had cost her a scholarship and this time nearly her life. Tonight at the bar when Cal told Houston—or who-ever he was—that he needed to break it off with a girl he'd been crazy about his whole life, Cal had been serious as a stroke. The best way to break it off with her was for him to leave Savannah and stay away. If he did she'd forget about him and give up on his connection with Dodd and the key. Everything would get back to the way it was.

If he left, Tripp would get back to normal, too. As long as Cal stayed around, he was a constant reminder of a lot of crap better off forgotten. He'd put out a few feelers for jobs in North Carolina and the Dirt Track Racing School seemed interested. He laughed. Him a teacher. Cal shook his head. The Lord had a great sense of humor. Cal just wanted to race. He wanted to kick ass. He couldn't beat up everyone out to get him but he could outrace them. He wanted one more time at the dirt track that kept him sane. He loved the track. It saved him in so many ways. When he was a kid and didn't fit in anyplace or with anyone he went out there. When he graduated and needed a job Silky had one for him. When he was in prison and thought about going home, the speedway was always home.

He went around to the back of the garage and pulled the tarp off the best Late Model he'd ever put together. He thought about selling her a couple of times but never got around to it, maybe because his heart wasn't in it. Rubbing his hand over the front red fender he could almost feel the metal coming to life under his palm. It was like that when he built a car himself. He was part of it, it was part of him. He got the keys from the rack in the garage, grabbed his hel-met and gloves then drove Ace of Hearts toward the race-track.

The roar of the engines vibrated under her feet and right up her whole body as Churchill elbowed her way through the crowds and wiggled her way up to Miss Ellie sitting in the top bleachers where she could see the whole track and all the cars at once. Miss Ellie had on a white ball cap, red blouse, and blue jeans. She was eating a hot dog and drinking a beer, a broken arm not slowing her down at all. "You look like the poster girl for USA Southern style. This place is packed tonight," Churchill said as she scooted in beside Miss Ellie. "Think everyone's here out of curiosity about the fire last night?"

"Oh I think that's a mighty big part of it. That and it's Championship Night, honey," she yelled over the engines. "Fifty laps, winner takes all. Cal's out there racing and all that publicity lately has folks curious as to what's going on with him."

Churchill felt her head spin. "Racing, as in driving a car for a long time and not just that qualifying stuff? What? Why? Is he nuts? They tried to run him over when he did that time trial thing and that was *before* he called Dodd a crook. They'll kill him."

"Not unless he gets them first."

"Oh terrific, this is about revenge? Revenge with big engines and going a hundred and sixty miles an hour! I think I'm having an aneurism."

"There's Cal right now, coming around the far turn behind the pace car. Number ten, Ace of Hearts."

"Ace." Churchill nearly fell off the bleacher but it was so packed the crowd held her in place.

"A couple guys are doing pit crew for him, and there's my Silky right behind that wall with them. He sure is a pistol all right. He can change tires and pump gas with the best of 'em. What a man."

The pace car pulled off the track, the green light popped on as the green flag dropped. Mud spewed everywhere and the deafening growl filled the night as the race started. Churchill grabbed Miss Ellie's arm. "What if there's one of those terrible wrecks? What if he gets hurt? I can't watch."

She slapped her hands over her eyes then slowly parted her fingers because not knowing what was happening was worse than knowing. "I'm going to kill him. I swear to God I'm going to kill him dead as Grant. Why didn't he tell me he was racing tonight?"

"Probably 'cause he knows you'd want to kill him dead as Grant and that you'd have your hands over your eyes. How did you know he was racing tonight?"

"I didn't. When I got home from the library he wasn't there so I figured he'd be out here working on a car or thinking how to rebuild his cabin. Then I came out here and found this going on. After getting cracked on the head last night you'd think he'd take it easy, but no, he has to try and kill himself again. Use up all those nine lives at once."

She watched the electronic lit board list the number of the cars in the order they were racing. Cal was in fifth place. Two laps down, forty-eight to go. Miss Ellie took Churchill's hand. "He's a gunner, a fast driver and he knows what he's doing. Taking it easy isn't exactly Cal's way. You know that. Cal's raced for a long time. His granddaddy had him out here when he was nine and he raced the midgets. He's got to do what he's got to do. You want him to be staying home sitting on a couch with the remote fused to his hand?"

"Yes! Great idea."

"Then he wouldn't be the Cal Davis you love. And you do love him or you wouldn't be turning instantly gray over him out there driving like a bat out of hell." Kicking up dirt, Ace of Hearts slipped by another car, number thirty-two and took fourth place. "He's scrambling for a transfer spot."

"I have no idea what that means but I'm guessing it has something to do with Cal not being content to be in fourth place. Of course he's not going to like being in third place either once he gets there."

"That's about it in a nutshell," Miss Ellie said on a laugh

as Cal squeezed by another car. Churchill's heart lodged permanently in her throat, as he came off a turn and took third place. Churchill grabbed the beer right from Miss Ellie and gulped it down. "You keep that up and you'll get sloshed."

"Now there's a plan." Then she remembered the gin plan and decided to pass. "Thirty laps to go."

Churchill watched Cal play car tag with number forty-five for the next ten laps then finally take second place when forty-five went too high on a turn. There was obviously some race jargon that fit that move but she had no idea what it was. Cal flew by him in a burst of speed and dirt to the cheering of the crowd. Much to Churchill's surprise she screamed and cheered, too. She jumped up and down and told everyone around her that she was the Ace in the Ace of Hearts and Cal was her man. Wasn't he great? Did she really just say all that stuff to perfect strangers?

"There's only five laps to go!" she yelled into Miss Ellie's ear because that was pretty much the only way to communicate over the people cheering and the loud engines. "Do you think he'll win? Second's pretty good. Do you think he'll be content with second?"

Miss Ellie looked at Churchill and broke out laughing.

"I know, but I had to ask."

"He's waiting for the right moment." Then as if he heard Miss Ellie, Cal took over first place, everyone in the stands yelling his name, stomping on the bleachers, and screaming. Churchill realized she was louder than anyone, standing in her seat cheering and jumping up and down as Cal kept the lead till the checkered flag waved in the air. The crowd went crazy. Ace of Hearts took a victory lap to more yells then pulled in to Victory Lane. Cal slid from the car and instantly five sexy girls in rhinestone short-shorts and skimpy glittery tops ran onto the track and hugged Cal, kissing him and draping themselves around him like a cheap suit.

"Who—who . . . ?" Churchill stammered to Miss Ellie and pointed because she truly couldn't get out the rest of the words. "Who are those women all over—"

"Your man? Those are the bar gals from Fanny's. It's one of those sports bars. They sponsored the race. This is all about the fun and excitement of the sport and they're just joining in."

"Well, Cal Davis sure seems to be enjoying himself and them to the fullest."

"Honey he just won a big race. It's pretty obvious that this crowd is a heck of a lot more in love with Cal and they don't give two hoots about Dodd. The girls are all part of the show. Giving him the winner's check and trophy, taking pictures, getting his name in the papers, on the radio and on local TV spots."

"Seems to me they're giving him a whole lot more than money and a trophy. Did you see that girl just pinch his butt? She really did pinch Cal's butt. I'll have you know that's my butt and a damn fine one it is, too! She kissed him on the mouth. That's my mouth and if I see one hint of tongue anywhere I'm going down there and break some heads."

"It's all part of winning and being in Victory Lane," Miss Ellie laughed. "I love that you're so jealous. This is the best."

"Me?"

"You."

"I am not jealous. I'm . . . I've got to go. I have to get out of here."

"You know, Cal would really like to see you. I'm sure of it. He'll be tickled you were here to see him take the checkered flag."

"I think he's doing just fine seeing all the girls out there on that track, taking anything he wants. There go two more out there now. They're just girls from the stands. Cal has groupies! Camp followers! The Rolling Stones have nothing on Cal Davis! I hope he gets fat lips." She could hear Miss Ellie laughing as Churchill wormed her way off the grandstand and stomped to her car thinking about the no-good rotten redneck varmint she slept with last night—many times slept with last night—who was smooching and pinching other females right this minute in front of an entire crowd for all the world to see.

She cranked over Tic Tac, hit the accelerator, and barreled down U.S. 80 hot and mad. A police car with lights flashing and sirens wailing appeared in her rearview mirror. Cal drove like a maniac, got swarmed by beautiful women, and got a big check; she drove fast, got pulled over by a potbelly, balding, with garlic breath, and got a hundred-dollar ticket. Life sucked!

After parking Tic Tac she made her way to her apartment, tore off her dusty, muddy clothes, and headed for the shower—the same shower she shared last night with Cal. The one they stood in together, where she took care to wash him gently so as not to hurt his burned skin. She could see the shampoo suds sliding over his face to his broad, tan chest and shoulders, then covering his firm abs, and dripping off his big thick hard erection. She swallowed, picked up the loofah, and washed her arms, then rubbed it over her breasts. She thought of Cal's hands there. She thought of his thumbs gliding over her nipples making them hard and sensitive to his touch, to his mouth, to his tongue as he licked and suckled. She thought of his hands running over her legs, his fingers easing between them to her clit, teasing and fondling, and how she nearly dissolved right there in the shower. And how he'd leaned her back against the wall, holding her derriere tight in his palms as he slid into her, taking her breath away, making every cell of her body aware of him as he took her again, then again.

Her body suddenly tensed at the thought of being with

Cal, of him making love to her in the shower. Her breath caught and ripples of climax ran through her like a hot current. She leaned against the wall her heart racing, her insides wanting him for real, and not just in a memory. She wanted his hands on her, his body pressed to hers, him inside her. She wanted him with her. But he wasn't there, of course. He wasn't there because he was with the speedway sequin sisters. If she found out he was sharing their shower she'd run him over with his own racecar! Blast the man!

Churchill finished in a rush. No more thinking about Cal and her together. She wound up her hair with a clip, yanked on jeans, and slid into her FORGET THE BOOKS, CHECK OUT THE LIBRARIAN sweatshirt. Grabbing her purse, pen, notebook, and Matilda—who she had on loan from Miss Ellie ever since the fire, Churchill headed for the library, the one place where she could forget about Cal making love to her in the EMS truck *and* the shower *and* in her bed. And that he was now at the track because he got a trophy. She'd give him a trophy all right, right over his big fat head. Then she'd cut off his dick and feed it to the alligators.

She unlocked the library, locked it behind her, and almost wished the creep who terrorized her came back because she was armed, pissed, and tired of men messing with her! She turned on all the lights, making the place bright as high Mass at St. John's church. She pulled the big books from the back reference section and sat at the checkout desk where she had a better view of the whole library. Nobody was sneaking up on her! She intended to lose herself in books the way she'd always done. When she flunked out of mountain climbing school she read *Emma*, when she ran away from white-water rafting school she read the *Count of Monte Cristo*. That took running away to a whole new level. When she hid in the attic for two days so Margo couldn't find her and make her go to cowboy school she read Barbara Cartland's *Angel and the Rake*. Lord knows that was a million times better than cowboy school could ever be.

Tonight it was back to books and the key. Reading let her forget about everything else—like Cal and that he was a really great lover. She could concentrate on why so much stuff had happened since that night Miss Ellie invited her over for a chat and started showing the key around. Churchill sketched it out, knowing instantly why she was a librarian and not an artist. Anything beyond a stick figure boggled her brain. A knock came from the front door. "Library's closed," she yelled.

"Open up. I got something you'll be interested in," Cal yelled back.

She stomped to the door and gave a yank. "Well if it isn't the speedway stud. If you think I'm interested in you because you have a great dick and I can't think of anything else besides it or can't survive without you, you are dead wrong. I'm doing just fine on my own, thank you very much. Go show your big old manhood off to those cupie dolls at the racetrack that were hanging all over you. I'm sure they'll be mesmerized by your attributes. In fact, you can screw the whole blasted female population of the greater Savannah area and beyond, for all I care. You couldn't possibly have anything that interests me, Cal Davis."

"Nice speech but that's not why I'm here." He held up the brass key. "What's with my manhood? Where'd that come from? What the hell have you been reading, Ace?"

"I should slam the door and forget this evening ever happened." Except he had the key, she wanted it, and her drawing was pathetic. She stepped aside to let him enter, then held out her hand.

"Don't I even get a *congratulations, Cal. Nice driving tonight?*"

"If you had any more congratulations out there on that race track people would have been yelling for you and your entourage to get a room."

"It's part of the hype. Girls, trophy, the check. That I'm the town bad boy just adds to it. It's all for show. Come on, Ace, I'm not the kind of guy who makes love to you one night and goes fooling around with someone else the next. You know me better than that. I'm sorry if I hurt you. That was not my intent. If you would have stayed around I would have brought you on the track with me and then there would have been some serious kissing going on."

She folded her arms and gave him a little smile. "You really mean that?"

"What do you think?"

She let out a resigned breath. "Nice driving. You scared the hell out of me, but nice driving."

He grinned, his eyes twinkling. "It was a hell of a lot of fun out there. I'm glad you came out to see it, even if it wasn't planned." He dropped the key on the counter with a clunk but put his hand over it. "It's yours, but there's a catch. I don't know what this key is all about and that's the God's honest truth but it's about something. Whatever it is and wherever it takes us, it stays between us."

"Us?"

"Somebody besides you and me is after this thing. I'm not leaving you alone with it so there is a definite us from now on."

"I'm not complaining, mind you but I've taken precautions." Churchill held up Matilda. "I now have protection."

Cal ran his hand over his face and groaned. "I've got to have a talk with Miss Ellie. I want your word that whatever we find you don't go to the police or the press with it. Or to Miss Ellie, or Silky, and not even Michelle. The only reason I'm giving you the key is that you nearly got killed last night in the fire. Maybe this key has some connection to it and maybe it doesn't. But it's gone way beyond idle curiosity now and you deserve an answer. Do you promise? Do I have your word?"

"And if I say no?"

"I toss the damn thing in the river and we're done with it."

She sat down on a stool behind the desk and studied the key. "Well I have to say it's all Greek to me. That's a little library humor. But a lot of it is Greek. We're thousands of miles from Greece and I cannot imagine what something like this is doing in Savannah. Some kind of college fraternity thing perhaps, but it looks a little fancy for college kids."

Cal touched the center etching of the key. "I think this is a magnolia blossom."

"Probably a lily. They're big in Greece, used in wedding ceremonies, made into a crown for the bride. We have an obelisk, an alpha and omega, some ivy leaves."

Cal flipped it over. "A sword and building tools that make up the teeth of the key and something that looks like a beehive in the middle."

"I think that's a mountain like in Mt. Olympus where the Greek gods lived."

"I thought it was a mountain too, till I saw this little chair when I came in tonight. I've seen the chair before but the beehive never registered till now when I had the key in my hand." Cal went to the children's section and grabbed a chair and pointed to the back. "See, it looks like this carving with curves on the sides more like a bee . . . hive," he added in a slow drawn out voice, his gaze fusing with Churchill's. "This beehive."

"It is exactly," she added in a whisper, looking from the chair to the key, then back again. Her heart was in her throat and goose bumps skated up and down her spine. "There are magnolia blossoms on the brass lamps, more blossoms are carved into the front doors, and the legs of the desks are made up of a square and compass just like the ones here on the key."

"And we have a sword," Cal pointed across the room to the glass case."

"The Richard Arnold sword. The one he gave to Sherman as a symbol when he surrendered Savannah."

Cal laughed. "Okay, we're both really tired and grasping at straws. We're making something out of nothing. A lot of public places, especially libraries in the South, have flowers on the front door, on the lamps, and on the planters out front. Every library has at least one Civil War sword in a case. We're reaching."

"Any Greek revival building in the city, like the Kehoe House and Trinity Methodist Church, is going to have those things so we're not any closer to figuring out where this key goes . . . except the beehive is a little unique, I have to say that. Someone wants this key to open the door to something or someone wants the key to keep us from opening the door to something. One thing for sure is that this key does not open this library door. I say we try the church tomorrow and maybe ask the pastor if it looks familiar. But for now, I'm starved. I want pizza. Do you want pizza? Pepperoni? And Ding Dongs? I could really go for a package of Ding Dongs." She kissed him. "That's not exactly a fit celebratory dinner for someone who just won a big race. Or did you do all your celebrating out at the speedway?"

"Did you know if you leave a pepperoni sitting out for a year it stays the same and ditto for a Ding Dong. The shelf life of both is eternity."

"That means they have them in heaven."

"How do you plan to make it to forty eating that crap?"

"This from the guy who drives around in circles at impossible speeds and calls it fun? *You're* giving *me* lectures on staying alive?"

"Fine, but I'm making the pizza."

"Are you going to have a nice, new, big kitchen in your cabin when you rebuild?"

"You never know." He kissed her and she kissed him back and said, "Thanks for coming to see me tonight and not spending it with the sparkle sisters. I love the library like this, all quiet and to ourselves. It's sort of a magical place when no one else is around. Especially this library with the balcony, open in the middle like it is, the winding staircase, and the stained glass. I think it's haunted. I've seen lights in here at night."

"That's what happens when you eat Ding Dongs."

"So, just how hungry are you right now?"

"Really hungry."

She went to the door, but instead of opening it she turned out the lights. "Really hungry for what exactly?" She went into the children's section and doused the lights there, then pranced up to him while sliding off her sweatshirt. "I think tonight is my turn."

"Your turn for what?"

"To get naked in the library, of course." Cal laughed and she kicked off her flip-flops, one landing on the counter with a thunk, one by the door. "Last time you stripped for me and you said the next was my turn. I think that's tonight. If you're up for it." She placed her hand on his crotch, the warm hard swell of his erection pressing against her palm. "You are so up for it." She pulled him across the marble floor to a sofa in the reading area.

"Now every time I look at this room I'll think of us making love here on this antique, blue brocade davenport with rosewood arms and legs and on this beautiful Oriental rug. This will be our little secret. When things get boring at the library I can think about tonight and how un-boring a library can be when you set your mind to it, or let other body parts get involved." She unclipped her bra and draped it around his neck bringing his face to hers. She kissed him deeply, her tongue in his mouth then his doing the same.

"I have to say this is one way to get me to the library more often."

She unclipped a quilt that was a wall hanging and had been in the library for as long as she could remember. She tossed it over the couch.

"What if that's some priceless heirloom quilt made by Betsy Ross?"

"Betsy Ross never lived in Savannah." Churchill gig-gled. She was completely naked and she lay down and stretched out across the quilt like a goddess. "But at least now the quilt has an interesting history. Us." She held out her arms to him. "Let's make history together."

Of all the things Cal thought he might be doing this night, making love to Churchill in the James Oglethorpe Library on Bull Street did not make the list. He pulled off his jeans and shirt and took out a condom. "Good thing these walls can't talk." He lay on top of her, her sweet scent washing over him. She wrapped her legs around his waist, pulling his body close to hers. His dick nuzzled the soft patch at her legs, his chest rubbing over her nipples. "You always surprise me, Ace. I brought you the key to surprise you, then you do something like this."

"I'm just a librarian."

"You are fantastic."

"All because of you. Only with you, Cal. When we're together everything is new and exciting and fun. Except at the fire. That wasn't much fun." She kissed him, one of those slow burning I'll-remember-this-forever kisses that seeped into his soul. "For me you're Christmas, the Fourth of July, and birthdays all rolled into one very handsome package. I can't get enough of you. When we're apart all I do is count the time till I'm with you again." She laughed. "I think it's been this way since that night in the Mustang. You've always been in the back of my mind like a very nice distant memory I couldn't forget and didn't want to."

Except she *had* gotten too much of him and nearly lost her life because of it. He wasn't going to think about that or that he was leaving. He wanted to remember making love to her right there in the reading room, next to the *New York Times*, the *Washington Post*, and the *Cleveland Plain Dealer*, on a quilt of colorful squares that must be hundreds of years old. Then he made himself part of her, memorizing how she felt next to him, the sensation of her legs around his back, her arms on his neck. Passion roared through him when she climaxed, her little cries echoing in the quiet room, filling his head and his heart. He smoothed back her hair.

She closed her eyes. "I've never been so happy or so tired," she said on a contented sigh. "My two favorite things, you and books, together in one place."

He turned, his back against the sofa as he cradled Churchill next to him. His body relaxed, feeling her drift off and fall asleep in his arms. Then he fell asleep too, knowing it would not last but making him treasure the moment all the more.

He wasn't sure how long he slept but it was still dark outside when he opened his eyes. Churchill wasn't beside him. The quilt was tucked over his shoulders as if she'd put it there to keep him warm but there was no sign of her anywhere. "Ace? Churchill? Where are you?"

Nothing. No sound or movement in the library at all. No light except the red glow of the exit sign across the room.

Everything was completely quiet except for an occasional car passing outside on a mostly deserted street late at night. "Damn." He pulled on his jeans and shirt. Churchill's clothes were not on the floor where she'd dropped them. At least she wasn't running around naked. Then again the thought of Churchill playing hide and seek in a dark library without a stitch of clothing was pretty damn intriguing. Maybe it was all just a game and she was hiding.

"Hey, Churchill, am I it or are you it?" he yelled louder. Making his way to the main hallway he turned on the lights flooding the place in brightness. He was holding out hope for the game idea until he saw that the key was not on the checkout desk where he'd left it. The main doors were still locked, her shoe still leaning against it from when she kicked it off. She couldn't have gotten out without moving the shoe. Churchill was there, somewhere, and she wasn't having fun with him. She was on the trail of finding what the key opened and obviously it was something there. Something she thought of during the night. Something she saw. What the hell had she found and where the hell was she?

He searched in the back of the library by the desk and the window where he'd surprised her the first time. He took the winding steps to the balcony, his footsteps the only sound. An uneasy feeling settled in his gut. The place felt dark and eerie whereas it had felt cozy and comfortable when Churchill was with him. Even the moonlight streaming across the old worn hardwood floor stained in dark and light squares didn't chase away the dread. Actually they weren't squares like in cubes but they were square spirals, like the pattern in the quilt he and Churchill had made love on downstairs. Is that what she saw? Was it the pattern on the quilt that was a clue? Why the hell didn't she wake him so they could look together?

He clambered down the wrought iron steps, and flipped open *Mysteries of History*, one of the books Churchill had on the desk. He turned page after page until he found what he was looking for—the pattern on the quilt and on the floor. The book showed it on the wall of a Greek temple. The pattern was called Greek Key and it was the symbol for unity. Why did people in Savannah need to be united? What union? "Oh fucking hell. The Confederate Union."

He looked across the library to the Confederate sword. Whatever was going on was all about the Civil War. If a racecar diver could figure that out a student of antiquities would have no trouble at all. But that didn't mean she wasn't in trouble. Whoever set all this up didn't want it found by just anyone. Whatever *it* was. A person had to be thinking about what they saw and how it linked together. Having the damn key was a huge help.

Churchill was in the library somewhere and Cal was looking at a roomful of clues that would take him to her. She put it all together and came up with the answer. And he had to do the same. He could pour over those books and it still might not make any sense at all. He couldn't cram all that Churchill knew into a few hours of reading, especially as slow as he read. He'd cursed his disability over the years but never more than he did right then.

Cal ran his hand over his face. He swore he'd never look back to what happened that day Dodd accused him of stealing the money. He didn't ask Tripp any questions; he didn't want to know. It was done with, all behind him. Cal did what he had to do at the time and he'd do it all over again in a heartbeat. It was the only solution.

Except Churchill was missing and he had no idea if she was okay or not. There had already been break-ins, a broken arm, and a fire. What part of all those things were connected to the key he had no idea. But since the night

Miss Ellie started flashing it around town and asking questions nothing had been the same.

He needed to find Churchill and for that he needed answers right away. There was one person who might have them. Taking a deep breath Cal picked up the phone behind the checkout desk and dialed. "Hey, we need to talk."

Chapter Eleven

Cal opened the library door to Tripp standing on the other side. "Hi."

"Hi? That's it? No questions? No *why the hell did you call me here at three a.m.?*" Cal closed the door.

"Nope."

"Tripp, I'm going to need more than one syllable answers.

"Then don't call me at three a.m."

"Churchill's missing. She has this key that Miss Ellie found in the Mustang, my Mustang, the one you borrowed and—good Lord, you got your hair buzzed." Cal ran his hand over his brother's fuzzy head. "I don't believe it."

"I gave it to Locks of Love. I was at the mall, they had a booth. It seemed like a good idea." Tripp folded his arms and leaned against the desk. "I always wondered what happened to that key. That was a cluster-fuck of a day if there ever was one."

"That's a phrase I never expected to hear come out of your mouth. What have you been smoking?"

"Sometimes that word just fits the occasion and that day was it."

"The problem is Churchill has the key and she's gone. We were here at the library and fell asleep. I woke up and she'd vanished. I know she's still in the library somewhere but she might be in trouble or hurt. When I call she doesn't answer. There are no signs of her anywhere. I need you to tell me where she is. I think you know what the key opens and I really can't believe you cut your hair to fuzz."

"I took a blood oath not to tell, Cal."

"How would you like a bloody nose to go with it? Look, I can appreciate whatever it is you swore to but Churchill's been missing for hours. Maybe she's fallen or trapped. The key goes to something in this library. Since you and I and Miss Ellie were the only ones to drive the Mustang one of us knows what it's about. I don't. Miss Ellie got roughed up over it. That leaves you. I won't tell a soul, I swear. I'll take it to the grave with me."

"You open your mouth and you might get to that grave faster than you intended. There are important people in this city involved who don't want anyone to know they're involved. The thing is when you got arrested I left all the key stuff behind. I don't know a whole hell of a lot."

Cal pointed to the Greek Key on the open page of the book he'd been looking at. "This pattern is in the hardwood floor upstairs and on an old quilt in the reading room. Unity. We have Arnold's sword of surrender. This place was built in 1862. The Confederate Union." He looked at Tripp who didn't look surprised at all. "That you knew."

"That much I knew."

"Tell me you're not involved in one of those fringe lunatic groups who think the Civil War is still going on."

"I can tell you that I know the Civil War is over." Tripp let out a deep sigh. "I can't believe I'm going to blab. A hundred and fifty years shot all to hell in one night. Not even Yankee invasions or St. Patrick's Day benders have loosened tongues."

"It's for a good cause."

"If anyone around here finds out they'll make me move

north, probably to some god-forsaken place like Massachusetts." Tripp sat on the desk and gazed out over the library. "Here goes. The magnolias on the front door signify
the South, the obelisk by the door is a symbol for enlightenment, a statement to all who enter, though I have to say
some members are more enlightened than others. The
compass and square on the desks are building tools like in
building together. The beehive is a symbol for everyone of
all walks of life working for the common good. The black
and white marble tiles in this hallway signify the passage
from dark to light, awareness of the truth that leads to the
spiral staircase, a path from lower to higher understanding.
The stained glass windows overhead light the way to the
great plan. The desk I'm sitting on is cypress, the everlasting
wood, preservation. The key itself is the shape of the checkout desk, the color is red. We are bound in blood—until
now of course because I just opened my big fat mouth and
spilled everything."

"That's a whole lot of shit going on."

"Personally I think they went a little overboard. But I
guess since you can't put a big old X on the floor to mark
the spot this is the next best thing."

"So where's Churchill?"

"How the hell do I know? After you got arrested I got
kicked out. I kind of botched the initiation. I'm probably
the only member to get booted. Dad was mortified. He
wanted me to be like him."

"Dad? Our dad, as in Ron of Ron and RuthAnn fame?
He was in?"

"Is. Do not rat me out."

"You were too young to get mixed up in this."

"I was too stupid. I wanted to be the big man in Dad's
eyes. I know books so I thought I knew everything. How
stupid is that?"

"Churchill?"

"Right. Okay, here goes. The best I can figure is that the marble floor you're standing on leads to the spiral stairs. We follow those to the stained glass windows that lead to the cypress bookcases upstairs in the back."

"And then what?"

Tripp slid off the desk. "Beats the hell out of me. Like I said, I was kicked out." He started for the steps and Cal took his arm. "You seem better. Not so morose. A little off the wall but not morose. Have you been taking mom's Zoloft?"

"Chocolate covered strawberries and champagne."

Cal followed Tripp up the spiral staircase to the big bookshelves across the back. "Do you see anything here that's a symbol that says Open Sesame?"

"Churchill?" Cal yelled.

"Cal?" Churchill answered.

"Where are you?"

"I'm in here."

"Where's here. Marco?"

"Polo. Look for the sign."

Tripp pointed. "There."

Cal ran his hand over a bookcase. "Did you find another symbol? Magnolias? A sword? Another beehive?"

"Fuchsia Post-it note. It says, *Cal, didn't what to wake you. It's unlocked. Push twice.* Then there's some *XOXO* stuff at the bottom. Well dang, what were you doing in this library, big brother?"

"Just push the damn bookcase, okay."

When Tripp did, the spring lock opened a door of books to a lit lamp and Churchill sitting on the floor of something that looked like a walk-in closet. Shelves were covered with hats, books, canes, an evening bag. There were jackets, guns, knives, pairs of shoes, scarves. Old stuff and new stuff.

"You found my Post-it. Isn't this neat?"

Cal picked up an old shoe. "A storage closet? Why would someone lock up a storage closet with a fancy key?"

Churchill got up and dusted herself off. "I've been looking at it for the last hour trying to figure it out. A librarian's paradise. Hi, Tripp. Nice hair. Are you a part of all this?"

"Was."

She handed him the key. "Then you'll know what to do with it. Someone is trying real hard to get it back. So, that's it. We can all go home now. We know what the key goes to. Tripp gives it back and it's over. No more breakins. No more roughing up Miss Ellie. That was a little over the top, incidentally. Someone needs to lighten up."

Cal said, "What is this place?"

"You don't want to know." Tripp sighed.

Cal gave him the big brother stare.

"Right." Tripp sighed again. "I am so getting sent to Massachusetts. Ever hear of Skull and Bones?"

"A secret club for the rich and spoiled."

"This is the Southern version. It's been around since the Civil War when it was for the privileged plantation boys to hang around together, meet the privileged plantation women. Scarlett O'Hara probably belonged. Rhett didn't. Then it was for those bound to preserve the Confederacy. Now it's for business, social, and political connections. Initiation has always been to steal something from an enemy." He picked up an old felt Union officer hat. "You get the picture."

"Amazing what's been stolen." Churchill picked up a Bible. "Most of the time I'd say the stuff was never even missed, but then sometimes it is. What do you think, Tripp?" She handed him the Bible.

"An initiation ritual, just a stupid, stupid custom." He put down the Bible. "Enough. We better go. It's going to be light soon."

"All this over a closet?" Cal said. "I thought there might be something . . . more. Something . . . Never mind."

"There's probably a big book hidden in here with pretty impressive names on the roster." They turned for the door.

"I'll get the light," Churchill volunteered, stepping back in, knowing she probably shouldn't do what she was about to do. When she walked Cal closed the cypress bookshelf. She took the Post-it note and stuck it to his shirt. "Sorry I worried you. You know me and questions. I woke up, started thinking and found the bookcase."

Tripp frowned. "Next time try Tylenol PM."

Cal led the way down the steps and out the library front door. Churchill locked it behind her and ran her hand over the carved magnolia blossoms. "I'll never look at this place the same way again." She eyed Tripp. "So, do I know any of the members?"

"Have you ever been to Massachusetts in the winter? That's where blabbermouths go."

"Thanks for coming to my rescue." She kissed Tripp on the cheek and headed for her apartment, leaving Cal and Tripp talking brother stuff on the sidewalk. She hurried up the steps and put the Bible she'd slipped under her sweatshirt under the couch just as Cal came in.

"Lose something down there?"

"I hope not." She stood and headed for the kitchen. "I'm so hungry my stomach thinks my throat's been cut."

"Wait a minute, Ace," he said snagging her around the waist and bringing her close. "You really did scare the hell out of me." He kissed her, warming her down to her toes and making her feel like a rat for hiding the Bible. But she wasn't sure what it was all about. When she flipped through it in the closet there were names in the front she recognized and then Tripp showed up. Maybe the Bible was nothing but Tripp had a look about him when he picked it up. Sadness? Regret? "Maybe I have a Ding Dong around here we can split."

Cal went to the refrigerator and opened it.

"Holy cow! I have eggs and bacon and tomatoes. And whole wheat bread and juice. I have steaks and sausage and carrots. I don't think my refrigerator has ever had a carrot in it. It's a carrot virgin. And sticky buns. How did sticky buns get in here?"

"The sticky bun fairy."

She slid her arms around him and smiled into his big blue wonderful eyes. "Would that happen to be the same as the egg, bacon, and sausage fairy?"

"Could be. He figured if he was crashing here he could add something to the larder. I'll go shopping more tomorrow. I ran out of time."

"Had a race to win?"

He tucked a strand of hair behind her left ear. "You are so beautiful, even at four in the morning."

"So are you." She kissed him, wrapping herself around him, loving the feel of his firm hard body next to hers. "We can eat, or make love, or take a shower. I don't have enough energy for all three."

"I'll whip us up an omelet and you run us a bath."

"Us?"

"We can eat and soak at the same time. That takes care of two. We can work up to the third."

She slid against him, her breasts to his front. Her hands found his fly as she kissed him again, her tongue sliding to his. Her fingers fondled him though his jeans. "Hurry," she whispered, then strutted away, twirling her glasses on her finger before tossing them onto the counter. She dropped her blouse and bra on the kitchen floor, her pink shorts in the hallway and draped her panties over the bathroom doorknob. "I'm waiting," she called.

"Trust me, Ace, I'm cooking as fast as I can."

She giggled and ran water into the tub, dumping in some bubble bath she bought for Michelle two days ago. She'd been walking down Bay Street, thinking about Michelle and Tommy Lee getting back together and ducked into a tourist trap. She'd picked up the bath salts along with candles and lotion. Not that she liked Tommy but if Michelle was hellbent on getting back together with the man at least she could enjoy some part of it because deep down inside Churchill couldn't imagine her enjoying much about the reconciliation.

The bubbles billowed up, the scent of pumpkin filling the room, spiced candles adding to the aroma.

"I don't know what you're doing in there," Cal called from the kitchen, "but now I'm starving."

She took a blob of bubbles and draped it over one nipple, then the other, then covered the dark patch between her legs. She pranced back into the kitchen and struck a pose against the doorjamb. "Hungry for what, big boy?"

Cal turned around and dropped the spatula and the loaf of bread. "I think I'm dreaming."

"All for real. All for you."

He yanked the skillet from the burner, turned off the stove, and discarded in seconds his shirt and shoes.

"I thought we were going to eat."

"I am, every delicious inch of you. Remember, you started this." He scooped her into his arms and took her into the bathroom. "You've outdone yourself."

"It was a get-back-together gift for Michelle and Tommy Lee."

"We'll buy them towels." Cal knelt down on one knee and slid her into the warm sudsy water, then turned off the tap. Steam circled around them. He took off his jeans, retrieved a condom, and stared down at her as she stared up, but only halfway up. "I have a face, you know."

"I'm overwhelmed by something else."

"Can't be that overwhelmed. You're getting to be good friends."

She looked at his face and smiled. "I know and I'm truly happy about it, about being with you. When you're not with me all I can think about is when I am going to see you again. I make excuses to go see you about something or go see Miss Ellie because I know you'll be there."

"You're the one who overwhelms me." He crawled in on top of her, his hands braced on either side, her legs circling his middle as her arms went around his neck. "I thought it was take a shower, eat, then we make love. What happened to our great plan?"

"We got our priorities straight."

She laughed, then kissed him as he settled into the water, her legs hugging him tighter. His erection pressed against her clit tantalizing her, setting her on fire. Then he slid into her, slowly, taking his time, letting her open to him, filling her, then withdrawing only to take her slowly again, a little deeper.

"You are a master of lovemaking," she said on a gasp, his size more than she remembered.

He pumped into her again, harder, a little faster, taking her breath away. Before she could catch her breath he took her again, then again, her body opening more. Her legs spread wider, her sex to his, her climax more powerful, more consuming than she thought possible as he possessed her body, mind, and soul. She belonged to him in every way and she loved it . . . she loved him.

The next morning Churchill eased out of bed so as not to wake Cal. Finding secret rooms and winning car races made for an exhausting day. Making love in a bathtub made for an exhausting night. She was tired too, but she was so curious she could jump right out of her skin.

She tossed on a skirt and blouse and tiptoed into the living room, got her purse and the Bible, then coffees from the beanery. Balancing, she hurried to the library. Michelle was already inside running the vacuum. Storybook was asleep on his blanket. Two scones were on the desk. Churchill put down the coffees, Bible, and purse, snagged a scone, then pulled the plug on the vac.

"Hey," Michelle looked back at her. "What's going on? Do you want to do the vacuuming that badly? Honey, that can be arranged. You do not have to turn the thing off to get my attention."

Churchill pointed to the ceiling. "You will not believe what is in the upstairs of this place behind a bookcase in the back."

"Okay, who blabbed? Silky? After three beers you can't predict what that man's going to do these days."

"You know? He knows? You both are—"

"I've lived in Savannah for thirty-six years and worked in this library for twenty of them. Silky's older than dirt and knows more about Savannah than anyone. Miss Ellie would have been a part too, but everyone knows she can't keep a secret to save her soul."

"But, but, what about me, huh?" Churchill poked her finger at Michelle's chest, standing tall and proud and hoping she looked especially Southern. "I live here too, you know. And I'm a librarian. I want in."

"You defected to Jersey. So, who told you? Bet it was one of those new Democrat converts with all their talk about disclosure. Everything's so blue around here anymore. Used to be you couldn't swing a dead cat in this town without hitting a redneck. They're getting to be an endangered species, I tell you. Right pitiful. Takes away all the local color. We might as well be living up there in New York City and listening to Charlie Rose."

"How did you get involved?"

"Great-great-granddaddy laid the cornerstone for the library so they thought I had a right. And with working here I can keep an eye on things."

"So what do you know about this Bible with a white cross on it?"

"It's Dodd's." She slapped her hands over her mouth and muttered, "Oh, shit, I can't believe I said that. What are you doing with it down here? I'm not saying anything more about it. No names, uh-uh, not me. I'm not getting sent to Massachusetts." Michelle put her fingers to her lips and made like turning a key there to lock her lips then throwing the key away.

"Last night Cal and I were in here late and I found the closet. Tripp showed up to help Cal find me. He picked up the Bible and didn't look any too happy about seeing it. What is Tripp doing with Dodd's Bible?" Churchill's gaze met Michelle's. "Oh my God, that was his initiation."

"You know, don't you? You got that look you always get when you got the answer to a question. Cal's going to get damned pissed if you get involved in this, Church. It's his business. He did what he had to do. You're going to go see Tripp, aren't you? You're going to go poke a stick right in a hornet's nest and stir things up the way you always do."

"Not always. How do you know what went on with Cal and Tripp and the Bible?"

"I know Cal and how he looks out for Tripp. Cal was accused of stealing Dodd's money. Cal's not the stealing type and Dodd is. I've always felt he was no good even if there's no evidence of it."

"Cal's innocent."

"Let it go. It's what Cal wants."

"Michelle, his life's been ruined. Everyone even his parents thinks he's a bum and rotten to the core. And there's the fact that it was my testimony that sent Cal to jail. There wasn't any Bible in Dodd's hand that night I saw him and Cal running, I just thought I saw it because Dodd carries the thing everywhere he goes. Me sending Cal to jail hasn't made me feel all warm and fuzzy these last three years and now that I know he's innocent you really expect me to do nothing and let it go?"

"Are you doing this for your sake or his? Think about that, Church."

"For the love of God, Michelle, I sent an innocent man to prison, a man I love. I'm not supposed to do anything now that I know differently? Let him keep suffering through life?"

"He'll survive. That's what Cal Davis does best. If you do anything his brother might go to prison for something Cal has already spent time for. That's not what Cal wants, his time behind bars to count for nothing. This is not your decision to make."

"But—"

"There are no buts this time around, honey. For once don't ask questions, don't look around. Just stay out of it. It's not your call."

"I hate this. You're right."

"Cal's a hero. He's not about putting himself first. It's who he is and why you love him."

There was a knock at the library door and Michelle made a face. "We open at ten. For crying in a bucket why can't they read the blasted sign? We're open ten to five. It's not ten yet." She peeked out the window. "Oh, Lordy, it's Tripp Davis. You don't look one bit surprised."

"I'm not the only one who can't live with sending an innocent man to jail. He was going to grow up sometime. This was bound to happen, and seeing that Bible last night had to trigger something."

Michelle took another peek. "What the heck happened

to his hair, not that it was all that terrific going in. Mostly looked like he got hit by lightning but at least he had some. I'm telling you the whole world is going haywire. Must be a full moon tonight."

Churchill opened the door and Tripp came in looking haggard. His eyes were bloodshot, his clothes looked slept in, like he'd done more tossing and turning than sleeping. "I came to get the Bible." He looked at the counter. "This one. When I confess to the police that I stole it three years ago, not Cal, I should have it as proof of the deed. Don't you think? I'm kind of new at this confession thing." He took the Bible off the counter and tucked it under his arm.

Churchill took the Bible back. "Cal will rupture a spleen if you go anywhere near the police."

Tripp grabbed the Bible back. "I can't have Cal covering for me any longer. Do you know what this has been like for me these last three years? I should never have agreed to his idea in the first place."

Churchill held Tripp by the shoulders. "What idea?"

"That he should cover for me. Take the blame. It was just a Bible, but Dodd said it was money. I was a twenty-year-old geek. I never would have survived prison. That's what Cal said but to tell you the truth I haven't survived that well these last three years anyway."

Tripp leaned heavily on the desk. "There I said it. You know it all, I know it all, it's out there. I cannot let Cal keep getting blamed for something I did. Everyone hating his guts, burning down his house, and ruining his business, when he's such a good mechanic and driver."

Michelle pulled a silver flask from her purse. "Well, they say the truth will set you free. Personally I think it's about to send everything straight into the toilet." She unscrewed the top, gulped, then smacked her lips in appreciation. She handed the flask to Tripp who drained it dry, Michelle and Churchill looking on in total wonder.

"You know, I do feel very free."

"Honey, what you feel is sloshed. A flask is for sipping whiskey."

Tripp burped. "I'll remember that next time."

Churchill said, "I'm going with him. He can't drive half bombed."

"Tommy's on duty. He might know a good lawyer who can straighten this out."

"How are you and Tommy Lee doing?"

Michelle gave a little smile that was more devil than smoochy-smoochy. "He and my cousin Houston, from Atlanta have bonded."

"And that's good?"

"Houston has a way with words."

Churchill parked Tripp's Volvo in the police station parking lot. "Okay here we are. Think about this, Tripp. Once you open your mouth there's no turning back. It'll be out there and the police will have to act on it. The Bible theft isn't the problem but the missing twenty-five grand is. Maybe you should run your idea by Cal. He needs to know."

"He'll talk me out of it. He'll say, 'Tripp, little brother, you're just a little brother. I'm the big brother and I'll take care of this'. For once I need to—how did DaisyLou put that—not be ten anymore. I can feel like a man so I need to act like a man."

"DaisyLou as in the gal at the speedway?"

"My therapist."

"I should have brought the flask." Churchill followed Tripp into the station. Tommy Lee waddled out and sat down at his desk. Tripp put the Bible down on the desk and hiccupped. "Cal followed me to Dodd's big tent because I stole his Mustang. When he saw what I was up to he sent me out one door and drew Dodd's attention to himself at the other door while I was getting away. Then he ran out and Churchill happened by and was an eye-witness even though she likes Cal a lot. That sucked for her. I can't live with myself any longer." He held out his arms for handcuffs. "Lock me up and take me away. I'm a no good son of a bitch. Well, technically, I'm not a son of a bitch because my mom's married to my dad—for quite a while now. Ron and RuthAnn. Maybe you know them?"

Tommy looked perplexed; usually he just looked stupid. "What the hell are you talking about? What the hell are you two doing here?"

"Cal didn't steal the money from Dodd, because there wasn't any money to steal. Just this Bible. The money was a cover to get more money out of his congregation because that's what Dodd does. Where did you think Dodd would get that much money in the first place? Did you ever think about that? I stole the Bible because Dodd's an ass and I wanted it—the Bible not Dodd's ass." Looking brave, Tripp held out his arms again. "Lock me up. I'm ready."

"Are you drunk?"

"A little."

"Oh for chrissake, this is some piss-poor way to start the fucking day." Tommy took a drink of coffee, slopping some on his shirt. "You're Cal's brother and this is Cal's girl. If you two think you can come in here and hand me some cock-and-bull story to try and clear him of all charges, you're both freaking nuts."

"I am not nuts," Churchill huffed.

Now Tripp looked perplexed. "It's the truth. I'm guilty of everything I just said, I swear." He put his hand on the Bible.

"And I'm the Easter Bunny and Churchill here is Mother Earth. Get yourselves out of here and don't either of you come back again."

"But—"

"Leave or I'll have you both thrown out. We've got better things to do than listen to false confessions to bail out assholes like your brother. He's guilty. Little Miss Librarian testified to it and Cal went to prison like he was supposed to. End of story. What did he do, send you here to get himself off the hook? Guess getting his place torched proved just how much people around here hate his guts."

"I don't believe this," Tripp said to Churchill as they came out of the police station. "Where is the justice system when you really need it? *Believe in the system*, that's what you're supposed to do. Here I am free as a bird when I'm guilty and supposed to be behind bars." He hunched his shoulders and hiccupped. "I'm a bad man."

Churchill draped her arm around Tripp. "Yep, bad to the bone, and totally blamed. I think we should send that confession to Woody Allen. He'd appreciate it."

"How am I going to make this right? I'm guilty and need to make amends. Everyone still thinks Cal's the one who's guilty. I don't know what to do next."

"It'll come to you."

"Really?"

"Promise. In the meantime go home and get some sleep. You should tell Cal what's going on. He needs to know."

"Maybe he won't find out. It didn't do any good. That policeman didn't believe me."

"Savannah loves to gossip and what just happened in that police department a few minutes ago is gossip dipped in chocolate."

Chapter Twelve

Cal got juice from Churchill's fridge and pulled out a piece of leftover omelet, a huge improvement over the blueberry pop tarts and frozen waffles from the day before. That Churchill lived to age thirty was a testament to the perseverance of the human body. He was mighty glad she made it. He smiled and thought of the unexpected bubble bath and how she made life fun, exciting, and different.

How'd he get so damn lucky? A lot of crap had come his way lately but Churchill had come his way, too. Not that it would last. Tripp had the menacing key and it would get back where it belonged so that was over, but Dodd and his followers hated Cal's guts. The rest of the city wasn't far behind. Sooner or later that would spill over to Churchill and he couldn't let that happen. She was the darling of Savannah and loved by everyone. He couldn't let that change because of him.

Cal downed another glass of juice, then drove out to the speedway. He was later than usual but that probably didn't have anything to do with the group of kids hanging around in front of the garage, TJ with them. Cal parked the Mustang. "What's going on?"

"These are my friends." TJ beamed. "When I told them

about the car you and I were going to build—well you mostly—they wanted to see what we were doing. This is Brian, Lamar, Forrest, Dillon, and Nancy. We mess around with cars together a lot. Brian and Lamar were here last night. I had homework. They said that was some hot race, Cal. You were in the groove."

"Thanks, I appreciate it. It was fun." They all grinned as if they knew the feeling, meaning they were dragging and racing off track somewhere illegally. That was dangerous as hell and a good way to lose kids. "You want me to tell a little about the Challenger and what we're going to do?"

They exchanged looks. "We want to help you build it," Dillon blurted. The others nodded, eyes bright, smiles hopeful. "Eco is the future but muscle cars are the bomb. TJ said the Challenger has both, or will have when you're done with it. *Popular Mechanics* is doing something like this and showing off their car at all the NASCAR tracks. You're doing it right here at the speedway. Dang, are we lucky or what?"

Cal was a god. Better than Superman, Batman, and Wolverine man. He was Car man. If there was a way for a mortal to be a god, that's who he was to those kids. Things hadn't changed all that much over the years, meaning they probably weren't the most popular kids. More like outsiders but they had each other and they had a love of cars. It was more than love. It was their life. He knew all about that. "All of you into this?"

"Nancy's a girl but she's good with transmissions. And you should see her drive!" If she had the respect from those boys she must be good.

Cal held up his hands in surrender. "No sexual bias here. My girlfriend would kick my ass." They laughed, easing the tension and giving him a second to think about what to do. He sat down on a case of brake fluid. "Look—"

"Nothing good ever starts out with that word." TJ's eyes lost their spark and so did the others.

"The problem is I'm leaving Savannah. Right now y'all are the only ones who know this. I'll be around for a few days. You can come out, and we can work on some cars together but that's it. I'm sorry." And he was, more than he could put into words. The kids would be great to work with. They were TJ times five.

The kids shuffled around, then walked off. "Hey, I'm not leaving today. There's stuff here to work on." He'd just gone from god to scum in one minute flat.

Dillon waved over his shoulder. "That's okay. We don't need your pity."

"Who drove out here? Need some work done on your car? I can help, maybe show you a few things. I'm free labor and if I have the parts you're welcome to them." Free parts was a sure sell. He remembered those days.

The kids stopped and turned. Nancy raised her hand. "I'm chasing down a rough idle problem."

"Then I'm your man. I have a scan tool and we'll check out the long and short term fuel trim first. A lot of the time that's where the problem is." A little more upbeat, the kids went to get Nancy's car. TJ hung back looking downright dismal. "Where are you going off to, Cal?"

"North Carolina. I'd appreciate you keeping this to yourself till I can tell Silky. I'm sure he'll keep you on, working around here." Cal ran his hand through his hair. "You know what's going on with me, who I am, and the trouble. I think it's best for me to get out of town."

"Thought you weren't supposed to run away from your problems."

"If there weren't other people getting hurt I'd agree with you. But my mistakes haven't just affected me. If I leave, people I care about won't be caught in the line of fire like they are now. I hate to see others pay for what I've done. There's a message there."

"You *can* run away from your problems?" TJ gave him a wise-ass look.

"Don't get into trouble."

Nancy drove her '95 Grand Am in to the garage to a spot not taken over by the Challenger. She popped the hood and everyone gathered round. "TJ," Cal said, "why don't you get us some Cokes out here. It's going to be a scorcher today." The kids nodded their thanks and Cal ducked under the hood taking in the engine. "Nice car," he said to Nancy as another car turned off 80 and onto the gravel road getting lost in the cloud of August dust as it came toward the speedway. Cop cruiser, Cal realized. It stopped and good old Tommy Lee Dempsey got out and waddled over. "Using cheap kid labor now, Davis? Not that I'm surprised."

"What do you want, Dempsey?" Cal needed to walk a fine line with the kids present. They didn't need to hear him mouth off to a cop, even a shitty one.

"I was in the neighborhood and—" He stopped dead, getting red in the face, anger bulging his eyes right out of their sockets but he wasn't looking at Cal. He was staring at something over Cal's shoulder. Cal turned to see TJ walking back from the concession stand. He was carrying Cokes. What was the big deal? He wasn't robbing the local gas station. What was Dempsey's problem? He was a Pepsi man?

"What are you doing here?" Dempsey bellowed.

TJ stopped and turned the color of the garage, Coke cans dropping onto the concrete, breaking open, spilling Coke everywhere.

"I asked you what are you doing here, boy?"

"He's working here," Cal answered. "What's it to you, Dempsey?"

"He's my goddamn son, that's what it is to me. He's supposed to have a job at an auto supply store, and this sure as hell ain't no auto supply store. You lied to me, TJ. All the while you've been coming here. You know I'd never let you work at the speedway especially with the likes of some lowlife criminal for a boss." Dempsey faced Cal. "I should haul your ass in for—"

"For what, hiring your son? Just for the record I didn't know TJ was your son, not that it would have mattered. He wanted a job, I had a job available and, no, I didn't know his last name. It never came up. Silky handles the paperwork. You aren't the only Dempsey in Savannah, so get over it."

Dempsey hitched up his pants, his extended gut pushing them down in front to the point where his belt disappeared under the layer of lard. He pointed to the rest of the kids. "You better get out of here, too. Your mamas and daddies don't want you associating with some ex-con."

Nancy put her hands to her hips suddenly looking more adult than kid. "My mama's home drunk and passed out. I haven't seen my daddy since I was three. I think I'm staying right here."

"Preying on kids now, huh, Davis," Dempsey said. "Trying to make yourself look good for a change? Is that why you sent your brother and Churchill to convince me you're innocent as a lamb? Like I was going to believe Tripp stole a Bible, you were some decoy, and there never was twenty-five grand stolen in the first place. You think I just fell off the cabbage truck? I'm not that stupid."

Cal felt as if he'd been sucker punched. "What?"

"Don't give me the innocent act. If you think for one minute that anyone would believe that you're not the one responsible for stealing from Dodd you are more of a freaking idiot than I thought and that's going some."

"Churchill and Tripp?"

"I came out here to tell you to your face everyone knows you're guilty. It's not going to change anybody's opinion so quit wasting my time getting your brother and girlfriend to deliver your trumped up story of you being a great guy and Tripp guilty. What a joke. That kid's nothing but a bookworm. Those two can go to jail for false confessions."

Dempsey pointed to the cruiser. "Get in TJ, right now. I'm taking you home. This time tomorrow you'll be cooling your heels in military school. Your mama's not saving you this time. You had your chance and blew it."

"I got a job and I'm passing school. That was the deal."

"Get!"

TJ headed toward the cruiser, turned, and came back to Cal. He held out his hand right there in front of his dad. Gutsy kid. "Great working with you, Cal."

Cal took his hand. "A real pleasure working with you too, TJ. Good luck. If you need anything—"

"TJ," Dempsey yelled. "Get in that goddamn car. You hear me, boy? I'm done fooling around with you!"

Cal was numb as he watched the cruiser head back to the highway. How could Churchill do that? She put together the pieces and somehow figured out he went to prison for Tripp. She must have confronted Tripp and convinced him to confess because it was the right thing to do. And after she swore to Cal she wouldn't, that what she found in the library would stay there. She stuck her nose where it didn't belong, again, and Tripp was right in the middle.

"Hey," Nancy called. "Do you want to forget about the car because of TJ and—"

"No," Cal said in a rush. He faked a smile and headed back to the car. He had to cool off. The kids were counting on him and he couldn't let them down twice. If he wasn't leaving he'd take them on. But he was leaving and if he had any second thoughts that he should stay in Savannah they were gone. He'd miss the speedway for sure but running into Churchill would be a constant reminder of how she betrayed him, went behind his back, and put Tripp in jeopardy.

It was nearly five when the kids left the garage. Cal had replaced the intake valve taking care of Nancy's rough idle problem. He was hot and tired, and still pissed as hell at Churchill. When he looked up, there she was.

"Hi." She stood in the doorway, the sun setting at her back. She was dressed in her librarian attire of black skirt and white blouse that always turned him on, except for now. "Helping the kids? I saw a carload leaving as I was coming in."

"Yeah."

"Like when Silky used to work with you, I bet."

"Silky taught me a lot."

She came further into the garage, her neat clothes looking out of place surrounded by car parts and the partially dismantled Challenger. The two of them were always out of place with each other and never so much as now.

"We need to talk."

"Seems you already have. Tommy Lee? Why'd you do it, Churchill? All I asked was for you to stay the hell out of my life. I said that right off when we were in the alley. When I gave you the key you gave me your word in the library not to go to the police about anything you found there. It took you less than a day to go spill everything and drag my brother with you."

"Tripp wanted to confess to the police and I went with him."

"Why the fucking hell didn't you bring him to me? I could have straightened him out."

"Because it's his decision to make. He can handle more than you give him credit for. He's not a kid, especially now. He can make up his own mind and you're going to have to let him. I get that you're pissed. You have that right and—"

"I don't need your permission. What I need is for you to stay away from me and butt out of things that concern my family. This is not your business."

"Oh but it is," she said in a low determined voice. A sick feeling settled in Cal's gut as she said, "When you ran out of Dodd's tent that night you headed straight for my car, my blue Bel Air. Unmistakable. No getting me confused with anyone else in this city. You wanted me to be the one to see and hear everything that went on with you and Dodd. You could have run around the back of the tent, into the park, in any other direction, to anyone else, but you wanted me as your eye witness, for there to be no question you were the guilty one. The librarian who's always in the middle of some shit storm was right in the middle of yours and the cops would believe me. You used me to get sent to jail and for no one to consider anyone else, especially Tripp. How does that sound for making it my business? Sound about right?"

Cal let out a breath that he felt as if he'd been holding for three long years. "Dodd said he'd drop the charges if I gave him the Bible. I didn't know what the hell he was talking about then. If I had, all this could have been avoided. I guess the twenty-five grand seemed like a better option than a cheap Bible and he went with that. The only winner in all of this has been Dodd."

"It sure isn't us." Churchill headed for her car and wished she smoked or did Jell-O shots or gambled or did something to get rid of the tension eating her up inside. For once in her life books weren't going to cut it. She climbed into the Prius and headed for Michelle's to get Storybook. She drove past the dirt track heading for 80, then suddenly she was heading back to the track, and then she was *on* the track. Why the hell not? A Prius wasn't a racecar but it could go over seventy. The question right now was, how much over seventy?

Her tires sliding on the dirt, she floored the accelerator feeling the tires spin, throwing grime and mud into the air. Neat! The tires caught and the Prius swerved off right, then left. She hit fifty, sixty, seventy then backed off going into a turn, but still too fast making her fight the wheel. Skidding as if on ice and out of control she almost hit the fucking wall!

But she didn't! Giving the car more gas coming out of the turn she took off. Physics wasn't her strong suit but she understood the basics of centrifugal force and was suddenly zooming down a straightaway, the far curve fast approaching. Going too fast again she hit the brakes, fishtailing the Prius. Sliding and skidding, nearly turning completely around, dirt doused the car and her. She swiped her hand over her glasses to clear the mud as she swung around the next curve. She ran too low and got into the grass but gunned the engine to get back on the track, then hit the accelerator again, climbing to eighty, then ninety. She was going to break a hundred. If they could throw a baseball that fast she could drive that fast and no cops were around to give her a ticket! How sweet was that?

She slid into the next curve and when she felt the car coming around the far side she flattened the accelerator to the floor. Eighty, ninety, ninety-five, but the next curve came too fast, again making her slow down, fishtailing around, then flooring the accelerator again and sooner. Eighty-five, ninety-five, one-hundred. "Yeeehaaaaaaaaa!" she screamed, sure that she had never screamed yeeehaaaaaaaa in her whole life. It felt good, really good, a bubble of bliss bursting inside. She grinned and licked her lips, tasting dirt. It tasted okay. It tasted like adventure! Not skydiving adventure or rafting the Amazon adventure but something.

She promised Tic Tac a detail job that she figured was the equivalent of a day at the spa as she drove off the track. In her rearview mirror she watched Cal staring at her, looking paste white. Even from where she was she could tell. At least he cared what happened to her. And she cared what happened to him. The problem was all the garbage in between.

When Michelle answered the door she stopped crying, choked back a sob, and said, "What the hell happened to you? The only clean spot you have is where your glasses were. You look like a raccoon."

"Cal and I had a fight."

"And you threw mud at each other?"

"There probably was some mud slinging but why are you crying," Churchill insisted, closing the door behind her. "You've got tears. Tears trumps mud every time. What's going on?"

Michelle dabbed her eyes and sniffed. "That job TJ had," she said in a wobbly voice.

"The great job? The one he loved. The one that changed him from Chucky to Ferris Bueller?"

"The job wasn't exactly at an auto supply store but more an auto speedway."

"He was working for Cal? I had no idea."

"TJ loved it and knew his daddy would never approve of him working out there at the speedway. Tommy found out anyway and now he's sending TJ to military school for sure." Her voice broke again. "TJ shouldn't have lied to us and I guess Tommy's right. Maybe military school will straighten him up, turn him into a man. I don't know what to do. I hate for him to go away but Tommy says it's time to get TJ off the tit. That's his rather crude way of saying I baby him too much. I keep making excuses every time he screws up."

"TJ's sixteen and sixteen-year-olds make mistakes. I know what it's like to not have a mom around. Margo was gone more than she was home. You and your mom saw more of me than she ever did. I hated it and I think TJ will, too. You two are close, closer now than ever and he has changed. Can't you talk to Tommy?"

"He says we have to be united in this and make TJ grow up. That the people at the military schools know how to do that. Tommy wants us to get back together and be firm and maybe this will work. Tommy is his father. He gets a say."

She put her arm around Michelle. "Where is TJ now?"

"With his dad. He said he was going over to try and talk to Tommy and reason with him. Apologize." She picked up Churchill's arm. "Now tell me about all this dirt you're wearing. Was Cal teaching you how to drive, is that it? Are you and Cal okay? Was he glad that Tripp didn't face the police alone?"

"Yeah, that's pretty much how it played out. We talked, I drove, he watched. I'm going over to the library for a little bit. This morning's escapade at the police station put us behind and there are end of month reports to get out. Call me if I can do anything to help."

"Honey?"

"Yeah?"

"Get a shower first. You'll dirty up the books."

Churchill clipped Storybook into his doggie seatbelt then drove the few short blocks to the library. She parked out front, then took the stairs to her apartment, and fed Storybook the rest of an omelet. If she tried to eat it she'd choke since she'd be thinking of making love in a bubble bath. Swearing off bubble baths and eggs forever she took a quick shower, then headed for the library. She wore jeans, no cute pink shorts that reminded her of Cal. No ribbons in her hair or flip-flops. She entered the library and let

Storybook run free, his leash trailing behind over the marble floor. As she turned to lock the door behind her the Reverend Dodd slipped inside. Just when she thought the day couldn't possibly get any worse.

"Well, my goodness now, this is indeed fortunate on my part. I was hoping you'd still be here this evening. I decided to go jogging and I find that your door here is wide open."

"Actually we're closed. I came in to finish up—"

"I won't take but a minute of your time. I'll be so quick you won't even know I was here."

Storybook came back to her side instead of flopping down on his red blanket to snooze. Was that a growl? She'd never heard Storybook growl, ever, even when Pinstripe one and two were around in Jersey. "What can I help you with this evening, Reverend Dodd?"

"Why now, I've heard you found my Bible and I was wondering if I might trouble you to return it to me. Somehow it wound up at your library for which I am eternally grateful. If you open it up you'll see a list of many of my congregation and their favorite Bible passages listed there. Makes that a special Bible indeed."

Why not just give it to him, she thought? The damn thing had caused more trouble than it was worth. Maybe getting rid of it would restore some good karma to the situation and everyone involved. "Sure."

"Wonderful." He smiled, his eyes shining.

She reached for the Bible she'd stashed under the desk after she and Tripp got back from their sojourn to the police department, then stopped. Tripp took it three years ago and Dodd was just asking for it now? Why not tell everyone it was missing right from the get-go? "I don't remember hearing any talk about you missing your Bible, Reverend Dodd. If folks had known they would have been keeping an eye out for it."

"Hated to be a bother. Everyone has so much on their minds these days."

She fiddled behind the counter for a minute. "How do you like your running shoes? I'm needing a pair and wondering what to get."

"Nike Trainer. Are you having any luck back there? I'm in a bit of a hurry. I have a meeting with the retirees tonight and don't want to be late."

Nike. She got a sudden case of the chills. Of course there were a lot of Nikes out there but probably not so many wanting an old Bible enough to sneak around a library in the middle of the night. "Well, I'll be. I don't know where it is." She came up from rummaging.

"Excuse me?" He looked pissed then immediately softened and gave another oily smile. "But I'm sure I heard that you had it this morning."

The phone rang. Churchill picked it up to hear, "It's Cal. TJ's with me and refuses to go home."

Churchill said to Dodd, "I need to take this. I'll have your Bible tomorrow. It's simply shelved in the wrong place. We have volunteers to help out and books don't always wind up where they should."

He paused, his eyes cold. "Tomorrow then." It sounded more like an order than a request. "You won't forget to look for it?"

What was with that old Bible? She waited till Dodd left, then said to Cal, "Okay, define refuse."

"Who was that?"

"Dodd. He wanted the Bible. I didn't give it to him. He's gone. Refuse how?"

"As in chained himself to my car."

"That's refusing all right."

"I thought maybe you could pick up Michelle and drive her out here. I didn't call her because I think this sort of information is better delivered in person and maybe she shouldn't be behind the wheel. Look, I know I told you to stay away but—"

"This is about TJ. This isn't about us. I'll swing by and get Michelle. And you better call Tommy."

"I already did. Oh and another thing. Some guys in a black Lincoln Town Car with tinted windows were here asking about someone named Benny who had a dog. The dog they described sounded a lot like Storybook."

"Benny left last week for parts unknown."

"And," he added, his voice closer to a yell, "what the fucking hell were you doing out there on that track this afternoon? Are you trying to kill yourself? Or were you driving like that to piss me off?"

"Not everything I do revolves around you. It's okay if you drive like a lunatic. Why can't I?"

"Because you don't know what you're doing! What are you thinking?"

"Well, right now I'm thinking of getting a motorcycle." She disconnected and laughed, wondering why she said what she did. Suddenly she wasn't laughing. She was serious. The yeeeeehaaaaa at the raceway was cathartic. It made her feel good, even downright happy after feeling rotten. Cal always made her feel good too, except now he was out of her life. She couldn't replace Cal with a motorcycle of course but both were gorgeous, strong, powerful, and fit nicely between her legs so it was a good start.

Chapter Thirteen

Michelle nearly jumped from the Prius before it came to a complete stop at the speedway. She ran to Cal's Mustang parked beside the garage, the periodic whine of a car circling the dirt track cutting through the summer night. TJ sat on the ground, a thick chain around his waist and fastened with a padlock, the other end around the front bumper of the car. A girl in ragged jeans, a T-shirt, and a baseball cap turned backwards sat beside him. They were sharing a Coke and a bag of potato chips and sympathetic looks.

"TJ, what are you doing?" Michelle came up to him. "Have you lost your mind?"

He looked up at her with sad eyes and ate another chip. "I'm not going to military school, Mom. I'll hate it there. It's all rules, uniforms, guns, and walking in straight lines. It's not me. Truth be told I didn't lie all that much. Just sort of fudged the truth a little. I'm sorry about that but I'm not sorry to be working here."

Michelle turned to Cal standing to the side, Churchill staying by her Prius. Obviously the mud they threw at each other earlier today stuck like glue. Michelle said to Cal, "I'm so sorry about all this."

"I'm sorry for you and TJ. He's a good kid, just a little

misguided at the moment." Cal pointed toward the high-way making Michelle look, too. "Here comes more trouble for you to deal with."

Michelle wrung her hands as the police cruiser, lights flashing and siren screaming, headed her way, a big black SUV with black windows following. "Three guesses who this is and he has an entourage."

The cruiser slid to a stop, gravel grinding under the big tires. Tommy Lee wedged out, face redder than usual, eyes a little wild. "TJ," he bellowed. "I'm mighty tired of your shenanigans, boy. You hearing me now? You're going to undo that there lock right this minute. If you don't I'm going to cut it off myself and have you hauled off to military school kicking and screaming if need be. I'm your daddy and I have the right. I've had it with you. You can go peaceful like or not. It's your choice." He pointed to the black car and two big gorilla-looking guys got out. They folded their arms and stood by the SUV.

"Who are these men?" Michelle looked from one to the other, feeling more nervous. "Leftovers from the SS?"

Tommy stood proud. "Intervention team from the Camp Hill Military Academy that is known for its strict ways, building character, making men out of mama's boys. That's what TJ is, nothing but a mama's boy."

"Dear heaven, Tommy, intervention from what?" Michelle asked, not quite believing what she was hearing. "TJ isn't into drugs, Tommy. He's into cars and Keith Urban. His hair's too long and it looks like he has a girlfriend but you don't get hauled off to military school for that."

"He done lied to us, Michelle and then chained himself to a goddamn car. He's completely out of control. The school will teach him about being a man, about guns and knives, about survival training and war. They'll cut his hair and make him shine his shoes and salute. The things that make a man a man. Not this here crap." He pointed to the speedway. "He'll be somebody I can be right proud of." If Tommy Lee stuck out his chest any more he'd pop a button.

"You want to haul our son off because he's out here working on cars and he doesn't like what you like?"

Tommy pointed to Cal. "He's an ex-con, Michelle. Look around. Your son is associating with criminals. Cal's ways are rubbing off on him. If we don't do something now TJ will wind up just like him."

"Going to school, holding a job, helping me out around the house."

"He's a damn sissy. He's an embarrassment."

"*You* are the embarrassment, and me too for letting this go on as long as it has. TJ is who he is, Tommy, and you're not sending him away because of it."

"He's sitting on the ground chained to a car and he lied. There's no denying that."

"The speedway sells car parts, it's off Highway 80. TJ's doing right well in algebra, not missed a class. I've been keeping in touch with his teacher. This is all about you, not him. What you want in a son, what you want for dinner, who you want to fool around with on the side when you think I'm not watching. I can smell the perfume, Tommy. I'm not an idiot. It's you wanting to be a big man through your son."

"I don't know what's gotten into you. I've been doing good by you, treating you with respect and all."

"Because a friend scared the bejeebers out of you. We're done, Tommy. TJ is not going to military school. He'll just up and run away again and then we may never find him. I'm not risking that because of your stupid pride or me just being too weak and pathetic to say something when I should."

"I'm his father and what I say goes."

Michelle gasped, yelped, and did a little jump.

"What in almighty hell was that all about?" Tommy growled. "You having some kind of seizure, woman?"

"Well my goodness, I think I just grew a set of balls all my own." Michelle wiggled her fanny. "And, Lordy, I think they're big brassy ones at that." To TJ she said, "You are grounded for three months for dragging good people all the way out here in the middle of the night because you're being a brat and wanting your own way. You're only leaving the house to work here and go to school. Your girlfriend can come over to the house on Sunday afternoons and have dinner with us right proper. You will do as I say because I'm your mama and control the keys to your car and pay your insurance. I will sign papers to let you race out here at the speedway as long as your grades are good and you mind your manners."

TJ's jaw dropped. "You're going to let me race?"

Tommy turned a vivid shade of blue. "What? What? Have you lost your mind?"

"Better Kart racing out here under supervision and rules and on a decent track than on Abercorn between traffic lights or some corn field and maybe getting himself killed."

Tommy spluttered, "I will not allow my son—"

"Who is my son, too."

"To race cars."

"Then we will go to court. I'm not afraid of court, Tommy Lee, and for sure I am not afraid of you. What I am afraid of is losing my son."

The next morning Michelle crept into TJ's room. It was only six o'clock and he was dead to the world. She said a prayer of thanks that statement was not a literal one. Her son was safe and she'd do her level best to keep him that way and to make him a responsible adult, as well. He was off the tit, like Tommy said. She would give Tommy Lee as much access to his son as he wanted. Maybe in time they'd find a common ground, something to bond over and if not, she would insist on mutual respect. This was the South and manners mattered.

But what was she going to do about a certain guy from Jersey who she was crazy about? How did she tell him that? How could she let him know she was interested and reconciliation with Tommy was off the table? It seemed a little forward and presumptuous on her part to just tell him, then think he'd be interested in her too, after she told him no way am I having anything to do with you.

What should she say? I want you not him? She'd think of something on her way to his apartment, maybe. She cut through Telfair Square and sat on the metal bench in front of Telfair Museum getting more nervous, her brain morphing into oatmeal. Two hours later she'd bitten off all her fingernails and was a hairsbreadth from tossing her cookies. She walked the rest of the way to York Street and Miss Ellie's apartment and stood on the little porch staring at the door when it suddenly opened, Benny on the other side.

"Hi." She smiled. It was one of those toothy ones that looked forced and a little deranged.

"Hi. Are you okay? You look funny. Something wrong? Is TJ okay?"

"Everything is okay. I'm okay, TJ is okay, you're okay. Good, yeah, things are good. Are you going somewhere? I mean here you are. You opened the door and I didn't even get a chance to knock."

"I was going for a run."

"I want to see more of you," she blurted. "I want to be with you and spend time with you. Tommy is history. I mean he's still alive and all but I grew a set of balls and told him to take a hike." She slapped her hand to her face and closed her eyes. She parted her fingers and looked through the crack. "I didn't actually for real of course grow . . . well you know. But Tommy and I are exes and going to stay that way forever. When I was picking out this new skirt I have on I was thinking of you and when I bought new shoes I was thinking of dancing with you. I want to be with you."

"You said that."

"I mean it." She bit her bottom lip because he was just standing there all firm and fit and tan, staring at her. "Say something."

"It's not enough." He ran his hand over his sandy-colored hair thanks to Miss Clairol. "What you said was nice and all but it doesn't work for me, Michelle." Then he kissed her on the cheek and closed the door leaving her on the porch staring at a brass knocker. Her heart sank and a tear slid down her face. He was gone. She'd lost him. It was the speech. She sounded like a spaz. Who would want to spend time with someone who couldn't string two intelligent sentences together? Slowly she turned and headed for the library, feeling sick to the core. She let herself in and sat down on the marble floor in front of the checkout counter.

Churchill stared at her. "What's going on?"

"I lost him."

"TJ? Again? We'll find him."

"Houston."

Churchill sat down beside her on the floor.

"I went to see him this morning to tell him I wanted to be more than friends but he wasn't interested. You see I told him I was getting back together with Tommy when I had plans of doing just that. Then I came to my senses and I know now I don't want Tommy. I want Houston. I bet he probably feels like my second choice."

"Your rebound guy."

"But he's not a rebound. He's my first choice. I can't think of a better choice. I really like him, Church." She sniffed and Storybook came over and sat beside her, putting his big doggie head in her lap, looking sad. "How do I tell Houston all that?"

"You say Houston, my man, I want your bod and I want it now."

Michelle laughed. "You always make me feel better but I think he's going back to Atlanta."

"Go after him, make him listen. If you care for him that's what you have to do."

"So does that mean if Cal leaves Savannah you'll go after him? There's talk that he got a job offer from some driving school in North Carolina. I can tell by your face you didn't know."

"Well, it's for the best. He needs a new start. I'm done with new starts. I like old starts, the old houses here, old furniture, old gardens. Savannah suits me just fine." Churchill hugged Michelle. "It's going to be a long day, honey. All this drama and it's only nine o'clock."

At ten o'clock Tripp parked the Volvo by the grandstand next to a truck for Southern Snacks and Refreshments. A delivery guy in jeans, a sleeveless T-shirt, with KILLER tattooed on his sizable bicep, hoisted boxes onto a dolly. Not much activity at the speedway in the morning. Tripp went to see Cal but first he wanted to check to see if his favorite therapist was in. With the delivery truck dropping off supplies there was a good chance. Tripp rounded the corner to the concession stand with its green awning up and windows wide open as if ready for business. Daisy-Lou was in red shorts and a blue top. Her hair was pulled back with a white scarf and she had on red high heels. Nothing sexier than skimpy shorts and high heels. Okay, they were a little on the trashy side but damn they were sexy as hell, too.

She was arranging Coke bottles in the glass refrigerator

case, bending over to pick up a few bottles at a time. Her incredible firm derriere was right there in front of him, her legs long, tan, and lovely. He walked right into a display of candy, knocking it on the floor.

"Well now, sugar," DaisyLou said as she turned, her electric smile making him dizzy. "What a pleasant surprise. I didn't even know you were here." She put the Cokes she'd had in her hand on the counter, stooped down to where he was, and helped pick up the mess. "Seeing you is a mighty fine way to be starting this day, I do declare." Her face met his and she kissed him on the mouth, one of those slow good morning kisses as if they'd spent the night together, just woke up, and were glad to see each other. A big part of him wished all that were true. That big part happened to be right between his legs and was becoming damn uncomfortable. They stood, Tripp in pain, Daisy-Lou looking wonderful. "You're getting ready."

"I sure enough seem to be getting you ready for something. All part of my job as a therapist." She glanced below his belt. "My, oh my, it is nice to be appreciated." She checked her watch. "I have an appointment soon so I'll have to be getting back to town. How have you been?"

"Better. Not always successful but better."

She leaned on the counter, her delicious cleavage right there for him. "The trick is to keep on trying, staying in the game, being part of life. You learn the ropes, get comfortable with who you are, and soon you're doing right well," she said, her beautiful face right next to his, her leg rubbing his. "You will do fine indeed."

"Do you have any available appointments this afternoon?"

"I'm afraid I'm all booked up."

"Bet you're not all booked up for me," came a guy's voice from the doorway. The delivery man wheeled in the cart of snacks and set down the dolly. "You two sure do look right friendly." He focused on DaisyLou. "What about spreading some of that fine sugar of yours around my way, to a big man who knows just what to do with a woman such as yourself."

DaisyLou grinned. "I don't think so. Now where do I sign for the shipment?"

"Why don't you come on over here so I can show you?" He winked and grinned.

DaisyLou's smile disappeared. Turning to Tripp, she said, "You're my type now, honey."

"This geeky guy is? Sweet thing, you need a real man in your life and I'm the one. I got the muscle. I got stamina. Stamina for lots of things I bet you'd find interesting and satisfying. I'm real good at satisfying."

"And you are very crude."

"Leave her alone," Tripp said, hoping he sounded braver then he felt, wondering what the hell persuaded him to open his big mouth. Then he looked at DaisyLou and knew. She'd been nice to him and helped him. Some asshole was giving her crap and he wasn't going to let that happen. DaisyLou deserved better.

"You're telling me what to do?" Delivery guy said with attitude.

Muscle man meets Math man. *Think, Tripp, think*! He took a bottle of Diet Coke from the counter. Diet was better because of the carbonation content. "I'm telling you to let the lady be."

"What are you going to do, runt, drink a nice cold Coke while I make out with your woman right in front of you? 'Cause that's what's going to happen." The guy gave an evil laugh as Tripp grabbed a pack of Mentos from the display he'd knocked over.

"I'm going to make your day, beautiful. You've never been loved unless Killer's been doing you." Killer grabbed DaisyLou and Tripp slid the mints into the bottle of Coke, shook and aimed. The force spewed Coke from the bottle and shock knocked Killer backwards, giving Tripp the chance to land one solid blow to the guy's jaw. Tripp winced in pain. Using his left hand he landed another punch at Killer's nose. The punch landed where the cartilage is most vulnerable and most likely to render the nose broken. Thank you Anatomy 101 and of course stupid chemistry tricks PhD students horse around with when bored.

Blood dribbled from Killer's nose, a stunned look on his face as he lay on the floor wondering what happened. Tripp got a towel and ice from the freezer and tossed it to him. DaisyLou signed the clipboard on top of the boxes of snacks and dropped the board on Killer's stomach. "You get yourself out of here right now and don't you ever dare come back to this establishment."

Holding the ice to his nose Killer stood and made for the door. "What made the Coke do that?"

"Take a chemistry class."

Killer left and DaisyLou smiled. She swaggered over to Tripp, gave him an appreciative look, then trailed one perfectly manicured red fingernail down the side of his face. "That is why I like smart men. You, Tripp Davis, are smart *and* brave." She kissed him on the mouth adding an educated tongue that made his insides sizzle. "I do believe someone is getting to know himself right well these days. And now that I think about it, sugar, I do have an opening in my appointment schedule. Say around five this evening? I'll get you acquainted with the pure magic of grilled oysters."

Cal came to the open window. "I just saw our delivery guy leaving here with a bloody nose. What the hell's going on around here?"

"He fell," Tripp said. DaisyLou wrapped ice in a towel and put it on his bruised knuckles. She kissed him on the cheek and added, "He fell right into Tripp's fist, imagine that. He got a little out of line and Tripp reminded him to behave as a gentleman should. Thank you, sugar."

DaisyLou strolled off and Cal looked bewildered. "The delivery guy is six-three and probably tips the scale at two-fifty. How did you—"

"Tsiolkovsky's rocket equation."

"If you say so."

"I sprayed him with Coke and decked him."

"Well, dang, Skippy, that's one way of doing it. What's going on with you lately? You're different." Cal lowered his voice. "What's with you and DaisyLou? You two got something going?"

"DaisyLou's my therapist."

"Therapist." Cal dropped his voice to a whisper. "Uh, little brother, I hate to be the one to break it to you but DaisyLou isn't a—"

"Let's just say she is." Tripp grinned and came around the stand to where Cal was. "You got a minute to talk?" He called out to DaisyLou, "I'll bring dessert."

"I'm looking forward to it. I truly am."

Tripp followed Cal to the garage and they sat down on two boxes, the sun toasting anything without a cover, birds and insects napping, waiting for the cool of evening. "When are you going to start rebuilding the cabin?"

"Not sure I am."

"I was afraid you were going to say that. For what it's worth I want you to stay in Savannah. I head back to school next month but I get here pretty often. I'd like you to be around when I come."

"Is that why you went to see Tommy Lee?"

"I didn't seek him out specifically but I did go to the cops. They didn't believe a word I told them."

"Tripp if they do believe you, you go to jail. That's a waste of your life."

"You gave up three years of your life for nothing. I get that but I'm at a better place now. I can handle what happens to me. I have to own up for what I did and get you off the hot seat with this town."

"You stole a freaking Bible for an initiation prank. We just can't prove all that was stolen was the Bible. Dodd was at the library last night wanting it back. Why the interest all of a sudden in the Bible?"

"He didn't know where it was before. Guess one of the holy roller cops told him. I thumbed through it. Nothing special like the Bible belonged to Robert E. Lee and is worth a lot of money. Just notes for sermons, lists of chapter this and verse that. Bible stuff. Sentimental value?"

"Sentimental? Dodd? Unless it's long, green, and has the picture of a dead president it's not likely." Cal draped his arm around Tripp. "If you go to prison the parents will not survive it. You are their great white hope, their dream. All the things I was supposed to be as their firstborn and never measured up. It's not their fault and or mine, it just is. Forget about confessing, Tripp, and get on with your life. Go out there and find a cure for something, a new fuel, gin that doesn't cause hangovers."

"What does Churchill think about you taking off?"

"We have communication issues." He grinned. "Maybe I do need to see your therapist after all."

"Go find your own therapist." He sucker punched Cal. "Go communicate with Churchill. She's always had a thing for you and I think it works both ways. You've both had this vibe for years. Do something with it."

"I sort of used her."

"She'll get over it if you ask her to."

Cal studied the concrete floor. "She's smart, Tripp, maybe almost as smart as you. What in the world does she see in me?"

"I could sit here and tell you you're a great guy. Churchill knows it. We all know it. Now you just have to believe it, too." He stood. "But right now, I'm off to find a superb bottle of wine, chocolate truffles, and flowers. I have a therapy session at five sharp."

"It's five o'clock," Michelle called to Churchill. "I'm locking these big old library doors for the day and we are out of here."

"I'll finish shelving these last few books and shut down the computers."

Michelle took out the master key as Houston Elliott the Third aka Benny-the-Book came in. Actually he strolled in, wearing a white felt fedora and a white suit. He had on wire rimmed glasses and looked like he should be running that house of ill repute over on Congress. "Well, my goodness gracious," he said sounding more Southern than Paula Deen. "It appears I just made it here in the nick of time." He handed Michelle a summer bouquet of black-eyed Susans, yellow and gold marigolds, white foxgloves, and sunflowers. "These here are beautiful Southern flowers for a beautiful Southern belle."

"You, you . . . But I thought—"

"When I said that your idea just wasn't working for me I meant that it wasn't enough. I can never get enough of you. I don't simply want to spend time with you, Michelle. So I've decided the best way for us to get to know each other better is for me to court you. The right proper way a man should pay attention to a lady." He bowed deeply. "Michelle, would you do me the great honor of allowing me to take you to dinner this evening?"

Heart swelling, she curtsied. "It would be my sincere pleasure."

"Perhaps a little dancing to commemorate our first time together right here at this library?" He pulled out an iPod and a waltz filled the library. Benny—Houston—swept her into his arms and guided her over the marble floor and in to the reading area, over the Oriental carpet then around the corner and back to the children's room, Storybook running beside them. Churchill watched, her eyes slowly getting bigger, then bigger still, as recognition set in.

Michelle giggled, feeling the world was perfect, romantic, and wonderful until she collided with two men in black pinstriped suits and black fedoras standing by the front door. Michelle tripped, Houston catching her. Churchill blanched dead white.

"We need to talk," Pinstripe one said, coming over to Churchill and leaning across the checkout desk. "Where's Benny-the-Book? Since you got his dog here I'm betting you know where Benny is. I'd think real hard before handing us a lie. It's not healthy."

"Benny was here and now he's gone," Churchill said in a rush.

"He'd never leave his damn mutt."

"Ever try being on the run with a dog? It's like wearing a neon sign around your neck."

Pinstripe two came over to Houston, Storybook sitting right beside him. "This dog sure likes you. Why is that?"

Sweat trickled down between Michelle's boobs and she nearly wet her panties. *Oh God! Oh God!*

"Well now, you see it's this way," Benny said, sounding perfectly at ease. "This here dog and I get along right well. I'm courting Michelle here. I bring her flowers and sometimes candy, not all the time bringing her candy, mind you, but now and then. Sometimes we even dance and I'll bring treats for the dog and—"

"Christ almighty. I didn't ask for your fucking life's history. just if you know the goddamn dog."

Benny straightened his bachelor button blue tie. "Do you happen to have a picture of this here person you're searching for? Perhaps I've seen him around."

Michelle slumped onto one of the children's chairs as Benny took the picture from Pinstripe two and held it up for a good look. "My, my he does look a tad familiar. A bit like me I should say, don't you agree? There are certain similarities." Benny turned, giving his profile and Michelle slid off the chair onto the floor.

Pinstripe two laughed, one of those laughs that sounded mean and cynical all at the same time. "This guy's Jerzee clear through. You got a white suit on and you're dancing in a fuckin' library." He turned back to Churchill. "Benny better be praying we don't catch up with him or he's a dead man. If you're hiding him around here you'll be one sorry dame."

Churchill folded her arms. "How could we hide someone like Benny in Savannah? You tell me that. How many times have you two been stared at since you've been here? In case you didn't notice, this is not the East coast."

Pinstripe one said, "You got a point. It's like the freaking circus came to town when we took a room at the hotel. Everybody stopping and staring at us. One lady asked if we were here to shoot a movie or something. That *Sopranos* show made us all look like a bunch of jerks who can't speak right. What the fucking hell was that all about, I ask you." Pinstripe one leaned across the counter to Churchill again. "If you hear from Benny, you tell him he can run but he can't hide. We're going to get him and when we do—"

"I ask you, sir," Benny said, making every bone in Michelle's body shiver, "if you'd kindly refrain from any further unpleasant talk here in the presence of these ladies. It's simply not done in these parts, you see."

"Christ almighty, we got ourselves a real live pansy." Pinstripe one studied Benny closely and Michelle felt her heart stop dead. "You look like somebody I know."

"That chicken Sanders person on TV perhaps. I get that a lot. Tourists have been known to stop me on the street and take my picture."

"Your taste in clothes sucks." The Pinstripe brothers filed out the door and Michelle flopped back on the floor, staring at the ceiling. "I'm having a heart attack."

Churchill was lying back on top of the checkout desk. "We could have been the headlines in tomorrow's paper. Shootout at the Oglethorpe Library."

Grinning, Benny helped Michelle stand. "But we're not headlines and I'm thinking Savannah is one fine city indeed. A perfect place for me and my pansy suit to settle down. And a perfect place to find a very fine lady, if she'll have me. What do you think, Storybook? You're the one who brought us together."

Benny clipped on the leash and offered Michelle his arm. "You're staying?" Michelle gushed. "After all that?"

"Sugar, I can hide but I can't run because now I have you in my life." He kissed her, the familiar kind that said I'm-going-to-be-around-for-a-while, and the three of them strolled in to the beautiful Savannah evening.

Churchill watched the happy threesome walk down the sidewalk and a small group of people, with Dodd right in the middle, come up the sidewalk toward her. She wanted nothing more than to slam the door.

"Evening, Miss McKenzie. I trust you've had a fine day. I'm here to pick up my Bible, like I said I would be. I brought along a few friends to help in the search for it if it's still gone missing in your library. I did just like you told me to. I told these good folks my problem about losing it years ago and they volunteered to help us out. Isn't that mighty fine of them? I am truly blessed."

Dodd's voice was all amicable and friendly while the look on his ratty little face said gotcha! Churchill hadn't counted on that. She'd looked over the Bible, found nothing, and thought she'd put Dodd off one more night for another go at it. She didn't have a choice but to hand over the Bible. It was right under the counter and the Bible posse would find it in a minute. "I already found it, Reverend Dodd. I came in early this morning just to look for it and found it right off."

Lying to a preacher was probably some kind of big no-no in the rulebook of getting to heaven but maybe that Dodd was crooked as a dog's hind leg would save her ass. She went inside the library, the little troop parading in behind her. She pulled out the Bible and placed it on the counter. "I did notice the names listed here in front. Some of the folks are right here with you now, Miss Emily, Miss Rose, Miss Delight. You have the chapter and verse of their favorite Biblical passage right by their names."

Dodd suddenly looked frazzled and tucked the Bible tight under his arm. What was unusual about the chapter and verse in a Bible?

"I do indeed. We've taken up entirely too much of your time, Miss Churchill. Come friends, we'll be on our way now. We have a potluck dinner down by the river before our Repent and Be Saved service this evening."

Dodd hightailed it toward the door, the others following at a slower pace. They were older, mostly widows. Dodd did befriend the elderly, she couldn't fault him for that. But he just outmaneuvered her in getting the Bible. The fact that Dodd went to such great lengths underscored that something important was in it and it had to do with the people and Bible verses listed in the front.

But what? She needed another look. Obviously she'd overlooked something, an important something. Dodd didn't do all that for kicks. How could she get another look? Dodd wasn't going to let that Bible out of his sight after three years of wondering where it was.

She needed a distraction to get him away from it—a big distraction—and no one distracted Dodd more than Cal Davis.

Chapter Fourteen

Churchill parked the Prius next to the garage, the fluorescent light on inside, Cal's head buried under the hood of what was once a car. He looked up, a surprised expression on his face. He wiped his hands and came her way. "If you're looking for TJ he's not here. He came to work and then left. He should be home by now."

"He probably is but this time I'm not here about TJ, I'm here for you. I know you're mad that I didn't talk Tripp out of going to the cops. I'm not thrilled you used me to get yourself convicted but right now we need to put that aside. I came here because I want to know how sinful you're feeling tonight."

He grinned and her insides did that familiar flip thing they always did when he smiled. "What did you have in mind?"

"Well, I'm thinking you need to repent, Cal Davis. You need to follow the path to righteousness and Reverend Dodd is just the person to show you the way."

"What in the hell have you been smoking? Or drinking? You shouldn't be driving like that, you know."

"Dodd's got the Bible and I need another look at it. I'm missing something."

"I thought you had it. How did he wind up with it?"

"I got bamboozled but the point is I need to look at it again. I think I'm on to something but I'm not sure and I never will be if I don't get the Bible back. How long do you think it will be before Tripp confesses to the police again? He'll keep it up till someone listens to him, and eventually they will. But if we can find out Dodd's scheme that will go a long way to discredit him. We can never prove there wasn't twenty-five thousand dollars but we can prove Dodd is a crook. The possibility that you didn't steal anything suddenly has a lot more substance."

"Why do you care?"

"Because I sent you to prison and I want your name cleared. And Dodd's preying on the elderly. Miss Ida, Miss Emily, and Miss Rose were sort of like mothers to me. When I needed cookies for a school bake sale I always had them. If I needed a hem shortened or ride to somewhere, I always had it. Now they come to the library and bring me cookies and pies and martinis, two olives."

"Martinis?"

"It's the Savannah way."

"Me repenting works into all this how?"

"I'm thinking the Bible is in the tent. If you get cleansed in the river, I can get the Bible."

"What!"

"It's part of the revival thing. That's why it's by the river. You repent of your terrible sinful ways and you get dunked in the river as a symbol of a new beginning in your life. You go in dirty, come out clean, sort of like an Oxyclean for sinners. While you're doing that I'll get the Bible."

"How about *you* get Oxyed and *I* get the Bible?"

She tucked her finger under his chin and smiled. "I'm not the sinner of Savannah, you are."

"How do you know Dodd will buy me being a repentant man? I'm not exactly the repenting type. I'm more of a hell-raiser with no regrets type."

"Because this will be so huge for Dodd he won't be able to resist. Just think of it. The guy who stole money from him is there in his very own revival tent to repent his ways. Dodd will imagine himself featured in the news, TV interviews, blogs, Twitter, Facebook, you name it. His ego will soak in every word you feed him. Cheer up, Cal. It's a hot evening. A dunking in the river will feel good."

She started to walk away and he took her arm, his touch reminding her of what they once had. It was good, so very good and she missed it.

"How come we can solve everyone else's problems and we can't solve our own?"

"Maybe the time has come and gone for us. We've been in each other's lives for years now and never made it stick. Maybe all we're supposed to be is friends." They may not end up together but what she felt for Cal was beyond friendship. She felt hot for him, always had and always would. She'd never think of Cal Davis as simply a friend to spend time with. He'd always be the guy in the back of the Mustang, the guy who made her sweat.

Cal parked his Mustang in the grassy field with the other cars and stared at the big white tent down on the bank, the last of the sun fading behind the line of river birches. What the hell had he gotten himself into? Dunking? What was he, a damn doughnut? But if Churchill was right and they could catch Dodd at his own game it would save Tripp from making a big mistake and keep Churchill in martinis. Both admirable goals. And it might get Cal off the hook as well. He'd like that for Miss Ellie's sake and for the parents and himself a bit, too. He'd been a misfit all his life, except on the speedway, and that part was okay. He got used to being an outsider, the dumb kid, the kid who couldn't read. But he always had integrity. His word was good. When he went to prison for stealing the money, he lost that and he wanted it back. It mattered that when he said something it was true and people trusted him.

As Cal approached the tent *Repent and Be Saved* floated out into the warm night air. He stood at the back of the tent gazing over the heads of the congregation. It was pretty much like the last time he was there, the choir to the side, Dodd already in front singing and waving his Bible, *the* Bible. Churchill was hiding in the bushes somewhere.

Okay, it was show time, like gunning for first place on the straightaway at the speedway. Put his foot to the floor and just go for it. He took a deep breath. "I do want to repent and be saved, Reverend Dodd," Cal called over the choir. The congregation whipped their heads in his direction, the choir and organ fading off, the whole tent falling quiet. "I am truly a sinner."

Dodd looked startled, a hint of skepticism on his face for a brief moment as their eyes met. Damn, Cal thought to himself. *I have to make this believable or Dodd will call my bluff.* "He said, I know I've done wrong and wish to change my ways. Turn from evil to good, make straight my path." He should not have cut Sunday school as often as he did. He didn't know repentance lingo.

"What has made you see the light, brother?" Dodd called back to him.

Churchill's big blue eyes made me see the light, Cal thought to himself. How could he say no to them? Instead he said, "You, Reverend Dodd, are an inspiration to me, to us all." How Cal managed to say that without gagging was a damn miracle. "I've seen you ministering to those in need. I want to be like you, follow in your footsteps. Tonight I want to be cleansed in the water of the river and lead a better life than the one I live now. Praise be."

Cal held his breath. Would he buy it? Would Dodd's overinflated ego actually make him think Cal was sincere in coming to him for forgiveness? *Come on you pompous ass bastard, bite!*

"Then come forward, brother, and wash yourself in the waters of hope and salvation." Dodd's eyes actually sparkled and Cal felt an instant sigh of relief. He was in! He walked down the center aisle, the choir doing an alleluia version of some song as Cal made his way to Dodd. Cal followed him out of the tent over a grassy path lit with lanterns to the river's edge. Dodd handed him a white robe. He slipped it over his head. If Churchill didn't get that damn Bible he'd wring her neck. He didn't care how pretty, slender, and lovely it was. Well, actually he did care.

"Enter the water. It will change your life, brother," Dodd instructed. "Wash away the stain of sin and follow a new path into goodness."

Cal went between two white railings and stepped in the water, shoes and all. He could feel the wood platform under his feet. Holding his breath he dunked under the water and prayed for real that he wasn't disturbing a nest of copperheads or water moccasins. He stayed there for a few seconds to look convincing as someone sorry for all the wrong he'd done and actually he was sorry. He promised to be nicer to Dempsey and Ron and RuthAnn. No need to waste a perfectly good dunking.

But when Cal came out of the water Dodd wasn't looking pious and holy the way Cal thought he'd look. He didn't look reverend or satisfied that he'd saved a soul. Mostly Dodd looked pissed because Churchill McKenzie was standing beside him clutching the Bible and an usher was talking to the police on his cell phone.

When Dodd said the water would change Cal's life he hadn't been kidding. Damn.

"I'll be taking that from you," Dodd said to Churchill, slipping the Bible from her fingers. His eyes were dark and angry as he looked at Cal. "You will burn forever in the eternal fires."

"Not unless I dry out first." Cal swiped his face and went over to Churchill, the wet robe clinging to him making it hard to walk. "Hey, Miss Marple, what happened?"

"Something that wasn't supposed to. There were lookouts. Dresses are not a good look for you. I'm so sorry I screwed up, Cal."

Dodd glared as sirens sounded in the distance. Red and blue strobing lights turned off the road heading for the tent. The crowd was quiet, mesmerized by the commotion and the two sinners in their midst. The cruiser stopped, siren off but lights still flashing. Tommy Lee Dempsey climbed from behind the wheel. Cal groaned. "This night just went from bad to terrible."

Tommy Lee hitched up his pants as he made his way through the crowd that parted before him like the Red Sea. "What in the world is going on here? This here is a prayer meeting. I'm not supposed to be getting called to prayer meetings."

"These two," Dodd bellowed as if St. Peter himself gave him lessons, "have come here to steal my Bible and—"

"Oh for chrissake that Bible thing again?" Dempsey huffed and ran his hand over his thinning hair. "Never knew a Bible to cause so damn much trouble in all my born days."

"Dempsey," Cal said. "There is no love lost between us, we both know that, but think about it. Why would I steal a Bible unless there was a reason, a big one? I just got out of prison. Why would I risk going back there over a Bible unless it was important?"

"Because you are a sinful man," Dodd roared. "The evil ways have overcome you."

Dempsey peered at Cal as if taking in what he said. "What do you mean?"

"Dodd's a crook and the Bible proves it." The congregation gasped and Dodd turned red with anger. Cal rushed on before Dodd could say anything. "You bring him down, Tommy, and you'll be a hero. I swear that is the truth. I'm playing straight with you here. My brother and Churchill both came to you over this thing. Something's going on. You said yourself you'd never seen a Bible cause so much trouble. It'll take five minutes of your time to prove me right or wrong. Five minutes to make you a hero."

"Attacking a man of the cloth is not the way to be a hero," Dodd huffed, clutching the Bible. But Cal could see the hero thing stuck with Tommy. He took the Bible from Dodd and Dodd took it back. "This here is mine."

"This here is evidence," Tommy said. "Y'all are the ones who called the police so we don't need no search warrant to look at things."

Churchill said, "There are names listed on the first page and they have chapter and verse references after them. See if they fit."

Dempsey opened the first page, then flipped through locating the references. "They are indeed chapter and verse, just as they should be."

Dodd beamed; Churchill looked ill. "How could I have gotten this so wrong? Some antiquities expert. I'm supposed to be able to decipher information, figure things out. I'm an idiot with a vivid imagination."

Cal draped his arm around her. "Hey, don't beat yourself up, Ace. You did what you thought was right."

"I could be responsible for sending you to prison again. How could I screw up like this, Cal? How can I do this to you again?"

"But," Dempsey continued, still looking in the Bible, "there were some notes in the margins, not that they make any sense. Just a bunch of letters and numbers. BOA in the margin of one, CCBT in the margin of another." He flipped the pages. "RB, CB, FCB."

"Banks," Cal said. "Bank of America, Regions Bank, Coastal Bank, Capital City Bank and Trust. I'm a business man, I know banks. They all turned me down when I tried to get a loan to buy the speedway."

"Coastal Bank is my bank," said Miss Emily.

"And," Tommy added, "they are followed by three numbers. 132, 108, 498."

"498 is my safety deposit box number," Miss Rose said.

"And 132 is mine," Miss Ida added. "After Elroy passed four years ago there was not nearly as much money in that there box as he told me there was." A scowl furrowed her already wrinkled face. She grabbed the Bible right out of Tommy Lee's hand and smacked Dodd on the head then on the shoulder. "How dare you use the sacred book for doing wrong and for ripping me off! You no good bastard!"

Dodd started to run off but the ushers held him in place. Tommy Lee pulled out his handcuffs. Churchill walked over to him and kissed him on the cheek. "Thank you, and I mean that from the bottom of my heart. Your son will be impressed and I think Michelle will be, too. I'm guessing if you check with these banks you'll find that Dodd's name is on all these safety deposit boxes and he helped himself to the cash savings there after the husbands died. He set up their finances and added his name to the safety deposit box list. He needed the Bible because that's where he kept the information. He could be writing in the Bible and carrying it around wherever he went and no one would think anything of it. A great cover. After all he is a preacher and who would steal a Bible from a preacher?"

Tommy looked from Churchill to Cal. "No one would. He just misplaced it and it wound up at the library. That's what must have happened. Can you please tell Tripp that's the story we're going with. I don't want to see his face down at the station again. We have more important things to deal with than a Bible that was supposedly stolen, but obviously wasn't stolen at all."

Chapter Fifteen

Cal entered the Pink House. He was there again but at his parents' insistence, and they did insist. A part of him felt he owed them that much. After all, the last time they were there it was the Davis family in disgrace. This time it was the public display of we-are-wonderful. Ron and RuthAnn needed the wonderful family image after three years of disgrace. He knew to order the wine right at the start and to tell the waiter to keep the bottles coming. The parents were easier to deal with after a glass or two of wine.

"Son," Ron said, coming over to meet Cal even before he reached the table. He wrapped Cal in a bear hug for all the world to see. Cal couldn't remember the last time his dad hugged him, period. Beaming RuthAnn kissed him on the cheek. "I knew in my heart a son of ours couldn't be a common criminal," she said in a voice a little too loud.

Cal exchanged looks with Tripp across the table. He had a double scotch in front of him.

They all sat and RuthAnn looked from Cal to Tripp and wiped away a tear that wasn't there but should have been. "I can't tell you how proud I am of you, Cal. That you took the time in jail to save your little brother is remarkable indeed. The faculty at the university can't talk about anything else. That was such a fine article in the newspaper," she gushed.

"And picture," Ron added with a huge smile.

Tripp saluted him with his drink. Well, at last Cal had made his parents proud for once. But strangely enough it didn't matter and deep down inside he thought it would. When he was little he dreamed of the day when the parents would look at him with pride and admiration and a touch of awe like they always looked at Tripp. It never happened of course.

"So how is that speedway of yours doing these days?" Ron asked.

Cal choked. He never expected that sentence to come out of his dad's mouth. "Fine. There are races scheduled tonight. It should be crowded and—"

"To think that we are all here today to celebrate this wonderful event," RuthAnn interrupted, ending the speedway conversation as fast as it started. She touched her napkin to her face for another invisible tear. "Cal has been exonerated of the charge and everything is perfect."

"Not quite perfect," Tripp said. "Cal gave up three years of his life for me. We all know I stole the Bible in the first place. That set a lot of stuff in motion, including Cal taking the fall for me. It wound up being so much more."

"Because that dreadful Dodd person lied," RuthAnn said in an indignant huff.

"Three years is three years and Cal will never get them back and I suspect Dodd burned down Cal's cabin to make him look guilty and Dodd a victim."

"You were young," Ron insisted. "You couldn't have handled prison. Cal did exactly what he should have done. His speedway ambitions would always be there but you had opportunity, promise, so much potential."

Tripp leaned forward suddenly looking more fifty than twenty-three. "Cal is the hero in this family. He does the right thing always, not for show, or fame, or for recognition but because it's the right thing to do. As parents it's about time you realize that."

Ron stammered, "We do."

"Darling," RuthAnn said in a hushed voice. "There's nothing to worry about now. It's all over."

"It's not over but I can't undo the past. But I can help the future. Pay it forward as they say and that's what I intend to do. I joined the army." He beamed, looking better than Cal had ever seen him look. "I'm going to build freshwater treatment plants, sewage plants in third world countries. Do some good that matters."

"What!" RuthAnn gasped loud enough to turn heads. "Have you lost your mind?"

"I think I found it. I had therapy, really great therapy." A sly smile drifted across Tripp's mouth and Cal lifted his wine in approval.

RuthAnn glared at Cal. "This is all your fault."

Ah, now the world was back in order. Things were just as they used to be. Nothing had really changed after all.

RuthAnn continued. "You made him feel guilty. You told him to do this to upset us. How can you be so cruel to your own parents?"

"Mom," Tripp said. "This is my decision, all mine. I am an adult, finally! Well at least I'm working on it. I imagine six weeks of basic training at Fort Benning will get me in tune with the more physical side of who I am."

"Basic training! Ohmygod! Ron did you hear that! Basic training! He's doing fox holes and guns. He's going to wear a helmet. Ohmygod, a helmet." RuthAnn flopped back against her chair in a swoon or something faint-like, making waiters rush around bringing her cold cloths and ice and giving Cal a look that said please-never-come-here-again.

Ron helped RuthAnn to her feet. "I think we should

go." He scowled at Cal and said to Tripp, "How could you upset your mother like this?"

"I didn't join the army to upset anyone but it is something I had to do."

"You are a stupid son of a bitch," Ron hissed under his breath. He looked from Tripp to Cal. "Both of you." Then he helped RuthAnn out the door.

"Well, gee," Tripp said, "that went really well, don't you think?"

Cal laughed then took the seat beside Tripp and ordered a pot of coffee. His need for wine just exited the building. "Are you sure about this army thing, kid? The parents are having a meltdown and for once I understand where they're coming from. You could get your damn head blown off."

"I'll duck. I can't just keep going on with my life, pretend nothing happened. Joining the army isn't going to fix anything but I can make something positive happen as a result. Make something good come out of it. That's what you should do, too."

"You want me to join the army?"

"I was thinking more along the lines of fixing things between you and Churchill. It's time the two of you got together and stayed that way. You got together long enough to straighten out this Dodd mess. When are you two going to get together permanently?"

"We've got baggage."

"Hell, who doesn't? It's how you handle the baggage that counts."

"How'd you get so damn smart?"

"I had therapy, remember?"

"The driving school in North Carolina is a good opportunity. I can start over. I'm out of here in two days. I can stay part owner of the speedway and Silky's going to hire a manager and—"

"No one ever starts over, Cal. We move on from where we are."

"Freud?"

"DaisyLou."

"You learned a lot from her."

Tripp took a long drink of his scotch. "You can't imagine, big brother. Then again, maybe you can. Go talk to Churchill, see how she really feels. You guys can make it work. I know you can. You're a match."

"Mismatch you mean. I'm not great with the reading and writing thing, Tripp. The woman's a librarian." He ran his hands through his hair. "And there's the little fact that I set her up. She had to live with that and it wasn't easy for her. It was a big reason she left here and went to Jersey. That alone is enough to never forgive me."

"Dyslexia doesn't define who you are. Churchill gets that. She always has. For the other part, make it up to her. Prove she's special in your life, not someone you take for granted, not a convenience but *the* one. The one you want to please and be there for and never leave. How do you win a race? Get that checkered flag?"

"Go for broke and don't look back."

"Then do it."

Churchill parked the Prius in the speedway lot, the roar of the cars signaling the races had started. Actually the roar was from a single car meaning the qualifying laps were going on. She headed for the bleachers and stomped her way up to Miss Ellie eating a moon pie near the top. "This is all your fault, you know."

"Honey, which fault are we talking about here? When you've lived as long as I have there are lists of faults."

"You got me involved with that key and that led to getting involved with Cal and now he's going to North Carolina. He's leaving. I'm here and I'm staying. This is home and I love home."

"Then tell him you want him to stay here."

"But this is his big chance to make it somewhere else. The driving school is one of the best in the country. He'll get a name, be respected, be known for something other than the guy who went to prison. The ex-con. If he stays because I ask him to he'll resent me for making him choose between me and the dream job."

"He might come back after a few years. You can always wait a few years."

Churchill gave her an evil look, sat down, snagged the moon pie from Miss Ellie, and stuffed the whole thing in her mouth at once.

"Go with him."

"I'll hate it. I hated every minute in Jersey."

"Honey, North Carolina is not Jersey."

"It's not Savannah either. No other place is Savannah." Churchill kissed Miss Ellie on the cheek. "How are things with you and Silky?"

"We're going to Maui as soon as the racing season's over. I'm going to teach him how to surf."

"You make it all sound so easy."

"Once you know what you want it is easy."

Churchill made her way down the bleachers and started back toward Tic Tac. There was a light on in Cal's garage, the Mustang parked in front. Her heart squeezed tight. She couldn't imagine not seeing Cal's car buzzing around town. She couldn't imagine him not being a part of her life. She didn't want him to not be part of her life and she only had two days to figure out what to do about it.

Another hot summer day Cal thought as he walked out of the bank. All his business was in order, everything signed and ready to go. He headed for the Mustang parked at the curb under a big oak and there was Churchill McKenzie sitting shotgun, her hair held back with a red ribbon that matched the car. She looked great in a convertible. It was made for her. So many things were.

He climbed in. "I was just coming to see you."

"To say good-bye? You're leaving today, right? It is today."

"You want to get rid of me that badly?"

"No, but I'd feel really stupid if I had my luggage in your car and we weren't going anywhere."

His heart stopped. "Luggage?"

"I can't wait another nine years, Cal. I can't wait period. I want to be with you always. You're going to North Carolina and I'm going with you, if you'll have me. I love Savannah. I always have. Why anyone lives anyplace else is a mystery to me. But if you're not here the very best part of Savannah is missing." She took his hand. "I don't want to be here unless you're here, too. I guess what I'm trying to say is I love living here but I love you more, a million times more. My home is with you."

A lump sat in his throat.

"Say something, anything. Do you want me to get out or—"

"No," he finally managed. "Don't get out. For the love of God, please don't get out." He fired up the Mustang, took Broughton Street to Price, and pulled into the weeded drive of an old derelict Victorian house with boarded up windows and plywood across the doors. The widow's walk hung off the roof and most of the front porch was missing. "What do you think?"

"It needs someone to love it."

Cal took her hand. "That would be us. I bought it for us. I love you, Churchill. I want this to be our home. We can fill it with all the old things that you love."

"You need to go to North Carolina, Cal. You need to

start fresh. It's only fair. It's your turn to be happy. For once you get to be happy."

"Then marry me and we'll start our lives fresh and new and wonderful together. You'll make me the happiest man on earth if you'll be my wife. I love you, Churchill McKenzie. I want to be with you always, here in this beautiful old city that was nearly lost, then saved, just like us. I never want to be away from you again, ever."

If you liked this book, try MISTRESS BY MISTAKE, Maggie Robinson's first book for Brava, in stores now!

Bay had done his duty. When news of his grandmother's illness arrived, he'd left immediately for Bayard Court, his oceanfront boyhood home. Grace Bayard had raised him, and he owed her everything. She'd been a little bit of a thing, but her tongue and wits were sharp and she'd done her damnedest to set him on the proper path. It was not her fault that he had strayed more than a time or two. She had wanted to see him settled again and a father, and perhaps one day he would be. But at present he had the divine Deborah Fallon waiting for him in his little house in Jane Street, the most exclusive enclave of kept women in London. Deb was the third mistress he'd set up there. The first, Angelique Dubois, had not been much of an angel of any kind or even French despite her name. His last lover, Helena Colbert, had served him well for a year but things had wound down to their natural conclusion. His friend Viscount Marlow was happy to take her off his hands, gushing his gratitude in disgusting fashion at every opportunity.

Bay had been ready for a change, and his choice was the most alluring Deborah Fallon. Those full lips, those fuller breasts, those tip-tilted blue eyes. She looked like a naughty cream-fed kitten. She had some wit, and if she were a bit of a prima donna, it was only because she knew her own worth. Her last protector had to reluctantly marry to further the family line, and nothing he could say would make Deborah part of a triangle. She had her standards—her lovers had to be rich, of course, and completely unattached. Along with several others, Bay pursued Deb for weeks before he persuaded her to move into Jane Street, and he hadn't gotten to warm the sheets even once before he was called away.

He'd stopped at his townhouse to make himself presentable after his long journey, pleased to see that someone had thoughtfully hung a mourning wreath upon the front door. He was truly sad that his grandmother had passed, but she had been nearly ninety-five, a very great age. He was three and thirty—and would be happy indeed to treble that if he remained as shrewd as his grandmamma up till near the end. She had fallen in her garden, tending to her beloved roses. The doctor thought she had a series of small strokes, and by the time Bay arrived, she was sleeping most of her days away. She had rallied briefly at the sight of him, then went to bed one night and never woke up. Bay had stayed to see to the disposition of her faithful servants and shut up most of the house for the time being. He was a city man now. One day he might try to raise a family again in the stone manor house, but now he meant to raise his spirits in Deborah Fallon's arms.

Perhaps he'd been foolish to ride back to London. Every inch of him hurt, but he was damned if he was going to wait any longer for Deborah. He wondered how she'd amused herself while he was away. He let himself in to the dark house with his own key and climbed the stairs. He could have been blindfolded and still have found Deborah's bedroom. She had changed her perfume to a delicious harmony of orange and lemons and her fresh scent filled his head. He stood by the bed, not wanting to startle her awake, dropping his clothing quietly to the floor. This was not how he pictured his first night with his new mistress, but he was stiff as a poker and could not wait to seduce her over champagne and strawberries.

Angeliques's revolting cherubs were still gleaming in the moonlight. Helena had been too superstitious to remove them and had actually acquired several more. Poor Deborah had probably waited for him to return before she made any changes. He fully expected her to make the bedchamber her own, although the rest of the house was exactly to his taste.

Their liaison had not gotten off to a good start. The carters had no sooner delivered Deborah's trunks before he'd left her in tears in the marble hallway. He had sent letters and flowers weekly, of course, and news of his grandmother's death. In a foolish fit of lust he had discovered a ruby necklace in his grandmother's jewel case and sent it to London, with the understanding that Deborah could wear it as long as she was his mistress. He was longing to see it around her white throat—it, and nothing else adorning her luscious body.

Grace Bayard was the rare woman who didn't care much for ostentatious jewelry, so he had never seen his grandmother wear it. He had buried her with the plain gold band his grandfather had given her eighty years ago before he made his fortune. Their marriage had not been an especially happy one. His grandmother had been practically a child when she wed, the fashion of the day. Her husband was older and ambitious, spending much of their married life outside England. Their long separation resulted in just one child, Bay's father.

Grandmama Grace had told him once his grandfather had given her the rubies to atone for some infraction. His grandfather, Bay thought, must have done something spectacularly bad, for the rubies were large and lustrous and very valuable, and the diamonds surrounding them not in-significant either. The collar with its enormous center drop was fit for a princess. Hell, fit for a queen. He hoped it had not been a mistake to gift them to Deborah temporarily. He'd have to tread carefully when he discussed the neck-lace on the morrow.

He encountered an amusingly virginal nightrail, which he made quick work of. She gave a pleased little sigh and wrapped herself around him. Her magnificent hair was in two schoolgirl braids—she certainly had not expected to entertain him this evening, and he was touched at her sur-prising modesty. And equally touched by her ardent, al-most thirsty kisses. She tasted of vanilla and wine and smelled like a Spanish summer. She cupped his balls and brought him to her entrance and he slipped in without any hesitation. She was wet but very tight. Heaven. If she was a schoolgirl, he was as randy as a schoolboy, and didn't last long in her pillowing embrace. He'd spend more time tomorrow morning tending to her needs. He was known as a considerate lover, one of the reasons Deborah had agreed to be his mistress. Even his wife had no complaints while they were married.

Thoroughly spent, he passed a delightful night in his lover's arms. And when the first rays of sun had the audac-ity to slip through the shutters, he feasted upon her breast as if it were a banquet of cream and honey. She gave a low groan, but he didn't think it was in protest. The faint light showed him his mistress was not quite as young as she ap-peared to be six weeks ago—there were a few silver strands in her unraveling ink-dark braids. No doubt she resorted to artifice and would have corrected this had she known he was coming.

And speaking of coming, he wanted to seat himself within her again. Last night had been heaven, and now that the empty day was spread before him, the devil in him intended to visit heaven again and again. No, he was not sorry he'd paid the exorbitant price to secure Deborah Fallon's favors. If last night was any indication of what the woman could do when she was half asleep, he would cheerfully beggar himself. He was a lucky man indeed.

He licked her nipple to taut, pale pink perfection, wondering idly if he'd get a child on her someday. He'd been fortunate with his mistresses thus far, but he would do his duty by her if she bore his bastard. He was a gentleman, and that's what gentlemen did. Somehow the thought of an infant suckling Deb Fallon's very tempting breast was unbelievably erotic. She would resemble a naughty Madonna, her black hair cascading down her ivory shoulders.

By God, she was making him lose his mind. The touch and taste of her was inebriating, clouding his judgment. One didn't keep a mistress for domesticity. One kept a mistress for sin, the darker the better. And if he knew anything about Deborah Fallon, she would complain loud and long caring for anything that was not her own luscious self. A baby? Preposterous.

As if she heard his thoughts, she stiffened beneath him. And then she screamed.

Ear-piercingly. Perhaps she had not recognized him when she awoke. But honestly, who could she be expecting? She was *his*.

He looked down at her, suspicious. She gave him a look he'd seen only in battle, when the other side was hopelessly outnumbered, pushed beyond recklessness and there was nothing left to lose. He hoped very much that she was not sleeping with a French bayonet beneath the mattress.

"You! You!" she sputtered.

"Yes, my pet, it is I. I know I gave you no notice, but thank you for your very warm welcome last night. It was worth every minute of the harrowing six weeks we spent apart." He set back to flicking her nipple again with his tongue.

She hit him on the head with a fist. "Get off me! This instant! You are much mistaken, Sir Michael. I am not Deborah."

And here's a sneak peek at UNDONE, the historical romance anthology featuring Susan Johnson, Terri Brisbin, and Mary Wine. Turn the page for a preview of Susan's story, "As You Wish."

Fortunately for the earl's pressing schedule, the night was overcast. Not a hint of moonlight broke through to expose his athletic form as he scaled the old, fist-thick wisteria vines wrapped around the pillars of the terrace pergola. The house to which the pergola was attached was quiet, the ground floor dark save for the porter's light in the entrance hall. Either the Belvoirs were out or already in bed. More likely the latter, with only a single flambeau outside the door.

He'd best take care.

Kit had described the position of Miss Belvoir's bedchamber—hence Albion's ascent of wisteria. Once he gained the roof joists of the Chinoiserie pergola, he would have access to the windows of the main floor corridor. From there he could make his way to the second-floor bedchambers, the easternmost that of Miss Belvoir. Where, according to Kit, she'd been cloistered for the last month, being polished by her stepmother into a state of refined elegance for her bow into society a few weeks hence.

Which refinements, in his estimation, only served to make every young lady into the same boring martinet without an original thought in her head or a jot of conversation worth listening to.

Hopefully, there wouldn't be much conversation tonight. If he had his way there wouldn't be any. He hoped as well that she wouldn't prove stubborn, but should she, he'd stuff his handkerchief in her mouth to muffle her screams, tie her up if necessary, and carry her down the back stairs and out the servants' entrance. It was more likely, though—with all due modesty—that his much-practiced charm would win the day.

Pulling himself over the fretwork balustrade embellishing the pergola, he stood for a moment balanced on a joist contemplating which window would best offer him ingress. His mind made up, he brushed himself off, navigated the vine-draped timbers, and reached the window. Taking a knife from his coat pocket, he snapped open the blade, slipped it under the lower sash, and pried it up enough to gain a finger hold.

Moments later, he stood motionless in the dark corridor. The stairs were to the right, if Kit's description was correct. After listening for a few moments and hearing nothing, he quietly made his way down the plush carpet and up the stairs. A single candle on a console table dimly illuminated the hallway onto which the bedrooms opened. Pausing to listen once again and distinguishing no undue sounds, he silently traversed the carpeted passageway to the last door on his right.

It shouldn't be locked. Servants required access if the bell pull by the bed was rung. For a brief moment he stood utterly still, wondering what in blazes he was doing here, about to abduct some untried maid in order to seduce her. As if there weren't women enough in London who would welcome him to their beds with open arms. Considerable brandy was to blame, he supposed, along with the rackety company of his friends who had too much idle time on their hands in which to conjure up wild wagers like this.

Bloody hell. He felt the complete absence of any desire to be where he was.

On the other hand, he decided with a short exhalation, he'd bet twenty thousand on this foolishness.

Now it was play or pay.

He reached for the latch, pressed down and quietly opened the door.

As he stepped over the threshold he was greeted by a ripple of scent and a cheerful female voice. "I thought you'd changed your mind."

The hairs on the back of his neck rose.

He was unarmed was his first thought.

It was a trap was his second.

But when the same genial voice said, "Don't worry no one's at home but me. Do come in and shut the door," his pulse rate lessened and he scanned the candlelit interior for the source of the invitation.

"Miss Belvoir, I presume," he murmured, taking note of a young woman with hair more gold than red standing across the room near the foot of the bed. *She was quite beautiful. How nice. And if no one was home, nicer still.* Shutting the door behind him, he offered her a graceful bow.

"A pleasant good evening, Albion. Gossip preceded you." *He was breathtakingly handsome at close range. Now to convince him to take her away.* "I have a proposition for you."

He smiled. "A coincidence. I have one for you." This was going to be easier than he thought. Then he saw her luggage. "You first," he said guardedly.

"I understand you have twenty thousand to lose."

"Or not."

"Such arrogance, Albion. You forget the decision is mine."

"Not entirely," he replied softly.

"Because you've done this before."

"Not this. But something enough like it to know."

"I see," she murmured. "But then *I'm* not inclined to be instantly infatuated with your handsome self or your prodigal repute. I have more important matters on my mind."

"More than twenty thousand?" he asked with a small smile.

"I like to think so."

He recognized the seriousness of her tone. "Then we must come to some agreement. What do you want?"

"To strike a bargain."

"Consider me agreeable to most anything," he smoothly replied.

"My luggage caused you certain apprehension, I noticed," she said, amusement in her gaze. "Let me allay your fears. I have no plans to elope with you. Did you think I did?"

"The thought crossed my mind." He wasn't entirely sure yet that some trap wasn't about to be sprung. She was the picture of innocence in white muslin—all the rage thanks to Marie Antoinette's penchant for the faux rustic life.

"I understand that women stand in line for your amorous skills, but rest assured—you're not my type. Licentiousness is your raison d'être I hear: a very superficial existence, I should think."

His brows rose. He'd wondered if she'd heard about Sally's when she mentioned women standing in line. She also had the distinction of being the first woman to find him lacking. "You mistake my raison d'être. Perhaps if you knew me better you'd change your mind," he pleasantly suggested.

"I very much doubt it," she replied with equal amiability. "You're quite beautiful, I'll give you that, and I understand you're unrivaled in the boudoir. But my interests, unlike yours, aren't focused on sex. What I do need from you, however, is an escort to my aunt's house in Edinburgh."

"And for that my twenty thousand is won?" His voice was velvet soft.

"Such tact, my lord."

"I can be blunt if you prefer."

"Please do. I've heard so much about your ready charm. I'm wondering how you're going to ask."

"I hadn't planned on asking."

"Because you never have to."

He smiled. "To date at least."

"So I may be the exception."

"If you didn't need an escort to Edinburgh," he observed mildly. "Your move."

"You see this as a game?"

"In a manner of speaking."

"And I'm the trophy or reward or how do young bucks describe a sportive venture like this?"

"How do young ladies describe the snaring of a husband?"

She laughed. "Touché. I have no need of a husband, though. Does that calm your fears?"

"I have none in that regard. Nothing could induce me to marry."

"Then we are in complete agreement. Now tell me, how precisely does a libertine persuade a young lady to succumb to his blandishments?"

"Not like this," he said dryly. "Come with me and I'll show you."

"We strike our bargain first. Like you, I have much at stake."

"Then, Miss Belvoir," he said with well-bred grace, "if you would be willing to relinquish your virginity tonight, I'd be delighted to escort you to Edinburgh."

"In the morning. Or later tonight if we can deal with this denouement expeditiously."

"At week's end," he countered. "After the Spring Meet in Newmarket."

"I'm sorry. That's not acceptable."

He didn't answer for so long she thought he might be willing to lose twenty thousand. He was rich enough.

"We can talk about it at my place."

"No."

Another protracted silence ensued; only the crackle of the fire on the hearth was audible.

"Would you be willing to accompany me to Newmarket?" he finally said. "I can assure you anonymity at my race box. Once the Spring Meet is over, I'll take you to Edinburgh." He blew out a small breath. "I've a fortune wagered on my horses. I don't suppose you'd understand."

This time she was the one who didn't respond immediately, and when she did, her voice held a hint of melancholy. "I do understand. My mother owned the Langley stud."

"That was your mother's? By God—the Langley stud was legendary. Tattersalls was mobbed when it was sold. You *do* know how I feel about my racers, then." He grinned. "They're all going to win at Newmarket. I'll give you a share if you like—to help set you up in Edinburgh."

Her expression brightened, and her voice took on a teasing intonation. "Are you trying to buy my acquiescence?"

"Why not? You only need give me a few days of your time. Come with me. You'll enjoy the races."

"I mustn't be seen."

Ah—capitulation. "Then we'll see that you aren't. Good Lord—the Langley stud. I'm bloody impressed. Let me get your luggage."

Mark your calendars! BEAST BEHAVING BADLY, the newest Shelly Laurenston book in the Pride series, comes out next month!

Bo shot through the goal crease and slammed the puck into the net.

"Morning!"

That voice cut through his focus and, without breaking his stride, Bo changed direction and skated over to the rink entrance. He stopped hard, ice spraying out from his skates, and stood in front of the wolfdog.

He stared down at her and she stared up at him. She kept smiling even when he didn't. Finally he asked, "What time did we agree on?"

"Seven," she replied with a cheery note that put his teeth on edge.

"And what time is it?"

"Uh . . ." She dug into her jeans and pulled out a cell phone. The fact that she still had on that damn, useless watch made his head want to explode. How did one function—as an adult anyway—without a goddamn watch?

Grinning so that he could see all those perfectly aligned teeth, she said, "Six-forty-five!"

"And what time did we agree on?"

She blinked and her smile faded. After a moment, "Seven."

"Is it seven?"

"No." When he only continued to stare at her, she softly asked, "Want to meet me at the track at seven?"

He continued to stare at her until she nodded and said, "Okay."

She walked out and Bo went back to work.

Fifteen minutes later, Bo walked into the small arena at seven a.m. Blayne, looking comfortable in dark blue leggings, sweatshirt, and skates, turned to face him. He expected her to be mad at him or, even worse, for her to get that wounded look he often got from people when he was blatantly direct. But having to deal with either of those scenarios was a price Bo was always willing to pay to ensure that the people in his life understood how he worked from the beginning. This way, there were no surprises later. It was called "boundaries" and he read about it in a book.

Yet when Blayne saw him, she grinned and held up a Starbucks cup. "Coffee," she said when he got close. "I got you the house brand because I had no idea what you would like. And they had cinnamon twists, so I got you a few of those."

He took the coffee, watching her closely. Where was it? The anger? The resentment? Was she plotting something?

Blayne held the bag of sweets out for him and Bo took them. "Thank you," he said, still suspicious even as he sipped his perfectly brewed coffee.

"You're welcome." And there went that grin again. Big and brighter than the damn sun. "And I get it. Seven means seven. Eight means eight, etc., etc. Got it and I'm on it. It won't happen again." She said all that without a trace of bitterness and annoyance, dazzling Bo with her understanding more than she'd dazzled him with those legs.

"So," she put her hands on her hips, "what do you want me to do first?"

Marry me? Wait. No, no. Incorrect response. It'll just weird her out and make her run again. Normal. Be normal.

You can do this. You're not just a great skater. You're a normal *great skater.*

When Bo knew he had his shit together, he said, "Let's work on your focus first. And, um, should I ask what happened to your face?" She had a bunch of cuts on her cheeks. Gouges. Like something small had pawed at her.

"Nope!" she chirped, pulling off her sweatshirt. She wore a worn blue T-shirt underneath with B&G Plumbing scrawled across it. With sweatshirt in hand, Blayne skated over to the bleachers, stopped, shook her head, skated over to another section of bleachers, stopped, looked at the sweatshirt, turned around, and skated over to the railing. "I should leave it here," she explained, "In case I get chilly."

It occurred to Bo he'd just lost two minutes of his life watching her try and figure out where to place a damn sweatshirt. Two minutes that he'd never get back.

"Woo-hoo!" she called out once she hit the track. "Let's go!"

She was skating backward as she urged him to join her with both hands.

He pointed behind her. "Watch the—"

"Ow!"

"—pole."

Christ, what had he gotten himself into?

Christ almighty, what had she gotten herself into?

Twenty minutes in and she wanted to smash the man's head against a wall. She wanted to go back in time and kick the shit out of Genghis Khan before turning on his brothers, Larry and Moe. Okay. That wasn't their names but she could barely remember Genghis's name on a good day, how the hell was she supposed to remember his brothers'. But whatever the Khan kin's names may be, Blayne wanted to hurt them all for cursing her world with this . . . this . . . Visigoth!

Even worse, she knew he didn't even take what she did seriously. He insisted on calling it a chick sport. If he were a sexist pig across the board, Blayne could overlook it as a mere flaw in his upbringing. But, she soon discovered, Novikov had a very high degree of respect for female athletes . . . as long as they were athletes and not just "hot chicks in cute outfits, roughing each other up. All you guys need is some hot oil or mud and you'd have a real moneymaker on your hands."

And yet, even while he didn't respect her sport as a sport, he still worked her like he was getting her ready for the Olympics.

After thirty minutes she wanted nothing more but to lie on her side and pant. She doubted the hybrid would let her get away with that, though.

Shooting around the track, Novikov stopped her in a way that she was finding extremely annoying—by grabbing her head with that big hand of his and holding her in place.

He shoved her back with one good push and Blayne fought not to fall on her ass at that speed. When someone shoved her like that, they were usually pissed. He wasn't.

"I need to see something," he said, still nursing that cup of coffee. He'd finished off the cinnamon twists in less than five minutes while she was warming up. "Come at me as hard as you can."

"Are you sure?" she asked, looking him over. He didn't have any of his protective gear on, somehow managing to change into sweatpants and T-shirt and still make it down to the track exactly at seven. "I don't want to hurt you," she told him honestly.

The laughter that followed, however, made her think she did want to hurt him. She wanted to hurt him a lot. When he realized she wasn't laughing with him—or, in this case, laughing at *herself* since he was obviously laughing *at* her—Novikov blinked and said, "Oh. You're not kidding."

"No. I'm not kidding."

"Oh. Oh! Um . . . I'll be fine. Hit me with your best shot."

"Like Pat Benatar?" she joked but when he only stared at her, she said, "Forget it."

Blayne sized up the behemoth in front of her and decided to move back a few more feet so she could get a really fast start. She got into position and took one more scrutinizing look. It was a skill her father had taught her. To size up weakness. Whether the weakness of a person or a building or whatever. Of course, Blayne often used this skill for good, finding out someone's weakness and then working to help them overcome it. Her father, however, used it to destroy.

Lowering her body, Blayne took a breath, tightened her fists, and took off. She lost some speed on the turn but picked it up as she cut inside. As Blayne approached Novikov, she sized him up one more time as he stood there casually, sipping his coffee and watching her move around the track. Based on that last assessing look, she slightly adjusted her position and slammed into him with everything she had.

And, yeah, she knocked herself out cold, but it was totally worth it when the behemoth went down with her.